THE LEGEND OF THE BLUE CLOUD

Charles Serio

St. DeSales, London 2019

St. DeSales First Edition 2019
978-1-9996159-0-1 (Print)
978-1-9996159-1-8 (e-Book)

Dedicated to William Simpson of Hove, East Sussex and Jerome Blake of Devizes, Wiltshire without whose generosity the writing of this novel would have been impossible.

CHAPTER
1

(1999)

'Stop your daydreaming, Mister!' Noah shouted down the hall. 'You'll be late for school again!'

Ben slowly emerged from his room, rubbed the sleep from his eyes, and sat down at the table.

'Make sure you come straight home from school today,' Noah said. 'I need you to feed and water the horses. I'm going over to the plant to see if they can give me some work. Don't leave the horses and let them get themselves in a state.'
'Okay, Pa,' Ben replied. 'I'll take care of them.'

They ate in silence both of them thinking about the day ahead. Noah sat and ate reckoning his chances of picking up some causal work and Ben fantasized about being a hero in his own made-up adventures.

A horn tooted outside. 'That's the bus,' Ben said as he grabbed his bag and headed to the door.
'Pay attention and do your best,' Noah called out after him. 'That's my boy. I'll be seeing you come dinner time.'

It had been a hard and unforgiving year-full of tragedy and worry. Noah had no steady work, since Grayson's food processing plant was bought out by a big outfit from California. All the locals were let go and replaced by teenagers and Latino itinerants who would work for next to nothing. There was no local union or public outcry to stand against it. There was not much other local work either. Grayson's was one of the few major employers in this part of Southern Idaho. Some folks fled over the border to Nevada and picked up some work at Cactus Pete's Casino in Jackpot, but Noah stayed where he was hoping for better days and refusing to give up on the area. Like the others in his community, he made a stand not to work on the cheap for the California outfit. But times were desperate and he thought he would stop there after the morning shift and see if they might have him back.

'Something is better than nothing,' he reckoned to himself.

Ben sat on the bus next to his best buddy, Carl.

'Hey, Ben! Did you see that thunderstorm last night? My dad said it was something strange. Lightning like great forks in the sky and sometimes shooting out straight down to the ground. Both our horses were stamping and kicking at the stable door. How did your Bess and Willy cope? Zeno was not too bad, but Dad said he'd never seen our Daisy Mae so spooked. My grandma thinks it could be a sign of something.'

'A sign?' Ben asked. 'A sign of what?'
'She didn't say... Did you see it?'
'No, I must have been dreaming,' Ben replied.

'Well, you'll get another chance,' Carl said. 'My dad says he heard they're calling for more big thunderstorms all week.'

Ben had grown progressively more silent and dreamy ever since his mother, Cora, disappeared. That was just over a year ago now. Mom had gone out for a trek in the Magic Valley on Willy, but only Willy returned- panicked and exhausted. The police and some of the neighbors went out looking, but there was not a sign of her. There was an official investigation, but nothing was discovered. Some gossips at the church said that she had run off, but Ben knew that was not so. He believed what Carl's dad, Police Chief Marty, had to say after they had given up the hunt.
'It's like she flat out disappeared off the face of this earth.'

Noah got into his pickup truck late that afternoon and headed over to the plant.
'Time to eat some humble pie, if they'll let me eat it,' he thought to himself.

As he drove along, he thought about Ben and how Cora's disappearance had affected him. His happy boy was no longer happy. He felt like he lost both his wife and part of his son too on that terrible day. Sometimes he would forget and think to ask Cora what to do about Ben or maybe about finding some work, but of course Cora was not there to ask. She was gone and his mind would play tricks on him like she was not. And every single time that mind-trick happened Noah would feel her loss again like it was only yesterday-fresh, raw, and sore.

At school that Thursday afternoon, just before the start of the week-long school holiday, there was a bit of a surprise. After lunch, all the students were called into the assembly room. They sat there giggling and fooling around until Principal Mavis called them to order.

'Today, we have a very special guest,' she announced. 'It is my pleasure to introduce an expert on genuine Native American medicine men. He's from the Shoshone tribe and he's going to talk to you about our local area and its history. Pay attention and welcome our guest, Edwin Greyhawk, Professor of Native American Studies at the State University.'

A tall, thin man ambled onstage. He wore a fringed-leather jacket and faded blue flannel shirt with bolo tie and jeans. His boots were weather-worn and an old battered baseball cap with a bent brim sat snugly over his long and scraggly hair. He did not look like what Ben imagined a genuine medicine man might look like. He looked pretty much like anyone else from the area. But despite the Professor's scruffy and unkempt appearance, he spoke with the fervor of a tub-thumping revivalist.

'Let me ask you a question, young people,' Greyhawk began. 'Does anyone here really know about this special and sacred place where we live?'

He looked around for a response, but there was none forthcoming.

'Then let me tell you that this here part of Idaho is revered by the Shoshone and the ancestors of the Shoshone people. We live in the land where the Great Spirit abides and can be summoned and called upon. Great medicine has been practiced here, since the dawn of my people. This is the land of miracles and healing. This is the land of mystery where all the fallen of my people dwell and where their spirits came to rest.'

Greyhawk dug something out from deep inside his jacket pocket. It was wrapped in soft leather. He held it aloft for all to see.

'I am holding here what is known as a Willing Stone,' he announced as he unwrapped its leather cover. 'It is one of a very few remaining examples now kept at the Shoshone Bannock Museum. They have generously allowed me to borrow this one and show it to you. Local Native American tribes have used one just like this for centuries to summon the spirits of those they have lost. It is a powerful totem used by shamans and medicine men who hold the 'Gift of the Stone' and can summon the spirit it contains. The Willing Stones of our ancestors hold great power for they are connected to the Great Spirit and can call on the Spirit to heal the sick and find what is lost.'

Greyhawk came down from behind the podium to where the students were sitting. He held the Willing Stone atop its leather cover in the palm of his hand.

He walked slowly along the front row holding out the Stone for them to examine it more closely. Carl was sitting next to Ben and when Greyhawk passed by, he glanced at the Willing Stone disinterestedly.

Greyhawk then abruptly stopped. He saw that Ben was staring at the Stone as if transfixed. He looked at Ben, held the Willing Stone out in the palm of his hand, and nodded at him.
'Go ahead, Son,' he said. 'Pick it up.'

The Willing Stone felt warm and smooth in Ben's hands like it had been handled many times and worn flat in the process. He kept running his fingers over the dull green Stone, when suddenly he was gripped in panic. He felt his hand close hard around the Stone. He could not unclench his fingers. His hand was no longer under his control and squeezed the Willing Stone into his fist.

He shook his head as he felt his vision start to blur. Everything kept going in and out of focus more and more rapidly. He shut his eyes for a moment, because he felt his stomach heave. Then he began to shake in convulsions.

When he opened his eyes again, he found himself transported to a place he did not know. He saw himself standing in a colorless valley landscape where everything around him was spinning in and out of perspective. The ridges surrounding the valley moved swiftly toward him and then just as swiftly away. He stood there in shock briefly and then took a few tentative paces forward, but found it difficult to walk.

His step was uncertain as the ground beneath his feet tilted up and down repeatedly in continuously changing angles. He stopped and blinked to clear his eyes. He looked down and saw the Willing Stone was still in his hand. When he looked back up, there, right in front of him, stood a woman in the swirling landscape. She had her back turned to him.

Ben saw a shadowy figure appear out of nowhere and approach the woman. Behind the shadowy figure, six more shadow-like beings appeared out of spinning columns of dark smoke that had descended from above. The shadowy figure crept nearer and nearer to where Ben and the woman were standing. As he drew closer, Ben caught just a glimpse of him and what he saw filled him with dread. A cruel, heartless, malicious, and white-eyed stare greeted him. The horrific figure was winged, but not with feathers. The wings seemed to be made of a hideous, brownish, papery skin. Like a moth's or a bat's.

Ben recoiled as the creature lurched at him and tried to snatch the Willing Stone from his hand. He stumbled backward and away from the creature's grasp. He felt so nauseous that he thought he would vomit. All his nerves were tingling in alarm.

The shadowy figure stared menacingly at Ben for a moment and then grabbed the woman by her hair and began to drag her away. Ben put out his hand to help the woman, but could not reach her. He tried to speak, but no sounds emerged. The woman turned to Ben with terror in her eyes as the creature kept pulling her roughly away. Ben saw her eyes pleading with him to come to her rescue, when suddenly he recognized her.

'No, no, it cannot be,' Ben said to himself. 'No,' he said to himself again while shaking his head. But no matter how much he tried to deny what he was seeing, there was no denying that the terrorized woman standing in front of him was his mother.

Helplessly, Ben watched as the shadowy figure and the six creatures in his service quickly disappeared with her and were gone.

When Ben snapped back from his disturbing vision, he found himself curled up on the floor. He heard himself shouting, 'Mom! Mom!' He looked around in confusion and saw that he was back in the school assembly room. A spasm of pain washed through him. He felt faint. His stomach was in knots. He thought he was going to be sick. The room started spinning. Greyhawk helped him back to his feet. He reached down to reclaim the Willing Stone from Ben's hand, picking it up by its leather cover, and instantly Ben began to feel more like himself again.

Greyhawk looked down at Ben and winked. 'Powerful medicine, Son,' he said mysteriously.

Principal Mavis and a lady from the nurse's office came rushing up to him. Everyone kept asking in frantic concern, 'Are you all right, Ben? Are you okay?'

Carl kept shouting, 'Back off! Give him air!' at everyone. Ben was both embarrassed and confused at the same time.

After Ben's collapse at Greyhawk's talk, the students headed back to class. As Ben and Carl walked along together, Carl said, 'Are you sure you're all right? You scared the bejesus out of me.'

'It was nothing,' Ben replied. 'Maybe I caught some tummy bug or something.'
'Spooky Indian and his mumbo jumbo,' Carl scoffed. 'I bet he really works at the casino in Jackpot.'
'I suspect so,' Ben said still a bit shaken.

When the final bell rang, Ben and Carl went out to wait for the bus and head home.

'Hey, Ben! Want to take the horses out for a spell?' Carl asked.
'Can't,' he answered. 'Chores.'

As Ben and Carl waited together, they saw Greyhawk walking over to an old Chevy Pickup. One of its side panels had rusted through.

'Bet that's still got more horsepower than anything his ancestors rode,' Carl joked. But just as Carl started laughing, Greyhawk turned away from the Chevy and began making his way slowly to where Ben and Carl were waiting. They stared uncomfortably as he made his way over to them. When he reached Ben, he looked down at him mournfully.

'I saw what happened when you touched the Stone, Son,' Greyhawk said. 'You have the Gift of the Stone. I know where you went. I know what you saw. I know where the one you lost is.'

CHAPTER
2

Noah sat in the cramped corridor along with about twenty other hopeful job applicants. He knew most of them. Most had worked at Grayson's before the California mob takeover. Most were like he was and refused to keep working at less than half their former pay. Two of those waiting, he did not know. One was a young man in a suit who kept talking on his new-fangled mobile phone. Another was a glamorous young woman dressed as if at a bank interview.

A woman came out of the office. Noah did not know her. She beamed a big toothy smile.
'We would prefer if you filled out the application online, but if you can't manage that, I have some paper applications here.'
She waved the applications in her hand at them.
'Anyone?'

Noah's and nearly every other hand in the corridor shot up. He waited his turn, stood up, and collected an application. All but the young man on his phone and the young woman did the same. The toothy woman walked over to the young pair and whispered something to them. She jotted down their replies on her clipboard and then they promptly left. Noah thought he saw a smile on their faces.

The toothy woman then said to the others, 'I'll be back

presently to collect your application forms. Thank you for your interest in working for Sunny Days Food Processing!'

Noah took out a pen and began completing the form. He had twenty years experience in food processing work. It was all he really knew. He wondered though if his past work experience at Grayson's would count against him. Maybe they would think he was a troublemaker. Maybe they would think he would stir up dissent. Maybe they did not need people like him anymore.
'I need to work,' Noah thought to himself. 'I'll be their good boy. Whatever it takes.'

The woman eventually came back out from the office and collected the completed forms.

'Thank you for filling in your applications. If you are to be recalled for an interview, we will contact you on the phone number you listed on your application form. Goodbye and have a nice day.'

She said all that with a frozen smile on her face and then turned on her heels and disappeared back into the office.

All the applicants looked at one another. One of them said, 'Have a nice day? Is she kidding? How are we supposed to have a nice day when we have no work?'

Noah got in his pickup and headed toward home. He shook his head back and forth as he drove.

'I should have guessed it would not be that easy,' he thought to himself. 'Companies just don't hire on the spot anymore. You have to jump through hoops these days, Noah. You don't get any job as easy as that. You got to grovel first and wish them a 'nice day'. You have to know what 'online' means.'

When Noah finally made it back home, he saw that Ben had already seen to Bess and Willy. He walked into the kitchen where Ben had started on dinner. He did not tell Ben what had happened at the plant, because there was nothing yet to say.

'I'm heating up the rest of the corned beef, butter beans, and potatoes, Pa,' Ben said. 'Is that all right?'
'That's fine… so how did you get on at school today?'

Ben just shrugged and said, 'Okay'. He decided not to mention Greyhawk and his lecture or the strange reaction he had when he touched the Willing Stone. His father had enough to worry about without his worrying him too. He thought it best not to share Greyhawk's eerie notion that he knew where his mother was either.

Both of them kept their worries to themselves for the sake of the other. They ate in silence.

Soon after dinner, the phone rang. Noah raced over to pick it up thinking it might be the California crew telling him to come in for an interview, but it was not. Instead he heard a familiar voice on the other end of the line.

'Noah? It's Annie. How are things? How's Ben?'

Noah had not heard from his sister, Annie, for quite
some time and he on his part had not bothered
contacting her. After Cora's disappearance, he had cut
himself off from everyone in his life. He had been
treating his phone like a stranger.

'As well as can be expected,' he said. 'How are you?
How's Stacey?'
'Good… good. Look, Noah, Stacey and I are thinking
about coming down for a visit. Do you think that
would be all right? We've not seen nor heard from you
and Ben since Christmas. That's a while.'
'When you thinking of coming?'
'This weekend, if that works for you. It's the school
holidays and maybe we can spend the week together.'
'Sure. That works fine. Ben will be happy to see you
two. So will I.'
'Well, see you both this weekend then.'

She paused for a moment and then asked, 'Noah? Are
you sure you two are all right? If you need anything,
don't keep it to yourself. After all, we're family.'
'You just get yourself down from Boise this weekend,
Annie. Don't you fret about me.'
They said their goodbyes and he hung up the phone.

Noah stood there for a moment and thought about
what Annie had sacrificed after Cora disappeared. She
gave up her job in the capital and came down to stay
with Ben. For a single mother, that was not an easy
thing for her to do.

She put her life on hold for them, when their own lives had been thrown into chaos.

'Ben!' he shouted into the next room. 'Your Auntie Annie and Cousin Stacey are coming for a visit.'

The following morning, Ben headed off to school. It was Friday and the last day before the week-long school holiday. He was still embarrassed about his swooning at the assembly yesterday. Some of the other kids poked fun at him, but he tried to let it pass.

'Hey, Ben Crenshaw!' one of his classmates shouted down the corridor. 'Did that bad Indian man scare you? Do you miss your mommy?' he asked while his buddies doubled over in laughter.
'Forget about them,' Carl said. 'Let them tease away. That's all they got.'

At lunch, Carl asked Ben if he told his father about what had happened during Greyhawk's lecture and his reaction when he touched the Willing Stone.

'No,' Ben said with a shrug. 'I don't want to be worrying him just now. He has plenty to worry about already.'

'Well, I told my dad about it and he thought it was mighty strange,' Carl said. 'He's heard about that Professor guy. He's some kind of expert on Indian rites and their religion he said. He told me he moved here a few weeks ago and has to commute to the university

now. My dad said that he heard he moved here to study some ancient Indian legend and be nearer to the spirits of his ancestors. Mr. Groves at the gas station told him so.'
'So?' Ben asked.

'So maybe you should go see the Professor and find out more. Maybe he knows something. Maybe he has the Indian magic in him. That's what my grandma said.'
'Didn't you call it spooky Indian mumbo jumbo?'
'Well, yeah, but it's *your* mumbo jumbo. That's what Grandma thinks. It's a sign. Your own personal mumbo jumbo.'
'You mean like she thought that thunderstorm a couple of nights back was a sign?' Ben asked with a laugh.
'Don't be laughing. There are signs Grandma says and we have to be on the lookout for them, because some of them may be signs for us.'

All that week, Noah kept leaping for the phone anytime it would ring, but it was never Sunny Days on the other end of the line. He finally accepted that he was not going to be one of the lucky ones who were called back in for an interview. They did not want him. His experience was poison to them, he reckoned, because he would know what the work was really worth.
'Better to give the work to the youngsters and the itinerants from south of the border than those of us who know the score,' he said to himself in resignation.

He walked over to a cupboard and started fishing around for something.

He dragged out some boxes of Christmas ornaments and bags of old clothing and some of Cora's things now consigned to storage.
When he finally found the item he wanted, he said aloud, 'There you are!'

He dusted off the metal detector. He thought while he had no work he could spend some time chancing his luck, looking for scrap metal, and selling it on. He had not used it for years. When Ben was just a little boy, Noah and Cora would ride out in The South Hills and the three of them would have a picnic together. Afterward, he would pick up Ben, help him hold the detector in his little hands, and they would walk together looking for what they told Ben was 'Old Cavalry Gold'. The thought of that made him smile. 'I could do with some old cavalry gold myself just now.'

He planned to rise early and spend a couple of hours with the detector before heading back and getting Ben ready for school.
'A shot in the dark is better than no shot at all,' he rationalized to himself.

On the weekend of Aunt Annie and Cousin Stacey's visit, Ben made sure all his chores were done long before their arrival. He walked down to the bus station, so he could greet them as soon as they arrived.

Since his mother's disappearance, Aunt Annie was the closest thing he had to a mother. She would hold him, when his tears would fall. He could let his guard down, when she was around. He did not have to be strong. He could let himself mourn and she would comfort him.

Finally, after waiting for over an hour, Ben saw a bus pulling into the station. It was the Boise bus. It was Aunt Annie's bus.

'Ben!' Annie shouted as she stepped down from the bus. 'How's my young bronco buster?'
Ben said nothing. He raced over to her and hugged her with all his might. He grabbed her and Stacey's bags after the driver had opened the luggage compartment.

'Are you our greeting party?' Annie teased him.
'Pa's at home,' Ben replied. 'He's getting the room ready for you.'

The three of them walked together to the house. Ben insisted on carrying all their bags himself. He had to stop every few steps to reposition everything.
'Give me my bag, Ben, before you drop it,' Stacey demanded.

Stacey was a year older than Ben and was flowering into quite a young beauty, but Ben was still too naïve to appreciate such things. He still thought of Stacey as a tomboy who liked to 'do stuff' as she would often say. That is how he remembered her and that is how she remained to his mind. She was like the big sister he never had, but wished he did. Someone he could really talk to and whose advice he would heed.

When they arrived at the house, Ben opened the door

and shoved against it with his shoulder so he did not have to put the bags down again.
'Pa! It's Aunt Annie!' he hollered.

After Noah got Annie and Stacey settled, Stacey told Ben she wanted to go outside.
'I've been on that smelly bus for hours. Let's get some fresh air.'

They first walked over to the stable and Stacey made a big fuss over Bess and Willy.
'Let's take them out tomorrow,' Stacey said as she stroked Bess gently.
'I missed you, Girl.'

They started walking side by side past the end of the property. They walked and talked about everything that had happened, since the last time they met, until they found themselves deep out in the surrounding Snake River Plains.

Ben shared everything with Stacey. Everything that is, except for what had happened at the school assembly. He wanted to tell her about Greyhawk. He wanted to tell her about his Willing Stone vision, but he did not know how to begin. He was trying to find the words, when Stacey interrupted his thoughts.

'This is nothing like Boise. There's space here. Space to think and breathe. In the city, there is always someone around. There's always someone who sticks their nose in your business. Here you have freedom,' she said.
'Here you can do stuff and nobody will bother you.'

Ben nodded in agreement. 'I suspect that's so, I guess.'

'And just listen to that, Ben!'

Ben looked around in confusion. 'Listen to what? I don't hear anything.'
'Exactly. There's silence here, Ben. There's quiet too. That's the sound of peace.'
'I never thought of it like that before,' he replied.

They carried on walking for only a few more minutes, when Stacey suddenly looked around at where they were and stopped.

'We better get back, Ben,' she sighed. 'The way Mom's been lately she'll commence thinking we were eaten by black bears. All she knows how to do anymore is worry over nothing.'
And then the tone of their conversation changed dramatically.

'Ben, don't tell Uncle Noah, but Mom needed to come here. Not just to visit. She needs a break from herself. She's worried all the time now. She worries about Uncle Noah, she worries about you, and she worries about me. She worries when my deadbeat dad doesn't send the money he's meant to. She worries about everything and everyone.'
'Pa's like that too,' he said.

'Don't tell what I said, Ben. But you should know. We have to be the grown-ups now. We can't be stupid little kids anymore.'

When it was time to sleep, Annie used the spare room and Stacey and Ben shared his room. He gave Stacey the top bunk where he usually slept and he took the bottom bunk. They kept talking and talking in the darkness.

'I have a boyfriend,' Stacey informed him. 'He's a senior at my high school. Mom doesn't know. His name is Gabriel. Like the angel.'

Ben said nothing and lay there in silence for a moment. 'You still awake, Ben?' Stacey asked. 'Are you asleep?' 'No,' he finally answered. 'There's something I have to tell you.'

He steeled himself and then began to share his story about Greyhawk and the Willing Stone incident. He tried to describe his disturbing vision as best he could. He thought perhaps Stacey could make sense of it all. She might only have been one year beyond Ben's thirteen years, but Ben trusted Stacey's take on things more than anyone else's opinion.

After he finished explaining what had happened at the school assembly, Stacey asked, 'And your friend, Carl, knows where this Professor lives?'
'That's what he said.'
'Then we have to go see him, Ben. I don't know if it's a sign or something like Carl's grandmother claims, but you have to talk to him. You have to find out if he knows something or is just plain loco. We'll go over to Carl's place tomorrow and see what he knows,' she advised.

'Don't you worry. I'll go with you to see this 'Medicine Man'. We'll get to the bottom of this. Me and you. Like detectives on the TV shows. You call your friend Carl in the morning.'

As they both drifted off to sleep, Ben felt like a great weight had been lifted away from him. He slept without tossing and turning. For the first time since his strange Willing Stone vision, those hideous, evil eyes of the shadowy figure haunting his dreams did not haunt him.

CHAPTER
3

Early the following morning, right after breakfast, Ben and Stacey saddled Willy and Bess and rode over to see Carl. As they rode along, Stacey kept asking more questions about Greyhawk and Ben's vision of his mother.

'Did you tell me everything? I won't tell anybody. Not even my mom. You only told your friend Carl and me? No one else knows?'

'Well, you're the only one I told about what I saw, but Carl told his mom and dad what happened at school,' Ben said. 'I wish he didn't. His grandmother too like I told you. His dad is the police chief around here. He's the one who led the search for my mom. I don't want him telling my dad,' he said full of worry.

'Okay,' Stacey replied. 'Don't you concern yourself about it. I'll set Carl and his parents straight.'

When they reached Carl's house, they dismounted, tied off the horses, and made their way to the door. Carl's mother answered.

'Hello, Ben!' she said cheerfully. 'Who's this lovely young lady in your company?'

'I'm his cousin, Stacey, from Boise,' Stacey said proudly.

'From Boise? My, my! A big city girl!' Mrs. Marty said with a smile.

Mrs. Marty invited them inside. Carl's grandmother sat at a table working on a picture puzzle.

'Mrs. Marty, is Carl ready?' Ben asked. 'We're all meant to go out riding this morning. Is he done with his chores yet?'
'Oh yes, he's out in the stable now saddling up Daisy Mae.' She handed Carl a paper bag. 'I made you all some biscuits for when you rest your horses.'
'Thanks, Mrs. Marty,' Ben said appreciatively.

Carl was lovingly brushing Daisy Mae, when Ben and Stacey walked into the stable.

'This is Stacey, Carl,' Ben said. 'Do you remember her? She came down to stay with us right after my mom disappeared.'
Carl blushed. 'Hi, Stacey,' he said shyly.

Carl and Stacey were the same age and he had been dreaming about her from the moment they first met. He never told Ben about that, but he had thought about Stacey countless times since. She was the girl of his dreams even if she knew nothing of it.

'Oh yeah, Carl,' Stacey said vaguely. 'Yeah, now I remember you.'

As Carl started to lead Daisy Mae out of the stable, Stacey said, 'Listen, Carl. You tell your folks to mind their own business about Ben and that Medicine Man. Ben's too quiet to let you know he doesn't want anyone telling his dad what happened. Got it?'

'Okay, Stacey,' Carl said. 'I'll tell them.'

Just to hear Stacey say anything to him made Carl's heart hop.

They rode slowly alongside one another in the hot morning sun and made their way to the Magic Valley. Several times they had to pull up on the side of the road as cars sped past.

'People have no respect,' Stacey seethed. 'The road is for all users. Not just the gas-guzzlers.'

They rode out along the canyon rim and watched for a while as the Snake River meandered its way far below. Ben then turned Willy away and led them inland. The ride out through the valley took them farther and farther into the wilderness until they found themselves completely alone. The sun was still low in the sky and the motionless air carried no breeze. When they found a mutually agreeable spot, they dismounted to rest the horses. They sat on the valley floor and ate some of the biscuits donated by Carl's mother.

'My dad says that Professor Greyhawk moved back to the area,' Carl shared with Stacey. 'My dad says the Professor wants to get back to his tribal roots. Mr. Groves at the filling station told him all about him.'

'Well, we'll all be seeing this Greyhawk guy presently enough,' Stacey said. 'Ben already told me you said he lives around here. We want to know what he thinks he knows. Do you know where he lives?'

'My dad says he bought a lot for his trailer just outside of town.'

They finished eating and remounted their horses. Ben took the lead on Willy as they rode deeper into the valley. Carl rode beside Stacey and stole glances at her, when he thought she was not looking. They continued to make their way in silence only punctuated by Carl's feeble attempts to engage Stacey in conversation.

'My dad says that Boise is a sophisticated place and their policemen have to be on the lookout for trouble all the time,' he said. Stacey said nothing in response and so Carl added, 'My dad says he wouldn't want to wear a badge up there.'

'Your dad says, your dad says! What do you say, Carl?' Stacey snapped back at him.
'Don't know,' Carl said shyly. 'I've never been to Boise before.'

Ben led them up a path that took them above the valley floor. The path was narrow and difficult to navigate on horseback. They had to continue in single file and rode past lichen-covered boulders and sagebrush.
Eventually the path grew wider and Ben cantered Willy for a spell to let him find his feet again. Stacey and Carl cantered behind.

Up ahead, Ben saw that the path forked and led back down to the valley floor. He kept riding at pace until the space opened up into a vast open flat vista.
'Beautiful!' Stacey shouted aloud. 'What a view!'

They stopped for a moment to take in the panorama surrounding them and then Ben continued to lead them forward.

He was some distance ahead of the other two, when he thought he saw something shimmering just ahead of him. It looked like a ripple of water in the low sky. It was there and then it was gone. Ben pulled Willy up short and held up his hand to signal the others. Stacey and Carl rode slowly up to where Ben was waiting.

'What is it?' Carl asked.
'Not sure,' Ben said. 'I thought I saw something.'
Stacey looked ahead and then looked back at Ben.
'Saw what?' she asked.
'Wait,' said Ben as he stared ahead.
'A rattler?' Carl asked nervously.
Shaking his head, Ben said, 'No, it's nothing. Probably just a trick of the sun in my eyes.'

They started to make their way forward again, but within a few paces Willy began to snort and balk. Despite Ben's coaxing, Willy refused to move.

'What's the matter, Boy?' Ben asked. He again tried to ride forward, but Willy just flashed his tail and would not budge.
'What's up with him?' Stacey asked in annoyance.

Carl suddenly started shouting.
'Wait! I see it too, Ben! I see something too! What is that?'
He pointed his finger directly in front of them.

'What do you see?' Stacey demanded.

'The sky is moving,' Carl said. 'Just over there. What is that? Do you see it moving?'

Ben got down out of his saddle and tried to walk Willy forward, but it was impossible. Willy stamped and snorted again and began to rear.

'Whoa. Easy, Boy,' Ben said soothingly.

Ben passed Willy's reins to Carl and walked forward alone to where he first thought he saw the shimmering ripple in the air.

'Don't you see it, Stacey?' Carl said. 'It's like heat vapor off the ground, but in the sky. You have to stare to see it. It comes and goes.'

Stacey turned away to look at Carl as they got off their horses. 'I see nothing. You two trying to play some trick on me?'

'It's not a trick, Stacey.'

They both grabbed their reins and turned back to look at Ben. But there was no sign of him. He was gone. Vanished right in front of them.

They both looked around in shock briefly and then Stacey shouted out wild-eyed, 'Ben! Ben! Where are you? It's not funny. Stop horsing around, you hear?'

She turned back to Carl. 'Where could he go? There's no place but flatland all around us! There's no place to hide!'

Carl grabbed Daisy Mae and Willy's reins and started walking forward to where they had last seen Ben. Stacey did the same with Bess, but as they reached the spot of Ben's disappearance, Willy reared with such passion that Carl lost hold of his reins and was flung to the ground. Willy turned in the opposite direction and bolted away as if on fire.

'Willy!' Stacey screamed after him. 'You get back here! I ain't fooling, Mister! I mean, right now!'
But Willy would not be stopped and all they could hear were his hooves pounding away from them into the distance.

After Stacey gave up on Willy's return, she and Carl both turned back to Ben's last sighting and began to inch forward to the spot again. But Willy's panicked escape spooked Bess and Daisy Mae and they too began to snort, stamp, and rear up.

'Whoa, Girl!' Carl coaxed. But they refused to settle down and go forward.

'We better go back for help, Stacey,' Carl said. He was going to add that he wanted to know what his dad would say, but he knew that would only draw a withering look from Stacey.

They both got on their horses and started riding back to Carl's place. Their worry and confusion tied their tongues and they rode on in utter silence.

CHAPTER
4

Police Chief Marty was still at work, when Stacey and Carl arrived back at the house. Mrs. Marty greeted them with smiles.
'I thought you'd be out a while longer,' she said.
She then craned her neck to look behind them.

'Where's Ben? Did he go home already? I was going to ask you all to stay for supper.'
When she saw the looks on their faces, she asked with concern, 'Is everything all right? Is Ben all right?'

Carl explained as best he could what had happened. Stacey added, 'Mrs. Marty, we don't know where he could've gone and Willy's run off too. We couldn't stop him.'

'Let me call your father, Carl,' Mrs. Marty said seriously. 'You two stay right here. You should not have left Ben out there on his own without a horse.'

Carl's father arrived home only minutes after his wife had called. He had his deputy with him. He walked straight over to Carl.
'Tell me exactly what happened. Tell me exactly where you rode off to. How long has Ben been missing?'

After Carl told him what he knew, Chief Marty said to his deputy, 'Get yourself over to Noah's place right away, Jimmy Junior. Bring him back here and we'll all go out together to search for Ben. Make it quick while we still have the light.'

'Okay, Orin,' Jimmy Junior said as he made his way back outside.

Chief Marty then looked over to Stacey.

'And young lady, you better go with him. We'll mind Bess. Don't you worry about that.'

Carl was settling Bess and Daisy Mae in the stable, when he heard the police cruiser return and pull into the driveway. Noah's Ford Pickup was not far behind. Noah, Stacey, and Annie got out of the car.

'I told you ten times already, Mom, we didn't leave him there!' Stacey said in exasperation. 'We couldn't find him and the horses were acting up. We didn't know what else to do.'

Carl walked over to Noah. 'We lost Willy, Sir. He ran off right after Ben disappeared. We shouted after him, but he wouldn't come back. I'm so sorry.'

'Stacey told us about Willy too,' Noah replied. 'He came home on his own sweating and in quite a state. We feared the worst even before Jimmy Junior arrived and told us what happened.'

'Jimmy Junior drive over to your place and get your horse,' Chief Marty directed him. 'We'll meet up on the edge of town outside your dad's filling station. Noah,

31

you and I will ride out on Bess and Zeno. And Carl, get Daisy Mae ready and show us where you last saw Ben.'

Stacey insisted on going along too, but Annie said, 'No, you stay right here, Stacey. Let them do their job. Carl knows the lay of the land far better than you do.'

They watched as Jimmy Junior drove off and Noah, Chief Marty, and Carl rode away.

While the women waited for the search party's return, Stacey decided to tell Annie about Ben's experience with Greyhawk and what she called 'The Magic Stone' and how he had a strange vision about his mother.

'Why didn't you tell me about this earlier, Stacey?' Annie asked. 'Maybe that's why Ben ran off.'

'He didn't tell Uncle Noah and I didn't tell you neither, because all the pair of you do nowadays is worry,' Stacey said. 'He didn't want his dad worrying about him. Anyway, he didn't 'run off'. I keep telling you that. Why won't you listen? He seemed fine before he went missing. We were all just having fun and then he was gone.'
'You still shouldn't have kept this to yourself,' Annie insisted.

'Don't you go pinning this on me, Mom!' Stacey cried with frustration.
'Carl knew about it too. He told his father. Ask Mrs. Marty, if you don't believe me. We were all planning to go see this Professor Greyhawk to see what was what.

It's why we went out riding in the first place. Carl said his father knew where Greyhawk lived and I wanted to find out more, because Ben was so anxious about what happened.'

Mrs. Marty made them all something to eat and drink. But Stacey could not touch a morsel.

It was dark by the time the search party returned. Chief Marty looked thoroughly drained with concern. He took his wife aside and spoke quietly so the others would not hear.
'There's not a sign of him.'

'Did Carl show you where they were? Couldn't you track Ben?'
'We did, but then the trail went cold. Marian, it's just like with his mother, Cora. It's like he up and vanished.'
'Oh my God, Orin, I can't imagine what Noah must be going through,' Mrs. Marty replied.

Carl was standing next to Stacey and whispered to her under his breath.
'I tried to tell them about the shimmering thing Ben and I saw, but they wouldn't listen. My dad said to keep quiet and keep my eyes peeled for Ben, but there was nothing out there except for a few elk.'

'You took them right to the spot where we lost Ben?' she asked.

'The exact same spot. But that shimmering vapor thing wasn't there anymore.'
'There weren't any signs of him at all?'
'Well, we did find his shoeprints. We followed them, but they didn't lead anywhere. They just stopped.'

'I told my mom what happened to Ben, when that Professor Greyhawk came to his school,' Stacey confessed. 'I didn't want to tell her, but I figured she needed to know. Mom thinks that's why Ben ran off.'

Carl shook his head. 'No, we know he didn't run off, Stacey. We were right there when it happened. We know he didn't run away. We would have seen him. I know you told me to keep my mouth shut about it, but I had to tell Ben's dad about Professor Greyhawk too.'

'Well, what did he say?'
'Nothing, but my dad says that maybe the Professor had something to do with it. My dad says he's going to talk to him about it.'
'Your dad says!' Stacey groaned while shaking her head.

'All right,' Chief Marty said to everyone. 'I'm calling this in first thing tomorrow morning and making it an official missing person's case. The State Troopers will join us in the search tomorrow. For now, there is nothing we can do. Noah, head back to your place. If there's any update before the morning, I'll be sure to get word to you. Let's all get some sleep and be ready to head back out to look for Ben come sunup.'

34

Before they left, Stacey whispered to Carl, 'Tomorrow, you and I are going to see that Professor. I want to talk to him before the police get over there and make him clam up. And don't tell your father!'
'Okay,' Carl said as he nodded bashfully.

Carl sprang out of bed early the following morning. He put on his best shirt, combed his hair, and then went into the bathroom where he applied an overly generous spritz of his father's aftershave. He wanted to look his best for his day out with Stacey. He quickly ate his breakfast and then rode Daisy Mae with Bess in tow over to Noah's house. By the time he arrived there, the search party had already been out for hours scouring the valley for any signs of Ben.

Carl tied off the horses and then rapped on the door. Stacey answered.
'There you are! What took you so long? Let's go. I want to see what this Professor Greyhawk guy thinks he knows,' Stacey said as they walked together toward the horses.

Stacey suddenly stopped and sniffed the air.
'What's that stink?' she asked with a scowl on her face.
'Did a cat piss on you, Carl?'
Carl's face flushed in multiple shades of red.
'I don't smell anything,' he said softly.

Carl climbed up on Daisy Mae and Stacey got atop Bess and the two of them rode off together.

'We'll head toward town first, Stacey, and ask Mr. Groves at the filling station where Greyhawk is living. My dad told me that he knows.'

'Of course, he does,' Stacey replied acerbically. 'Obviously, your dad knows everything.'

Groves Gas Station was just outside of town. They saw the large old enamel sign that read '*James Groves Sr. Auto Services*' and rode up just outside the garage door. Mr. Groves came out to greet them.

'Carl, I hope you don't want me to fill those up with hi-test!' he joked. 'Who's your pretty lady friend?'

After Stacey told him who she was and why she was in town, she gave Carl a sharp nudge in the ribs.

'Go ahead, Carl, ask him. What you waiting for?'

'Something on your mind, young man? You looking to be working for me?'

'No, Mr. Groves,' Carl said timidly. 'It's not about that. Not about work. It's about... um, uh...it's uh... well, my dad said...'

'Oh goodness gracious me!' Stacey blurted out. 'We hear you know where that Professor Greyhawk is living. Is that so? Do you know where he lives?'

'We're hoping he might know something about my friend, Ben, Mr. Groves,' Carl added.

Mr. Groves looked at them both sadly.

'Yeah, I heard about young Ben going missing. My Jimmy Junior's out with Orin and the rest of search and

rescue right now. Terrible for poor Noah.
Makes you wonder why such badness would keep
visiting a family.'

'Yes, Sir,' Carl said and then he asked again, 'Do you
know where Professor Greyhawk lives?'
'I do, Sonny, I do. He had some trouble starting his car
right after he moved back here. I went over to his place
to get him going. I was telling your father. Greyhawk
moved in at the trailer park east of town.'

'Do you know which trailer?' Stacey asked.
'Sure do,' Mr. Groves replied. 'You can't miss it. He's
put Indian hex signs all around his trailer. Not sure
what the neighbors think about that!'

As Carl and Stacey started to ride off on Bess and Daisy
Mae, Mr. Groves teased after them. 'Wait! Would you
like me to check their oil before you head over there?'

When Carl and Stacey reached the trailer park, they
dismounted and walked the horses with them. Not far
away, they saw the trailer Mr. Groves must have
meant. Native American animal totems and symbols
surrounded the trailer.

'This has to be the place,' Stacey said. 'What a mess!'

A simply rendered turtle carving stood on one side of
the entrance to the trailer with a roughly-drawn image
of a bear painted on a bark-stripped log on the other
side.

Suspended on the roof just above the entrance, hung a primitively carved image of a wolf.

As Carl found a place to hitch the horses, Stacey marched up to the trailer door. She knocked on it loudly, but there was no response. She rapped on the door again and hollered.
'Hello? Anyone in? Hello!'

'He's not home?' Carl asked when he rejoined her. Stacey just shrugged and continued knocking at the door as she shouted.
'Professor!'

Eventually, they could hear someone stirring inside.
'Professor Greyhawk?' Carl called through the door.
'Professor, we need to talk with you about Ben, Sir.'

The door finally opened and Greyhawk stood there in his bathrobe, pajamas, and slippers. He let out a yawn, pulled the visor of his baseball cap down over his eyes to block the morning sun, and stood there for a moment staring at them.
'Come on in, Young people. I was expecting you.'

Greyhawk led them into the cramped trailer.
'Sit yourselves,' he said as he cleared away some books from two chairs at his kitchen table.

'Professor,' Carl began. 'We want to talk with you about Ben. You know, the one who got sick at your talk.'
'He wasn't sick, Young man. Well, maybe travel sick.'

'What do you mean 'travel sick', Mister?' Stacey asked.
'Never you mind, Young lady,' he said. 'What can I do for you?'

'My cousin Ben is missing,' Stacey told him. 'And Carl says you might know what's going on. We were out riding yesterday and he plum vanished. Out in the Magic Valley.'

Greyhawk walked over to the sink in the tiny kitchenette, filled a kettle, turned on the gas ring, and started to make some tea.
'Yes,' he muttered softly. 'I feared something like this might happen.'

He poured the boiling water into a teapot and brought it and three mugs back with him to the table.

As he began pouring the tea, Greyhawk said, 'I came back to this area to study a local legend I stumbled upon during my research at the university. I read a few stories about it written down over the years from tribal oral tradition. The local tribes call it The Legend of the Blue Cloud.'
He stopped for a moment and sipped his tea.

'I thought it was just another of their dream myths, but when I saw what happened to Ben after he touched the Willing Stone, it seemed to match some of the stories I'd read. They spoke about similar 'transportations'. According to the Legend, your Ben was marked by hostile spirits once they discovered he had the Gift of the Stone.'

'These spirits hope to lure those with the Gift through the Blue Cloud. He was spotted there, when he touched the Willing Stone at school, and these malevolent creatures then looked for their chance to trap him.'

Stacey glanced over in confusion at Carl. 'Do you know what the hell he's talking about?' she muttered at him. Carl just looked at her blankly, shrugged his shoulders, and had a sip of his previously untouched tea. Stacey gave him a disapproving look and then turned her attention back to Greyhawk.

'What the hell are you talking about, Mister? What exactly do you know about my cousin, Ben?'

'Young lady,' Greyhawk replied. 'There are things your Western world does not know and refuses to know. There are dark things all around us hoping to do us mischief and torment us whether you want to believe it or not. Your Ben has the Gift of the Stone. I saw it there that day at school, because I have read much about it and know the signs. The Legend claims he was then transported through the Blue Cloud where these vile things were sent by the spirit guides of my ancestors.'

'When your settlers and cavalry soldiers invaded our lands, they brought more than death and disease with them. They brought old and powerful dark forces from their European lairs with them too. This is why I guard myself with the symbols of protection for my people. These symbols protect the land from evil spirits transported here from what you call the Old World.'

40

'The 'agwai' or bear symbol beside my door is a sign of protection for this abode. The wolf sign above my door is another example of symbolic protection from dark spirits. They represent the Great Spirit who protects us from the malicious spirit forces brought here by the European invaders. Like the one my people call White Eyes.'

Carl sat there stunned. He did not know how to react to what he was hearing.
Stacey, on the other hand, knew exactly what she thought.

'Who the living daylights is White Eyes?' she asked with a frown. 'And what the heck is Blue Cloud? Do you speak any English? You ain't making any sense at all, Mister.'

Greyhawk smiled briefly at Stacey and then had another sip of his tea.

'There is more sense than you know about, Young lady,' he continued. 'There's more than your Western sense. Your Ben has the Gift. He touched the Willing Stone and it transported him to White Eyes' den. This malignant creature plots to ensnare all those who possess the Gift and imprison them in his domain. White Eyes is the name my ancestors gave to the most powerful of all the dark spirits brought to our lands by the Westerners in their arrogant ignorance.'

'The Legend states that the spirit guides of my people caged White Eyes and the spiteful spirits in his service in an alternate world behind the Blue Cloud. The Willing Stone is the key to gain entrance to and exit from this world via the vision it evokes.'

'The Blue Cloud phenomenon is a deadly danger to all of us. Innocent people can wander right through the Blue Cloud and become marooned there without knowing, because it is not easy to see. Folks think they see clear blue sky and do not notice the Cloud, the disturbance, and walk or ride straight through.'

Carl gulped nervously. He had another sip of tea before he said, 'Ben and I saw something in the sky right before he vanished. It looked like some kind of sparkling vapor in the air. We couldn't get a fix on it though. It seemed to move and come and go.'

'I didn't see anything,' Stacey said dismissively. 'Sparkling or otherwise.'

'Like I say,' Greyhawk replied. 'Not all can see it. That doesn't mean it isn't there.'
His tone then changed gravely.

'I fear no one will find your Ben on this side of the divide. You tell Ben's people to come and see me. I fear their son is in great danger. Those with the Gift are a threat to White Eyes, because they can warn others of his evil intent. If he has his clutches on Ben, he won't willingly let him go. White Eyes and his followers, who my people call the Grinning Dogs, are vain, arrogant, and heartless. Like the cavalry soldiers they infested.'

'These are beings who exult in their own power. They only exist to destroy what is good. It is their pleasure to do so. Go. Bring Ben's parents here. Tell them to hurry. Time is of the essence.'

Carl decided that he better tell Greyhawk about Ben's mother and her disappearance.
'It was just over a year or so ago,' he told him. 'It's just like what happened to Ben. She was out riding on her own and never returned.'

'Then this is far worse than I feared,' Greyhawk said with a shake of his head. 'White Eyes may have been plotting to get his hands on Ben for some time. It is possible that he has been using his mother like a candle luring a moth.'

'Wait,' Stacey said. 'Hold your horses. I don't understand. Are you saying Ben's with my Aunt Cora?'
Greyhawk looked at her and nodded somberly.

'He may be. At this moment, I am still unsure. It would be rash of me to say more now. Tell Ben's father to come and see me. I will try to explain my fears about the fate of Ben and his mother.'

Carl thanked Greyhawk and then he and Stacey went back outside, remounted Bess and Daisy Mae, and began their journey home.

Carl was unsure what to do about what Greyhawk had told them. He was just about to ask Stacey what she thought, when she interrupted him.

'I hope you really didn't drink any of that tea, Carl! That guy is a total whack job. I sure as hell didn't drink any of his witch's brew!'

Carl said nothing while trying his best not to look concerned. He quickly changed the subject.

'So what do you think, Stacey?' he asked as they rode along together. 'How can we tell Ben's dad what Professor Greyhawk said? Even if it is true, how could we explain it to him? I'll ask my dad what he thinks, I guess.'

Stacey glared at Carl and shook her head.
'Maybe this is the one time in your life, Carl, when you don't tell your father every single, blasted thing. I want to get my head around what this batty professor had to say before you start blabbing to the adults. You keep this to yourself. You hear me? I think that's what Ben wants too.'

CHAPTER
5

Ben walked cautiously toward the strange ripple in the sky glimmering in front of him. He could hear Willy snorting anxiously behind him. He reached out his hand toward the ripple as he heard Stacey speaking with Carl.

'I see nothing. You two trying to play a trick on me?'

'It's not a trick, Stacey.'

Ben took another step forward and suddenly felt his head spinning. He bent over, shook his head to clear it, and then looked back up. Panic rushed through him. He shook his head again afraid to believe what he was seeing. He looked around frantically at where he was in terror. He trembled with fear that he was back in the monochrome, sepia-tinted world he had seen in his vision at school.

Ben spun around to look for Carl and Stacey. He could just about make them out as they went in and out of focus. He heard Stacey shout, 'Ben! Ben!', but her words sounded muffled and faint. 'Ben, where are you? Stop horsing....' And then he could no longer see or hear them. It was as if he were swallowed in an opaque bubble. He was alone.

He took a few tentative steps forward. It was easier to move than it was when he had his vision. Then everything was distorted and he was unsure of his footing, but now he could move around easily enough. Every single thing was as colorless as before, like a nineteenth century tinted photograph, but the landscape seemed more stable. The ridges of the valley were not moving toward him and then quickly away like they were when he held the Willing Stone. He did not feel sick to his stomach like he did then, but he was as frightened and uneasy as he was during his vision. He did not know for certain where he was, but to his mind it appeared to be the same disturbing place he had visited in his trance at the school assembly.

He glanced down at his feet and saw he was standing atop a hill. He stood still for a moment to try to make sense out of where he found himself. He scanned the horizon. In the distance, what looked like a herd of buffalo were wildly stampeding out of control. Overhead, a kettle of vultures circled screeching in alarm. A mother bear and her cubs appeared out of nowhere and raced past him as if they were trying to escape from something. They ignored Ben's presence as if he were not there.
Like he was invisible to them.

He had just started to make his way down the hill, when without warning two teenagers on mountain bikes hurtled right at him. He dived out of the way before they ran him down.
'Where did they come from? Why couldn't they see me?' he thought to himself as he dusted himself off.

Nothing made any sense. He kept seeing different groups of animals and birds as he walked. They were racing and flying around in panic like they had all gone mad. None of them paid any notice to Ben even if they were close enough for him to reach out and touch.

Ben patted his head and chest to check if he was still physically present. He nodded to himself that he was actually there and not some invisible phantom.
'What is this place? Where am I? Why didn't those two bikers and those animals see me?' he asked himself in confusion.

He continued to walk and went down a steep path that took him to this other-worldly valley floor. He tried to calm himself and breathed deeply. He decided to keep making his way forward. Maybe he would see someone who could tell him where he was and how to leave. Then he stopped dead still as an awful thought washed over him. Maybe those winged creatures were lying in wait for him. Maybe the one with the dreadful, malicious eyes was there with them.

He tried to compose himself as he carried on walking along the valley floor to explore this inexplicable place, when suddenly he heard loud shouting coming from behind him. He turned around quickly to see what it was and froze in shock. A hundred of more braves in war-paint and on horseback were galloping fiercely at him. He ran over to the face of the ridge to get out of their way as they whooped their way past him.

But just like with the animals, birds, and bikers he had encountered earlier, it was as if the war party could not see him.

He sat down and watched the braves race off together down the valley until they were out of sight.

'What is going on?' he asked himself. 'There haven't been any tribes on the warpath around here for over a century.'
But then he remembered that he was not on home ground. He was not home. He was in this strange place. This was his home now.

He sat there resting against the face of the ridge for he did not know how long. Was it safer to stay still? Should he keep moving? Should he look for cover? He did not know what to do. As he sat there, he looked up to the dull and soulless sky as more flocks of birds flew by helter-skelter looking for direction. He could not guess how long he had been in this place, but the sky had not grown any darker in all the time he had been there.

'Maybe I should go back to where I started,' he thought. 'Maybe I should have stayed put.'

He got up to retrace his steps, but everything seemed different somehow. He could not find the steep path that had brought him down to the floor of the valley. He went this way and that, but wherever he went nothing seemed familiar. It was as if in trying to find out where he was and getting back to the spot where he was last with Stacey and Carl, only succeeded in making him more disoriented.

He thought he had no choice. As terrified as he was

about coming across those winged monstrosities with their evil-eyed master, he began to shout aloud.

'Hello? Can anyone hear me? Is anyone there? Hello!' He cupped a hand to his mouth and called out loudly in every direction. But there was no response. He felt somewhat relieved however that he could hear the sound of his own voice.

He started to lose all track of time. Nothing seemed to change. The light, the sky, the stationary clouds, they all remained just as they were as when he first arrived. Everything stayed the same as if time had stood still. And yet when he tried to find his way, everywhere he walked seemed new and unfamiliar. A shudder went through him.
'What if I am alone here?' he wondered. 'What if I am lost here forever?'

He began to panic and cry out in fear.
'Mom! Can you hear me? Ma! Are you here? It's Ben, Mom! Help me!'
He started running as he shouted until he was out of breath. He dropped his head and began to sob.

He stood there crying and sniffling back his tears, when a voice whispered in his ear.
'Be quiet!'

He jumped back in shock and fearfully spun on his heels to confront the voice. There in front of him stood a small Native American boy dressed in clothes made of stripped tree bark and fur.

'Be quiet,' the boy said again. 'They will hear you. They want you to show fear.'

'Where did you come from?' Ben asked cautiously.
'Who are you?'

'I am Bird-Who-Hops,' he answered. 'You must not shout. They can hear like a bat. You must show no fear. If you do, they will come. Fear to them is a strong scent and they can follow its trail. Like a snake to the eggs.'

'Who will come?' Ben asked.
'They will. They will come.'

CHAPTER
6

At first light, Police Chief Marty rapped hard on the trailer door. Jimmy Junior stood beside him.

'Professor Greyhawk!' Chief Marty shouted. There was no response and so he continued knocking on the door. 'Professor, it's the police. I'm Police Chief Orin Marty. We have a search warrant for your premises. Professor, please, this is a police matter. Let us in!'

Greyhawk blinked in the sunlight as he opened the door.
'What's this all about?' he asked with a yawn.

As they entered the trailer, Chief Marty said, 'I am the police chief in these parts and this is my deputy, Jimmy Groves Junior. We are here in the matter of the disappearance of young Ben Crenshaw.'
'Did you say you had a search warrant?' Greyhawk asked.
'Yes, Professor, we do.'

Jimmy Junior brushed past Greyhawk and immediately began to search through the trailer as Chief Marty motioned for Greyhawk to sit down.

'Professor, my boy, Carl, told me what happened at his school when you were there. He said you told Ben that you knew where he went and knew who he lost. And

now he's lost. You can understand why we think you may know something about why he's gone missing.'
'Am I under arrest?' Greyhawk asked anxiously.
'No, Professor. But you are a person of interest in our inquiries.'

As Greyhawk watched Jimmy Junior rummaging through his property, he said, 'Chief, please tell your deputy to be careful. I have some very old Native American artifacts here. Some are quite fragile.'

Chief Marty stood up and called Jimmy Junior over to him.
'Go easy,' he said. And then he added under his breath, 'Check every drawer, every cabinet, look for anything that might belong to Ben or Cora Crenshaw.'
Jimmy Junior nodded and went back to his search.

Chief Marty sat down again and turned his attention back to Greyhawk.
'So, is what my boy said true, Professor?' he asked.
'Yes, what your son said is so. I did briefly speak to young Ben after his strange reaction during my short talk to the students. I have heard of such things before.'

'What things, Professor?'
'There are some who are strongly affected by Native American totems and symbols. I believe Ben is such a person.'

'Professor, I know about your work at the State University. Mr. Groves told me about you after the two of you met. I make it my business to find out what I can about new-comers to the area. He said you claimed to be a respected authority on local tribal rites and their religion. I can appreciate that, but I think you need to consider what effect sharing that knowledge with youngsters might have. They are impressionable. Ben especially so, since his mother, Cora Crenshaw, disappeared.'

Jimmy Junior walked over to where they were sitting. He whispered in Chief Marty's ear. 'Orin, there's nothing of interest here. About Ben or Cora Crenshaw anyway.'
'Okay. Thanks, Jimmy Junior. Go ahead and wait in the patrol car. I won't be long with Professor Greyhawk. I'll be along in a few minutes or so.'

After Jimmy Junior left the trailer, Greyhawk said, 'Officer, did your son tell you about what I had to say, when he and his young lady friend paid me a visit?'

A look of surprise crossed Chief Marty's face.
'My Carl came here to see you? Funny that he didn't mention it to me. Or to his mother as far as I know. That's not like him.'

'That may be so, but he was here early yesterday morning with that young Stacey girl. From what they told me about Ben's disappearance, I fear something mysterious and rather worrying may have happened to Ben. What they told me fits the facts of an old Shoshone tribal myth called The Legend of the Blue Cloud. I have been studying this and other Shoshone dream myths and I expressed my concern about what they told me.'

Chief Marty gave Greyhawk a disapproving look. 'Professor, this is what I was just saying to you. You have to be careful what you say to young people. Now tell me exactly why you think this mysterious thing has happened to Ben?'

'As for why, I am not yet sure. I told Carl and Stacey that this was an urgent matter and Ben's father needed to come and see me right away. I told them Ben may be in danger.'

'In danger? In danger from what? In danger where? Are you saying you know where he is?'
'I believe I might. I believe it does have something to do with what happened to Ben on the day I came to his school.'

'And you think you may know something about the disappearance of Cora Crenshaw as well? My son told me that you claimed you knew where the one Ben lost is. Do you know where she is?'

'Perhaps I do. I know this all may sound rather fantastical to you. I think though that it is important that Ben's father, you, and anyone else involved in this situation meet and discuss it together. I am hoping you may be willing to arrange just such a meeting. Soon. There may be something going on which is beyond the powers of the police to solve.'

'All right, Professor,' Chief Marty said after a pause. 'We'll leave it like that for now. I only want to find Ben. That's my only interest. If you are willing to share everything you think you know, I will get everyone together. In the meantime, please do not leave the area. Once I've contacted Ben's father, Noah, I will get back to you.'

'Finding young Ben is my only interest too,' Greyhawk replied.

Chief Marty got back into the patrol car. He sat there silently for a minute or so trying to size up Greyhawk.

'Orin?' Jimmy Junior asked. 'What did he say? Did you find out what's going on? Does he know anything about Ben Crenshaw?'

'Never you mind for now, Jimmy Junior. We have some work to do. Drive us over to Noah's place.'

CHAPTER
7

'Who will come?' Ben asked Bird-Who-Hops again.
'You know. If you touched the Stone, you saw him and his Dogs. They will come.'

Ben swallowed nervously. He thought again about his Willing Stone vision and the monster haunting his dreams.
'I'm Ben,' he said while trying not to panic. 'When I touched the Stone, I had a dream of this place. But what is this place? Where are we?'

'Through the Blue Cloud of course. Do you not know?' Bird-Who-Hops then looked at Ben suspiciously.
'You are not of my tribe. How did you come to touch the Stone?'

Ben began to tell Bird-Who-Hops about Greyhawk and all that had happened that day at the school assembly. He shared with him what he saw during his unsettling vision. He told him about his terrifying nightmares, since the day he held the Willing Stone in his hand. He did not really know why he felt so comfortable sharing his story with a little boy, but Bird-Who-Hops seemed so self-assured and confident that he felt safe in confiding in him. He felt some relief in finally telling someone who might be able to explain what it all meant.

'Then I was out riding with my friends and saw this strange sparkling wrinkle in the sky. I put my hand through it and the next thing I knew I was here. What about you? How did you come to be here?'

Bird-Who-Hops let out a long, sad sigh. He struggled to remain calm as he remembered.

'Our medicine man once showed me the Stone. When I touched it, I had a vision of this place. I saw terrible things just as you did. Then one evening, Pony Soldiers came and raided my village. They were hunting for Chief Pocatello and his braves. They drove their horses through our grass houses and burned our lodge. Then they ran their horses through our elders and trampled our children to save their bullets. Many died badly. I ran away to hide from them and did not notice the Blue Cloud in front of me. And so I am here.'

'Pony Soldiers?' Ben asked. 'When was that? When did Pony Soldiers come to your village?'
'Soon after the War between the White Men began,' Bird-Who-Hops answered softly.
'You mean the Civil War? You've been in this place since the Civil War?'

Ben's mind was spinning. 'This is impossible,' he thought to himself. 'I must be dreaming.'
Then he said aloud to Bird-Who-Hops, 'How long do you think you've been here?'

'I do not know. Time does not pass here. We do not eat. We do not sleep.'

Ben did not know what to make of what Bird-Who-Hops had said. How can someone live if they do not eat or sleep? But he did understand that Bird-Who-Hops knew this surreal world. Maybe he could make some sense of it too.

'I don't understand what's real and what isn't real in this place,' Ben said. 'I saw a tribe of braves on the warpath earlier, but they acted like they didn't see me. The animals and birds too. They don't react to me. It's like I wasn't there.'

'No,' Bird-Who-Hops said quietly. 'They do not have the Gift of the Stone. They do not know they are lost. They do not know they are through the Blue Cloud. They carry on with whatever they were doing, when they passed through. Only those with the Gift of the Stone are aware of where they are.'

Bird-Who-Hops gestured at Ben to follow him.
'To speak aloud in the open is very dangerous. Like all the Pales, you speak too loudly and too much. Come. I take you to our Gathering Place. There are others like us there.'

As Ben followed along behind Bird-Who-Hops, he asked, 'How can you find your way around here? I just keep going in circles, whenever I try to go anywhere or retrace my steps.'

'Do not believe your eyes,' he answered. 'Follow your nose instead. Look to the sky. It never changes. That will show you the way.'

They continued along together in silence for quite some time. After they had made their way up and down yet another rocky hill, Bird-Who-Hops stopped suddenly, sniffed the air, and held his hand up to signal Ben to stop and listen.

'Blue Coats,' he whispered softly.

He pushed Ben to the side of the path they were taking.

Ben looked around, but could see nothing. He then heard a faint sound ring out in the distance. The sound grew louder and closer until swinging around a bend, a troop of cavalry soldiers appeared. With their bugles blaring, Ben watched as the troop charged forward with their sabers drawn. He could see the blood-thirsty look in their eyes as they galloped past just a few feet from where they were standing.

'They chase what they imagine they see,' Bird-Who-Hops said as the troop rode off into the distance. 'I have seen them countless times before. They sound their bugle calls and charge forward again and again and again. They think they are on the trail of the hunt for their prey.'

'And if they ever did come across their prey?' Ben asked. 'What would happen?'

'Nothing,' he answered. 'Nothing at all. They would not see one another and just pass through unharmed and unaware. Like the shadows of two squaws crossing one another's path.'

Bird-Who-Hops then warned Ben that his fate would not be the same.

'We've lost many who failed to find cover in time and were crushed to death. Those with the Gift must get out of the way,' he said as he began to lead them on again.

Ben kept his eyes firmly fixed on Bird-Who-Hops. He feared that if he lost sight of him, he would never find him again. It was difficult to keep up. Bird-Who-Hops moved very quickly and stealthily. Ben had to race to stay up with him.

'We must hurry!' Bird-Who-Hops commanded. 'Can you not hear? White Eyes has heard your cries of fear and he is coming!'

'Who's White Eyes?' Ben asked nervously. 'I don't hear anything.'
'Can you not smell him then? Soon, you will come to know his scent. He is coming! Quickly! Look! The dark plumes are in the air!'

'Plumes?' Ben asked perplexed.
'Yes! Hurry!' Bird-Who-Hops said already on the move.

They both began to run and after jumping down from a ledge not far off the ground, Bird-Who-Hops led Ben into an area strewn with loose rocks and many large and broken boulders. He jumped from one large boulder to the next with Ben scrambling behind. Ben saw there was a narrow gap between two of the largest boulders. He watched as Bird-Who-Hops squeezed himself through the crevice.

'This way!' he said as he disappeared down the hole.

Ben followed Bird-Who-Hops into the tight space between the boulders and wriggled his way down. He could barely see and had to feel for his footing with his feet.

'Keep going,' he heard Bird-Who-Hops call out in the darkness below him.

After a few yards in the cramped space, the gap widened and Ben kept climbing down until Bird-Who-Hops called out from beneath him.

'Jump!'

Ben closed his eyes and jumped. He landed in a heap onto a flat and rocky surface.

'Come. Follow me,' Bird-Who-Hops said.

They walked along the rocky floor in silence until it opened up into a wide open space. Ben looked up and saw the fallen boulders formed a sort of canopy above them which allowed some light to shine down on where they were standing.

'We are here,' Bird-Who-Hops announced.

Ben looked around and saw four other people were already there. He could not make out their faces in the dim light. Three of them came out from behind the shadows and greeted Bird-Who-Hops.

'He is coming,' Bird-Who-Hops said to the others. 'I found this New One, Ben, crying out in fear. He does not yet know. White Eyes has surely sensed his fear and will come. Hide away now!'

Ben looked on as Bird-Who-Hops and the three who had greeted him scurried away into the shadows.

'Wait! What do I do?' Ben called after them.
'Where do I go?'

'Come with me, Ben,' a voice from the shadows said.

Ben blinked his eyes to try to focus in the dim light.
'Who said that?' he asked.

'It's me, Ben,' someone said as they emerged from the gloom.
'It's Mom.'

CHAPTER
8

That evening, everyone committed to finding Ben met together at Chief Marty's house. Carl's grandmother helped Mrs. Marty make some coffee and Carl brought it out to the living room. Everyone looked apprehensively at one another. Three days had now passed and there still was no sign of Ben.

Greyhawk got up on his feet. He looked around the room for attention.
'What I am about to share with you may sound beyond believing. I only ask that you hear me out.'
'Go ahead, Professor,' Noah said.

'As I told Carl and Stacey when they came calling, this rippled or shimmering phenomenon that they claim they saw is what is known as the Blue Cloud. In my tribal culture and tradition, a medicine man can contact the Great Spirit and create via certain rites and ceremonies a sort of warp or tear in space and time. It is used to banish dark spirits away from our world. From my research at the university, I learned my ancestors believed an especially belligerent and wicked spirit came to this area brought here by early European settlers, soldiers, and traders. This spirit is known as White Eyes in my tradition. The Hebraic tradition refers to it as Remiel, a malignant spirit with wings. Many world cultures refer to this being. He is always described as winged and hostile in intent.'

'He has many servants who do his bidding. In the ancient Hebrew texts, these are referred to as the Grigori. In the tradition of the local Native American tribes, they are called the Grinning Dogs.'

'Come now, Professor!' Chief Marty interrupted. 'Grigori, grinning dogs, and dark spirits! Please! How does this help us find Noah's son? We don't need a school lecture. What we need are facts. What do you know that is useful in finding the boy?'

'Orin Marty!' Carl's grandmother called out from her rocking chair. 'How many times have I told you to keep an open mind over matters? There are strange things that we do not know. There is more than one way to skin a cat. Haven't I always told you that?'
'Yes, Mom,' Chief Marty said a bit embarrassed.

'There are all kinds of strangeness, Orin,' Carl's grandmother said. 'Don't you forget that. Now you let the man speak.'

'Chief, I do understand,' Greyhawk said patiently. 'I know we need to find Ben. It is important though that you let me explain to everyone what I think is going on here.'
Chief Marty shrugged at him to continue.

'I am telling you this, because what I saw happen to Ben at school that day and what I was told happened, when he vanished, matches precisely some of the historical accounts and records I have studied,' Greyhawk explained.

'Centuries ago, when the first Europeans came to this area, legend has it that the local medicine men from all the surrounding tribes convened. There was famine and disease all around this part of Idaho. The tribal elders decided that these plagues were the result of an unclean and previously unknown dark spirit brought here by these European outsiders. They called for a gathering of the medicine men to drive this evil entity out. They created the Blue Cloud as a trap, an alternate reality, which would bind White Eyes and lesser unclean spirits in league with him forever. To do this, the myth states, they cast their magic into ceremonial stones and drew in the sky with these enchanted stones to form, for want of a better phrase, a time and space anomaly. These stones became known as Willing Stones. The gathering and rites of the medicine men willed, by drawing with these stones, the Blue Cloud to come into being and for this entity, White Eyes, to be trapped within it. This is the Legend of the Blue Cloud according to our folklore.'

Everyone looked around at one another. No one knew how to react to what Greyhawk was saying. Finally, Chief Marty stood up.

'Professor, we are simple and, I hope, honest folk. Let me see if I have this straight. Are you saying that Ben Crenshaw is in this Blue Cloud warp thing you just described? You must admit. It all sounds a bit whacky.'

'I fear he may be lost beyond the Blue Cloud as mad as that may sound to you. These Willing Stones allegedly have a power all their own for those who hold the Gift.'

'Believe me,' Greyhawk continued. 'I thought all this was myth and legend myself. I go to many schools. I show them the Willing Stone. I tell the same story. Nothing ever happened before.'

'But when I saw Ben affected as he was, when he touched the Stone, with his writhing, cramps, and confusion, it was right out of the folklore. The Legend mentions this Stone as a key to gain entrance, via a vision, through the Blue Cloud. These stories describe the dark world where White Eyes is trapped. They talk about people and wildlife obliviously unaware that walk through this split in the fabric of space and time and are never seen again. They describe those with the Gift of the Stone who can observe this dark world and return. Noah, I believe your Ben has the Gift of the Stone. I saw it there that day at his school. I believe he then walked through the Blue Cloud, when out with his friends, and that is why he is nowhere to be found.'

'And what about his mother?' Noah asked. 'Is she there too? Isn't that what you told Orin?'

'I do not want to build false hope, but she may well be. I think he saw her there. He called out for her as he was coming back from his vision.'

'So how do we get them back home?' Stacey asked thoroughly fed up. 'What good is all this yakking, if we can't get Ben and Aunt Cora back? Is it possible or isn't it?'

Greyhawk nodded. 'There may be a way.'

CHAPTER
9

Cora led Ben deeper into the shadows of the Gathering Place where Bird-Who-Hops had taken him. She whispered, 'We must be still and silent. The ruler of this world feeds on fear and confusion. You weren't to know. Try to remain calm. If you show no fear, they cannot sense you here. We are together now, Ben, and I won't let anything happen to you.'
And they held one another close, mother and son, together.

Suddenly, above them, they heard a fluttering of wings. 'Be still, be silent,' Cora said in hushed tones. 'Think of us together and don't be afraid.'

Ben watched, trying his best not to be frightened, as a dark-winged figure appeared on top of the boulder canopy. Instantaneously, he saw six more of these creatures materialize behind him. They were the same terrifying creatures he had seen in his vision with the Willing Stone.

'Where is the one known as Ben?' the dark-winged figure bellowed below. 'I heard his cries. I know he is near. Do you think you can hide him from me? You of the absurd Brotherhood who still refuse to fear me? In time, you will all fear me. I will sense his fear and claim you all.'

The creature and his entourage then opened their wings and lifted their noses in the air. Ben struggled not to cry out in fear. Cora tried to calm him by holding him closer to her.

'I can pick up no scent, My Lord,' one of the creatures behind their dark-winged leader finally said.
'Nor I,' another of the six added. 'I sense no fear.'

Their master then lowered his wings and the others with him immediately followed suit.

'Know this, the one known as Ben,' their leader sneered contemptuously. 'You dare spy upon me with that vile Stone? For that disrespect, your suffering will be greatest. You do not know what pain means, Child. I will teach you. I will make you squeal in agony beyond all endurance. You have fallen through my door and into my domain. The Brotherhood of the Gift protecting you from me will not save you. I have you now. I have your mother. I have the other hapless fools here who hold the Gift of the Stone. Soon, I will lure all with the Gift from your world to mine and then I will be free to venture forth again away from this prison. Then all will be at my mercy. All will be mine as before.'

The others with him began giggling in malevolent glee. Their empty, mirthless laughter filled those hiding below with dread.

The creature and his retinue then morphed into black pillars of smoke. The dark and spinning pillars rose slowly upward and then in an instant were gone.

One by one, they all came out from their hiding places and gathered back together in the wide open space beneath the canopy.

Ben's heart was racing. He was panting to try to catch his breath. He turned and looked to the others.
'Who were they? Was that White Eyes? Why couldn't they see us? They were standing right above us,' he asked still in shock.

'They cannot see us, because White Eyes and his Grinning Dogs cannot see,' Bird-Who-Hops explained. 'I don't understand. They're blind? They can't see?' Ben asked trying to grasp what he was hearing.

'No, at least not in the way we see,' Bird-Who-Hops replied. 'They have no eyes. Only large, white gleaming beads where their eyes should be. But they can hear the slightest sound. Their sense of smell can find anyone who betrays their fear. It is why we must not speak loudly or be afraid. Then they can 'see'. Then they can count the hairs on your head. Anyone they find, who has the Gift, is driven to madness. We have lost several to him in this way.'

Ben nodded nervously at what Bird-Who-Hops had to say.
'And what about the Brotherhood of the Gift?' he asked. 'What did White Eyes mean? Who's the Brotherhood?'

'In this diabolical place, we are,' someone in the Gathering Place grunted.

'All who share the Gift and do not serve White Eyes make up the Brotherhood,' Cora said. 'White Eyes plots to lure all with the Gift here. Then he can break the bonds of this world and turn our own world into his domain. He and his minions never tire boasting of that in their vanity.'

'All of us here have the Gift,' a man dressed in buckskin and wearing a fur hat said. 'Some of us knew, because they touched the Stone and visited here. Like your mother. But others of us here did not know about the Stone or that we possessed the Gift until we came here through the Cloud.'

He cleared his throat and announced proudly, 'I am Henri Cherbot, the French explorer and cartographer. Surely you have heard of me?'
Ben smiled and nodded even if he had never heard of Henri.

'I was given a Royal Commission to map the unexplored lands of the New World. Guides from the local tribes assisted me. One day, we were all out in our canoes, when I saw a glistening ripple just above the river. I signaled for my guides to wait and paddled forward to examine it. I thought it might be a new natural feature unknown to us in Europe. One of my guides shouted a warning to me, but I ignored him and took my canoe through it. This is how I found myself here in this place.'

'Welcome to the Brotherhood, Ben,' a sunny voice said.

Ben turned to the voice calling to him and an exquisitely attractive young woman with a beaming smile strolled over and wrapped him in a hug.

'So you're Cora's son, Ben?' she asked excitedly. 'I'm Mei-Ling. I'm so pleased to meet you! Your mother has told me so much about you! I feel like I already know you!'
She kissed Ben on both cheeks. He blushed brightly in his embarrassment.

'I'm from China. Mei-Ling is my stage name. I'm a dancer and performing artiste. I was on my way to San Francisco to entertain the miners, when our wagon train was captured. The local tribe took us to their camp. Their medicine man showed me the Willing Stone. I don't know why, but I was utterly entranced by it. I felt compelled to pick it up. I held the Stone in my hand and had a frightful vision of this place. Then one summer morning, when I was out with the other women picking berries, I saw the sky shift and sparkle. When I walked over to it to see what it was, I found I was transported here.'

Behind Ben, a deep and low voice said, 'You will show no fear. If you do, we're all at those monsters' mercy.' Ben turned to see who was talking to him and a giant of a man stood before him.

'The name's Frank. I was an Indian trader. I have the Gift of the Stone too. Not that I knew it,' he grumbled. 'Early one evening, after trading for animal pelts, I was heading back to my cabin when I saw the sky shaking.'

'I went over, like a fool, to have a closer look. The next thing I knew I was in this godforsaken place.'
Then he added, 'This is no place for a child. You must not act as one. Like Bird-Who-Hops does not act as one.'

Ben looked around at the others. He was still shaken by White Eye's appearance. His only thought was to leave this place.
'Is there no escape from here?' he asked. 'Are we all going to be trapped here forever?'

'We all hope for escape,' Cora replied. 'You must never give up hope, Ben. There may be a way.'

'But has anyone ever escaped before? Do you know someone who did?'
'In time, I will explain everything to you,' Cora said. 'But for now, it is important to remember that you must not give up hope. Hopelessness leads to fear and fear is our greatest enemy here.'

Cora then took Ben aside. She looked at him with her eyes still tearful at seeing her son again and cuddled him close.

'Tell me, Ben. Tell me how you came to be here. White Eyes said that you saw him through the Willing Stone. Is that so or was that another of his lies?'

'Don't you remember, Mom? I did see him. I saw you too when I was here. I saw White Eyes and his flying Dogs. He grabbed you and I couldn't do anything about it. Did he hurt you, Mom? You looked so terrified. I kept seeing you and White Eyes in my dreams. His eyes! I couldn't get them out of my mind. I was afraid to sleep. Every time I did, I had nightmares.'

Cora stroked his hair and kissed him.
'No, Ben,' she said softly. 'No, he didn't harm me. Anyone who has the Gift of the Stone and has a vision of this place only sees what White Eyes wants them to see. You saw this place and then you saw the thing you feared most. He feeds on our fears. What you saw was not real. He didn't capture me, but he wanted you to think he had to terrorize you. Everyone who has a Willing Stone vision of this world says the same thing. White Eyes only allows us to see the things he wants us to see.'

'Is that what happened, when you had your vision?' Ben asked. 'You touched the Stone too. Isn't that what Henri said?'

'Do you remember when I went upstate to visit your Aunt Annie just before I disappeared?' Cora asked. 'We drove down to the Shoshone Bannock Museum in Pocatello. I saw the Willing Stone in a display case there. I remember feeling strangely hypnotized by it. It was almost as if I were dreaming. I couldn't take my eyes off of it. I remember a Native American man standing beside me. He kept smiling at me and nodding at the Stone. He whispered at me to pick it up.

I don't know why, but my desire to touch the Stone was irresistible. I reached into the display case and put the Stone in my hand. The next thing I knew, the museum room started spinning. I tried to let go of the Stone, but my hand wouldn't listen. I couldn't let go of it. I closed my eyes, because of the cramps in my stomach. I thought I would be sick. When I opened my eyes again, I saw this place. I saw White Eyes and the unspeakable visions he put in my head. Afterward, I found myself lying on the museum floor. I thought I must have fallen down and bumped my head. I thought I must have hallucinated the whole thing and it was just some awful nightmare.

When I got back home, I took Willy out for a ride. I thought it would clear my mind from the revolting things I saw. We were riding along, when I noticed something odd just ahead of us. It looked like a patch in the sky was bubbling up and glistening. As we got closer to it, Willy jibbed and threw me. I watched him race off. When I got back to my feet, I walked over to the strange sight. I put my hand against the wrinkled sky and suddenly found myself here.'

'That's what I saw too,' Ben said. 'That's what happened to me. It was like the sky sparkled and was wrinkled.'

Ben then told Cora about Greyhawk and everything that had happened, since that day at the school assembly.

'Professor Greyhawk knew what I saw, Mom. He understands about the Willing Stone. I think he knows about this place. He said he knew you were here.'

'That is wonderful news, Ben,' she said. 'Wonderful! If this Greyhawk knows of this world and the door into it, he may also know a way of helping us escape. This gives us all hope. The others will be very excited to hear about your Professor Greyhawk.'

'But, Mom, I don't know if Greyhawk heard about what happened to me.'
'I'm sure your father told him. I'm sure they are all out looking for you right now. Don't worry.'

Ben looked at his mother and let out a long plaintive sigh.
'No, Mom. I didn't tell Pa about Greyhawk and the Stone. I couldn't. He's been so sad ever since you went away. All the time. I hear him crying in his room sometimes, when he doesn't know I'm listening. I couldn't worry him about what happened to me. I couldn't tell him about my nightmares.'
Cora hugged Ben and said with a smile, 'Don't you worry. Your father knows, Ben. I'm sure he does.'

'Come on, everyone,' Frank said. 'We better go look for any New Ones before White Eyes and his hounds get to them first.'

Ben looked around in confusion. 'What are New Ones?' he asked.
'You,' Bird-Who-Hops said. 'New Ones who only just came here and don't know anything. Like you.
New Ones put us all in danger. They are like the baby buffalo who wanders off to the wolf pack.'

They all scrambled out from the Gathering Place through the gap in the boulders above and began walking together.

'Keep your eyes open, Lad,' Frank said to Ben. 'Listen. If you hear cries, it may be another New One.'

'Smell for signs of fear,' Bird-Who-Hops added. 'That's how I found you.'

CHAPTER 10

'Do you know a way to get Ben back or don't you?' Stacey asked irritably. 'Stop talking in riddles, will you? What do we do? How do we do it?'

'I said there may be a way,' Greyhawk replied. 'Young lady, I can only share the myths and stories that I have come to know. Much of this is conjecture. Old tales passed down by my ancestors from generation to generation. It is not a guidebook.'

'And what have you learned about getting someone back from this Blue Cloud world you described?' Noah asked.
'That's what we all want to know,' Stacey agreed.

'I have read tales claiming that people can be retrieved from this place,' Greyhawk said. 'One of the myths I came across referred to 'The Brotherhood of the Gift' and a possible escape for someone trapped in the world through the Blue Cloud. It claims one who holds the Gift can cross the divide via a Willing Stone vision and return with another with the Gift trapped there. They must make contact and then touch the Willing Stone together. However this myth warns that such a feat is extremely dangerous. If White Eyes touched the Stone with one of this Brotherhood, then they would be trapped there themselves in White Eyes' world.'

Chief Marty started shaking his head dismissively. 'How is this a plan of action?' he asked. 'Even if it were true, how would we know who had this Gift you speak about? You said yourself you showed this Stone artifact at many schools before and nothing ever happened. Do you have this so-called Gift?'

'No,' Greyhawk said.

'Then this doesn't do us much good, does it, Professor? I thank you for what you've shared, but I think we'd all be better off continuing our search here in this world with our feet firmly on the ground.'

'Orin,' Noah said, 'we've been searching high and low and so have the police. For three days. Ben's nowhere to be found. Carl and Stacey say he just disappeared right in front of their eyes. Your son took us to the spot where they last saw him. We found Ben's shoeprints there and they led nowhere. We saw the prints going forward and then they just stopped. How can you explain that? How does reason account for that? Reason isn't making any sense here. Maybe we're looking for a rational explanation, when there isn't one. Maybe what the Professor is telling us makes more sense than we know.'

'I may not have the Gift,' Greyhawk interrupted, 'but I think we may know someone who does.'

Everyone turned and looked at Greyhawk as he slowly made his way over to Carl.

'When you and Stacey came to my trailer, didn't you say that you saw the sky shimmer like Ben did?'

'I didn't see anything,' Stacey said. 'Carl did though. He even pointed at it.'

Carl nodded. 'Yes, I saw it, Professor. It was like heat vapor suspended low in the air. But it wasn't there anymore, when we went back to search for Ben.'
'No, that doesn't surprise me,' Greyhawk said. 'From what I understand, the Blue Cloud entranceway does not stay in the same place for long.'
'So where did it get to?' Stacey asked.

'It could be anywhere in the former lands of the indigenous people of the area. Do you remember the news reports a few years ago about that teenage couple out riding their mountain bikes in the Craters of the Moon Preserve? They both just disappeared without a trace. Just like what happened to your wife, Noah, and to Ben. Craters of the Moon is miles away from where Ben vanished. The story is the same. The police hunted for the teenagers and found absolutely no sign of them. I remember thinking at the time that the story matched The Legend of the Blue Cloud.'

'You believe this Cloud thing is responsible for those two missing as well?' Chief Marty asked.
'I think so,' Greyhawk replied. 'The Legend states the Blue Cloud is a trap for White Eyes and keeps him and his kind out of our world. He is banished there, yes, but he himself can also use it as a trap. It is his jail and his domain.'

'Like the bird in the gilded cage?' Carl's grandmother asked.

'I suppose, in a way, it is. Our myths explain that White Eyes will seek to capture all with the Gift in his realm behind the Blue Cloud. He targets them. He knows who they are. Some reveal themselves to him by visiting his dark world via a Willing Stone vision. Others, who do not know that they possess the Gift, are also targeted by him. Like your wife, Noah, and perhaps those teenagers. White Eyes can move the Blue Cloud entrance. He tricks them into stepping through unknowingly. He puts it in their path. I believe this is what has happened to Ben.'

'And what's meant to happen once this White Eyes captures everyone with this Gift?' Noah asked.
'From what I understand in the folklore, the Brotherhood of the Gift will be broken and White Eyes will then be free to cross back through the Blue Cloud and wreak his havoc here on our side.'

'So how are we meant to find this Blue Cloud thing again and rescue Ben?' Chief Marty asked.

'I don't believe it's necessary to find the Blue Cloud,' Greyhawk said. 'What we need is to find someone with the Gift to gain entrance via a Willing Stone vision and retrieve Ben in that way. Maybe his mother too. And that brings me to you, Carl.'

'To me?' Carl asked nervously.
'Yes,' Greyhawk nodded. 'Would you be willing to assist me in a little experiment?'

CHAPTER
11

Henri and Mei-Ling led the way as the Brotherhood began their search for New Ones. They stayed in one group and looked for signs of any new arrivals. Frank lifted Bird-Who-Hops up on to his shoulders so he would have a wider view.

As they walked along the valley floor, Cora whispered to Ben, 'We mustn't think only of ourselves. Imagine how Henri and the others must feel. They have all been here for a very long time. This is even more difficult for them than it is for us.'

They walked together in silence for a few moments, but Ben's curiosity would not allow him to be silent for long.
'Mom, do you know which one of them came here first?'

Cora reminded Ben again that he must speak quietly. 'Never speak in your full voice here, Ben. It is very dangerous. You must remember.'
'I will, Mom,' he whispered.

'Henri's been here the longest,' she said softly. 'He is often confused by what comes through the Blue Cloud to this place. He once saw a dirt biker roaring past us. He had no idea what it was. But despite his confusions, he's always cheerful and hopeful.'

'He imagines that if we do escape, we will all go back to the exact time and place where we passed through the Cloud. He thinks no one will even realize we had gone missing. We all have our own notions about what might happen if we did get away from here.'

'So no one really knows if we can escape this place?' Ben asked.

'Remember what I told you, Ben. You must never give up hope. One of the Brotherhood who arrived here once told us that we could all be saved. She said it was possible, if someone passed through the Blue Cloud with the Willing Stone. She told us much of what we now know. But then one time, when we were all out looking for New Ones, she stumbled and fell when we were running away from a rockslide...'

Cora stopped speaking for a moment. She swallowed and blinked back a tear at the memory.
'None of us really know. Try not to ask too much about escape. It is hard for the others to think about it.'

Bird-Who-Hops tapped Frank on his head to signal him to stop walking. 'Look,' he said as he pointed.

On the high rock bluffs on the far side of the valley, a young man pranced around in circles and began declaiming melodramatically.

'To be or not to be! Romeo! Romeo! Wherefore art thou Romeo?!'

'Friends, Romans, Countrymen! Cry havoc and let slip the dogs of war!'

He then burst into deranged, hysterical laughter and repeatedly bowed to the imaginary applause of his audience.

'The time is out of joint. O curséd spite that ever I was born to set it right!'

'It's Mad Tom,' Frank said.
Ben looked and saw a young man dressed in a frilly shirt, breeches, hose, and a tricorn hat.
'Hide,' Bird-Who-Hops told everyone as he climbed down from Frank's shoulders.

As Mad Tom turned in their direction, he exclaimed with his arms held wide, 'In time we hate that which we often fear.'

Cora grabbed Ben by the hand as they all raced for cover behind a rocky outcrop.
'Who's Mad Tom, Mom?'
'Hush,' she said.

They all stayed hidden away until Mad Tom began to skip out of view. As he did, he continued his delusional solo performance from the top of the ridge.

'What devil art thou that dost torment me thus? This torture should be roar'd in dismal hell,' he recited with passion until his voice faded away.

As they made their way back to the trail, Mei-Ling said to Ben, 'Tom was once with us. He's an actor from England.'

'He's dangerous,' Frank said dismissively.

'I did so enjoy his company,' Mei-Ling said. 'A fellow entertainer and so amusing. I do miss him.'

'What happened to him?' Ben asked.

'Poor young chap,' Henri said. 'He was always highly strung. He could not control his fear. White Eyes did this to him. He sensed his fear, captured him, and drove him to this madness.'

'He was a lovely young man. He did not deserve his fate,' Mei-Ling sighed.

'None of us deserve our fate,' Frank grunted in reply.

'But his fate is my fault,' Mei-Ling lamented.

'You see, we were on the same wagon train heading to California, when we were captured by the local tribe. They took us both to their village. When I wandered by accident through the Blue Cloud, Tom ran through the Cloud too to try to find me. That is why he ended up here in this loathsome place. I am to blame. I am the reason he was trapped here. Now he's lost to us and it's all my fault.'

'It's all White Eyes' fault,' Frank said. 'Not yours. If you're looking to someone for blaming, blame him.'

'How I wish I could help my charming Tommy!' Mei-Ling despaired.

'Don't pity him,' Frank growled. 'He can still see us and, if he does, he will betray us to his new 'Master'. Remember that.'

'Tom is not the only one,' Cora informed Ben. 'There are others here who we once called friends and who now serve White Eyes.'
Mei-Ling sighed again and nodded. 'Yes, they are our fallen comrades.'
'They are Betrayers,' Frank insisted. 'They are part of the enemy now.'

They continued hunting for new arrivals with the Gift, but had no luck in locating one. At one point in their search, they moved off the path as a Conestoga wagon began to pass them by. Ben watched as a young man with his wife and children drove their wagon slowly forward. They looked like they were in the midst of a long journey. Homesteaders on the Oregon Trail on their way to what they hoped would be a better life. Ben followed their progress with pity.

'They don't know they're behind the Blue Cloud. They don't know their journey will never end,' he thought to himself.

As the homesteaders continued on their way, a teenage couple on mountain bikes quickly rode up on either side of them. The boy was showing off to his girlfriend. He was popping wheelies and riding with no hands on the handlebars.

Ben looked on astonished as the boy cycled straight through the wagon and back again as if it were not there.

Neither the homesteaders nor the cyclists paid the slightest heed to one another. Both of them simply carried on as if they were on their own.

Ben could not tear his eyes away from the spectacle unfolding in front of him. He braced himself awaiting the expected crash every time the cyclist bore down on the wagon.

'Yes, it does take some getting used to,' Henri whispered to Ben. 'They are there and they are not there at the same time. They see only what they want to see. They do not know they are here nor are they affected by what happens here.'

'I saw those mountain bikers before,' Ben said to Henri. 'They nearly crashed into me right after I first came here.'
'What's a mountain biker?' Henri asked.

'There are no New Ones here,' Bird-Who-Hops finally decided. 'I see no one new. I hear no cries. I sense no fear.'

'I hope you're right,' Mei-Ling replied. 'And White Eyes did not find them first.'

CHAPTER
12

Greyhawk looked at the others for their attention. He asked them all to sit down before he began to speak.

'I propose we do a simple experiment to see if my hunch is correct or not. The Legend states that people who can see the Blue Cloud often have the Gift of the Stone themselves and, Carl, you did see it. It is possible that you yourself have this Gift.'

'Whoa there, Professor!' Chief Marty interjected. 'I'm not for a moment saying I am convinced by any of this, but if for some Twilight Zone reason it is true, you are definitely not going to use my boy as a lab rat to find out.'

'Orin, how many times over these many years have I told you to keep an open mind over matters?' Carl's grandmother said with a shake of her head. 'You go ahead, Professor Greyhawk,' she added. 'What sort of experiment are you talking about?'

'As I said, a simple one. I want Carl to hold the Willing Stone and see what happens. There should be no danger. If he shows the signs that he is having a vision like writhing, cramps, or discomfort, I will remove the Stone from his hand and he will be instantly returned to us.'

Stacey nudged Carl and whispered in his ear, 'This is your chance, Carl. Tell them you're not a daddy's boy anymore. Show them you're not a scaredy-cat.'
She gave him a little shove to get up on his feet.

Carl paused for a moment as he remembered Ben's painful twitching on the school assembly room floor during his Willing Stone vision. Then he stood up, took a deep breath, and said with conviction, 'I want to try. If I can, I want to try to rescue Ben and Mrs. Crenshaw.'

'Now just slow down for a minute, Carl,' Mrs. Marty said. 'Professor, are you certain it's safe? I mean, if Carl has this Gift, he wouldn't end up lost there himself, would he? Are you sure, Professor? Are you one hundred percent sure?'

'Once the Stone is taken from his hand, he will be back with us,' Greyhawk reassured her. 'Just like Ben at the school assembly after I retrieved the Stone from him.'

An air of nervous silence filled the room, until Chief Marty asked, 'This is what you want, Carl? This is what you want to do?'

'I'm not a little kid anymore, Dad. I'm fourteen years old now. Nearly fifteen. If there's any chance to get Ben back, I need to try. I need to do this.'
Stacey smiled and patted Carl on his shoulder.

'Orin, Mrs. Marty, we don't yet know if anything at all will happen when your son holds the Willing Stone,' Greyhawk reminded them.

'As I say, it is an experiment. An experiment with no risk really.'

Greyhawk looked Carl in the eye.
'Are you certain that you want to do this, Son?'
'I am, Professor.'
'Excellent. Wonderful. Do not worry. I will be with you every step of the way.'

Greyhawk shook Carl's hand and then said to everyone, 'I had to return the Willing Stone to the museum. I'll drive up there tomorrow and see if they are happy to let me borrow it again. I hope they may be willing. If so, Orin, I will call you from the museum and we can all meet again tomorrow evening. Then we'll see if Carl has the Gift or not.'

CHAPTER
13

The young woman's eyes darted around wildly in terror. She was petrified and trembling with fear.

'Please don't hurt me!' she squealed. 'Where am I? Who are you? What do you want?'
'Quiet! How dare you speak!' one of White Eyes' Grinning Dogs raged as he slapped her hard and shoved her to the floor.

'My Lord Remiel, we found this Defiler wandering in fear in your domain,' the Grinning Dog said. 'We have brought the Defiler here to your Court to deal with her as you wish.'

Two of the winged creatures dragged the young woman forward and flung her roughly at the feet of White Eyes.

'Have you come to visit me, my dear? How sweet and thoughtful of you,' White Eyes said with wicked relish. 'Who are you?' the woman asked again. She looked around in panic. 'What is this place?'

Another of the winged servants kicked her until she groaned in pain.
'Shut your foul mouth, Defiler.'

White Eyes rose from his throne and knelt down over

the woman moaning on the floor. He cradled her head in his hands.

'Tell me, my dear,' he said with mock concern. 'Are you not comfortable? Come. Sit here beside me. Let us talk together, shall we?'

White Eyes stood back up and sat back on his throne.

One of White Eyes' servants grabbed the woman by her hair, lifted her up from the floor, and threw her into a seat next to White Eyes' throne.

'There! That is better, is it not?' White Eyes asked. 'Tell me. Have you come here before via that vile Stone? Ah, I think not. I would have remembered you!'

'Answer him!' One of the Grinning Dogs spat out. 'What stone? What are you talking about?' she asked in a stutter.

'All will be revealed soon enough,' White Eyes said with a frozen grin on his face.

He nodded to two of his servants and they approached the woman. They each grabbed her under an arm and stood her back up to face White Eyes.

'We shall now see what you do know. We shall see what you do fear most,' he said.

White Eyes then rose and put a hand on either side of the woman's face. He pressed his face to hers.

'Show me,' he said.

As he did this, the woman instantly began screaming in agony.

'Ah! A child! Yes, I see! You have a new-born, do you not?' he asked. 'Yes, I believe you do. Here let me show you the fate of your miserable brat.'
White Eyes blew softly in the woman's face and stepped back away from her.

Immediately, the woman started to shake with convulsions. Froth and spittle began to escape from her mouth and her eyes rolled to the back of her head.

'My baby!' she blubbered. 'Stay back! I'll never tell you where I've hidden her! I'll keep her safe from you! You will never find her… No! No! Don't go in there! Get back! Take your hands off of her! Leave my baby be! Put her down!' she screamed as White Eyes sat back on his throne and looked on in pitiless pleasure.

'No, give her back to me! What are you doing? Keep her away from the fire! My God, no!' she screeched in despair.

White Eyes and his servants watched happily as she suffered in her trance.
'You monsters! No! Put that spike down! Are you insane? No! Stop! Keep your filthy paws off of her! Don't put that through her! Get away from her!'

The young mother tore at her eyes to blind herself from the horrors that White Eyes had put into her mind.

'What are you doing? Murder! Murderers!' she wailed and howled in horror. She began to run in circles and screaming all the while.

'You butchers! Maniacs! My baby! You're roasting my baby alive!!!'

The young mother continued to run wildly, tearing at her eyes, and lost in her abominable vision. White Eyes' dark-winged servants spat and kicked at her as she ran past them over and over again.

Finally, after taking his pleasure from the appalling spectacle he had created, White Eyes nodded to two of the Grinning Dogs. They grabbed the shrieking woman forcibly and stood her in front of their Master. White Eyes slapped her firmly across the face. She stopped her wailing and stood motionless.

'Tell me how you came to be here,' White Eyes commanded the now expressionless woman.

'Yes, My Lord,' she answered vacantly. 'I came through the sparkle in the sky when my partner and I were out walking in the valley. I was carrying our baby when I saw the sky twinkling just over some sagebrush. I reached out my hand to touch it and the next moment my baby and I found ourselves here.'

'I see. I have work for you then,' White Eyes said smiling repulsively. 'You do have the Gift, do you not? But you did not know? Is that not so?' he asked.

'Yes, My Lord,' she replied blankly as little rivulets of blood began pouring from her eyes.

'Good. There are others here, who also have the Gift,

but they hide from me. They hide their fear. Go! Walk freely in my domain. Look for these upstarts. Hunt for this so-called Brotherhood. Find them. Tell me where they are and you will be rewarded.'

She bowed and said tonelessly, 'I will, My Lord.'

White Eyes shoved the young woman away from him. He signaled to one of the Grinning Dogs who then dragged her away from White Eyes' Court and out into his colorless world.

'Get out!' The Grinning Dog shouted after her. 'Go! Do your Master's bidding.'

White Eyes listened with pleasure as the woman again began to squeal inconsolably as she ran out into his dismal realm. He smiled smugly at her howling and screaming. The sound of her agony and misery seemed to fill him with dreadful delight.

White Eyes looked so pleased and self-satisfied with the horror he had visited upon her. Like he had just eaten a fine meal.

'What's that noise?' Ben asked nervously. 'Is that someone screaming?'

'He has taken one with the Gift. He tortures a New One now,' Frank said in disgust.

'Yes,' Cora said. 'Try not to listen. It is part of the wickedness he does to make us reveal our fear as well. Be calm.'

After the shocking, frightful screaming had at last faded away, Frank shook his head in resignation.

'That's another New One those bastards got to before we could,' he said to the others. 'White Eyes is trapping more and more with the Gift here all the time. He keeps moving the Blue Cloud doorway to catch them. In time, he will trap us all.'

'No, he will not,' Mei-Ling shot back. 'Don't you hold any hope at all, Frank? I will never give up hope. Cora says, 'hope is our only hope' and she is right.'
'I hope she is,' Frank replied.

'You did well, Ben Crenshaw,' Bird-Who-Hops said. 'I did not sense your fear. When White Eyes does his evil spirit magic to drive captured New Ones to madness, he makes certain that we can hear their screams. But you were not afraid. You are strong like I am. You are brave like the braves from my tribe.'

Henri walked over to Frank. 'What do you say, Man-mountain? If you're right and more and more New Ones are trapped here by White Eyes, if more and more of the Brotherhood are arriving, then let's go out and find them before his Grinning Jackasses do.'

Frank nodded and stood up. 'All right,' he said with a shrug. 'I could use some new company. Let's go find some.'

CHAPTER
14

Noah drove his pickup off to the side of the road and stopped.
'I think it's just over there, Jimmy.'

Noah and Mr. Groves got out of the pickup and grabbed their metal detectors, headphones, and shovels out of the back.

'Noah, this is just like old times. We've not gone detecting together, since I don't know how long.'
'Don't know, Jimmy. Must be five years or so, I reckon.'

That morning, the State Police had called off the daily search and rescue team hunting for Ben. There was still no sign of him just like there was not a sign of Cora when she disappeared.

'Noah, my Jimmy Junior says the State Police chopper is needed elsewhere. There's a flash flood up in the Owyhee Mountains. He said they hadn't given up on Ben though. He wanted you to know that,' Mr. Groves said trying to offer him some comfort.

He then started chuckling quietly to himself.
'Jimmy Junior told me he wanted a peaceful life after he came home from Desert Storm and his time in Kuwait and Bosnia. He didn't want any more heroics. That's why he came back and worked for Orin,' he said.

'But with your Ben and Cora missing and all the craziness around here lately, my boy's not getting much of a quiet life, is he?'

Noah nodded, but said nothing in reply. Mr. Groves sensed Noah's hopelessness. 'Jimmy Junior promised he'd be sure to reach us, Noah, if Professor Greyhawk contacts Orin about that Stone thing he's trying to fetch. Don't you concern yourself about that.'

They both slung their detectors over their shoulders and started walking.
'It should be just up over there, Jimmy, according to the library map,' Noah said to change the subject.

On the day Noah dragged his metal detector out from the cupboard, he had gone into town and did some research at the local library. He was hunting for information on the locations of old cavalry camps during the Bannock War in the latter part of the nineteenth century. He found what he thought might be a good lead to a cavalry camp, while looking at some area maps of the time.

After returning home, Noah called Mr. Groves and asked him if he wanted to go out and see if they could find it and, if so, try their luck in unearthing something worthwhile.
Then Ben disappeared and everything was put on hold.

Noah decided to call Mr. Groves again right after the meeting with Greyhawk at Chief Marty's house.

Annie encouraged him to do it.

'Noah, you get your mind on something else for a while,' she suggested. 'There's nothing to be done until Professor Greyhawk contacts Orin. Stewing and worrying won't help Ben.'

Mr. Groves was surprised when Noah rang.

'You sure, Noah?' he asked. 'You sure you want to go out there detecting with all that's on your mind?'

'I am,' he replied. 'My sister says to get my mind on something else and she's right. Pick you up first thing in the morning.'

The two men continued walking until they reached the bottom of a large circular mound. Noah took out the piece of paper onto which he had scribbled down the location from the library map.

He looked toward the top of the mound.

'This looks like the spot, Jimmy.'

'Then let's get these old bones of ours up there,' Mr. Groves said with grin.

They made their way up to the top of the mound. When they got there, they stopped for a moment and looked around at the landscape that greeted them.

'This surely is God's Country, Noah,' Mr. Groves sighed.

'Amen to that,' Noah said.

They decided to split up with Noah working one side of the mound and Mr. Groves the other.

'I'll be sure to let you know, if I strike gold,' Mr. Groves joked as he walked away.

Noah readied his detector and then walked slowly and in a clear pattern, so as not to miss a spot. He kept his eyes down and focused on the detector in his hands.

An hour or more passed in silence. Noah tried to forget, as best he could, about Cora and Ben, but his loss kept forcing him to remember. He was exhausted in his worry. He took a deep breath. He hoped, if only for a moment, that he could breathe again freely without the weight of his world upon him.

He looked down and saw his hands were trembling. He paused his search briefly to calm himself down. 'Fresh air will clear my mind,' he kept repeating to himself, but he could not keep his worry at bay. He felt his eyes well up in tears and mumbled softly, so Mr. Groves would not hear.

'Please,' he called out to the sky. 'My wife has been taken from me. And now my son. My work is gone. Everything and everyone I care about has vanished. If only for a few minutes, please give me some peace of mind.'

Only someone who had lost all they had themselves could possibly know how deeply Noah grieved. But then his brief, prayerful reverie was abruptly shattered.

'Noah! Get yourself over here!' Mr. Groves hollered.

'Damn it all! Look at that!' he continued to shout.

Noah rushed over to where Mr. Groves was standing.
'What is it, Jimmy? Did you find something?'

'Look!' Mr. Groves said as he pointed down to the plain
below them. 'What the hell!' he added in amazement.
'What do you see, Jimmy?'
'Look, Noah, look!' he shouted as he kept pointing
down.

Below them, a herd of wild horses were running by.
Noah watched as the lead horses and those following
them ran and then disappeared into thin air right in
front of his eyes.

'Where the hell did they go?' Mr. Groves asked looking
at Noah. 'Must have been a dozen of them disappeared
before you came over. Look! They just keep
disappearing!' he said unable to stop pointing down to
the impossible sight below.

They both stood there in shock and confusion as the
entire herd raced ahead and then vanished without a
trace.
'Damned, if I ever saw a thing like that, Noah! What the
blazes?!'

Noah pulled Mr. Groves around to face him.
'Jimmy,' he said seriously. 'This could be important.
We got to get ourselves back right away. We'll walk
down there, have a quick look around, and then we
have to go. Maybe it's that Blue Cloud thing. We need

to tell Professor Greyhawk exactly where we saw it. It could be a clue to get my boy back. You understand? You help us remember the exact spot where those horses disappeared.'

'Sure I will, Noah,' he said in a daze. 'Better call Jimmy Junior about this too.'
'Do that, Jimmy, as soon as we get back.'

They walked down the side of the mound to the spot where they had just seen the horses vanish. Noah observed that the hoof prints all stopped appearing along the same line.

'You see that, Jimmy?' he asked. 'Where'd they go?'
'I don't know, but damned if I can see anything that would explain it,' Mr. Groves said as they scouted the area together. 'Do you?'
'No,' Noah said. 'I don't see a damn thing.'

Above them, a turkey vulture circled high in the sky. As it looped over where they were standing, it too vanished in mid-flight.

'Did you see that, Noah? The sky is swallowing up everything! What in the Sam Hill is going on around here?'
'I wish I knew, Jimmy. I wish I knew.'

Mr. Groves stopped in his tracks. He looked around cautiously at where they were standing and then looked over at Noah.

'We best not get ourselves vanished too, Noah,' he advised. Noah nodded in agreement.
'Yeah, Jimmy, we best not.'

And together they slowly backed away from the line of the horses' disappearance.

Noah dropped Mr. Groves back off at his garage. He watched for a moment as Mr. Groves ran inside to call Jimmy Junior.

He drove back home not knowing what to think. As he got to his door, he could hear the phone ringing. By the time he had fumbled with his keys, opened the door, and run in, Annie had already picked up the phone.

'Orin? No, I'm sorry he's… wait. Here he is. He just came back in this second.'
Annie passed Noah the phone.

'What is it, Orin?' Noah asked anxiously. 'Did you hear back from the Professor?'

'He just rang me from the museum. They're letting him borrow that Stone thingamabob again. He says he has some news to share. I told him to get back down here and meet us over at my place tonight.'

'Good. I have some news to share myself,' Noah said. 'Jimmy Senior and I went out metal-detecting just now. I'm not sure, but I think we just saw Professor Greyhawk's Blue Cloud.'

CHAPTER 15

The Brotherhood set off together on yet another search for New Ones. Frank, with Bird-Who-Hops perched on his shoulders, led the way. Ben and Cora were walking directly behind them.

'Mom, how are we safe in the Gathering Place? I don't understand. White Eyes knows we're there.'

Cora put her arm around her son. 'We are safe, because we are together. We're safe, because each of us helps the other not to be afraid. Together, we can be brave and show no fear. To be together makes us strong. It gives us hope. It's only when we are separated and show fear that White Eyes can take us.'

Frank began to scoff while this exchange took place.

'Or if we get caught out here unawares and scream out in shock and fear,' he said. 'Or if we speak too loudly. Or if a Betrayer points us out to that white-eyed fiend. Or when the land shifts under our feet again and we find ourselves hanging off some cliff... Safe, Cora? Why tell the lad that?'

Cora let out a sigh. 'You really should keep some hope for yourself, Frank,' she replied with a smile.
'She's right, Frank,' Mei-Ling laughed. 'It would do you good!'

As they continued looking and listening for signs of New Ones, it suddenly dawned on Ben that he had not eaten anything or had anything to drink or slept for that matter, since he came to this place. He was not hungry though. He was not thirsty. He did not feel tired. Finally, a thought came to him.

He turned to Henri. 'There's no time here, is there?'
'No, no time, my young friend. Time does not pass here.'
'But our bodies…they're real, aren't they?'
'Yes, they are real enough,' Henri said.
'But we don't eat or drink,' Ben said unable to comprehend.
'No, we do not. We do not have that pleasure. We do not have the peace of sleep and yet we still live.'

'I told you this, when I first found you,' Bird-Who-Hops said from atop Frank's shoulders. 'Did you not believe me?'
'I didn't understand,' Ben replied. 'I think I do now. This has all been like a single day that never ends, isn't that so?'
'Like a single moment that never ends,' Henri replied.

'It's not all bad,' Mei-Ling said trying to lighten the mood. 'No need to wash or bathe. No need to change our clothes. Dirt just seems to fall off of us and our clothing. I do miss my wardrobe though. And all my lovely costumes too.'

'I don't understand. We don't need to wash?' Ben asked. 'We don't need to rest?'

'No, we do not. It's as if we were constantly restored to the state we were in when we first passed through the Blue Cloud,' Henri posited. 'Even our bruises and scrapes heal quickly. They're still painful in the obtaining, but are gone moments later. There is no time here. Without time, nothing can change. Not even the Brotherhood. That is what I believe.'

Ben thought for a moment about what Henri had said. He felt at last like he was beginning to understand this place and he wanted to know more.

'When I first met Bird-Who-Hops, he told me to look to the sky to find my way. But, Henri, I don't understand. Everywhere I go seems unfamiliar to me. Even when I try to retrace my steps.'

'Yes, we look to the sky,' Henri answered. 'It never changes. But this land above ground is in constant motion. A ridge we pass when looking for a New One may have shifted elsewhere upon our return. But the sky is fixed. We follow a line in the sky to find our way. If we look to the terrain, we will be lost. Instead we look up to the sky. I have a theory as to why this is so.'

'Great balls of fire!' Frank interjected with a laugh. 'Don't get him started or he'll philosophize until your ears fall off.'

Ben was just about to ask Henri more about his theory, when a faraway sound distracted him. A low, loud rumbling roar off in the distance began to grow closer and closer.

'Do you hear that?' Ben whispered apprehensively. 'What is it?'

The Brotherhood stopped and turned to face the uproar heading their way. They stood there together staring, when out of a cloud of dust a herd of stampeding buffalo appeared and bore down on them.

'Over here! This way!' Henri urged them as he raced off the path and headed toward the ridge rock face. Bird-Who-Hops quickly jumped down from Frank's shoulders and followed Henri. Frank stood there and motioned the others forward while he took up the rear. 'Go, Go, Go!' he shouted as he waved them by.

The Brotherhood sprinted past Frank and gasped for air as they raced ahead. Their pace was so frantic that it was difficult for them to keep their balance.

Mei-Ling was trying to catch up with the others, when she stumbled, tripped over her own feet, and tumbled headlong onto the dusty valley path. She scrambled to stand back up and keep running. But as she tried to get to her feet, she fell over. She looked down at her ankle. It was red and swollen. She grunted as she struggled to get up again and run, but she could put no weight on her sprained ankle. She could not move and sat there helpless and unable to escape. She turned around anxiously and saw the stampede's dust cloud and heard the rumbling beasts charging nearer.

The rest of the Brotherhood had been running ahead of Mei-Ling, when she fell, and were long gone. Only

Frank had been running behind her. She looked around again in panic, when she saw Frank suddenly burst into view. He was haring around a bend and running for his life with the rampaging herd in hot pursuit.

As he was tearing by, Mei-Ling waved frantically to get his attention. She saw Frank glance over at her and then, without breaking stride, he swerved off the path to where she had fallen, scooped her up with one arm, and threw her over his shoulder. He carried her like that as he ran at full throttle with the panicked herd bearing down on them.

'Hang on tight,' Frank warned her as he continued racing forward.
Bounding like an antelope, Frank then jumped off the dusty track, hurdled over the mass of loose stones and rocks that bordered the pathway, and raced to where the others were taking shelter just as the terrified beasts rushed wildly past them and away from the constant threat they imagined.

'Phew! That was close,' Mei-Ling said still draped over Frank's shoulder.
'Too close,' Frank said as he struggled for breath.
'Are you hurt, Mei-Ling?' he asked.
'My ankle's sore, but it'll heal soon enough. I'm fine, Frank. You can put me down now,' she giggled.

'Stay on your feet next time, will you?' Frank grunted gruffly as he lowered Mei-Ling back down to the ground.

Mei-Ling began to hop up and down on her one good foot as she started to dust off her clothes and hair. She was covered in dirt from head to toe.

'I must look a sight,' she sighed.

'Don't worry yourself,' Frank reassured her. 'You're still as pretty as you always are.'

'Frank!' Cora said with a grin. 'Who would have guessed? You're quite the romantic, aren't you?'

Ben stood there amazed as he saw all the dirt and dust covering Mei-Ling quickly fade away in front of his eyes. Her swollen ankle seemed magically healed too. She quickly stopped her hopping and stood upright on her two feet again. In just a matter of moments, there was no sign at all that she had fallen to the ground.

Henri saw Ben staring with his mouth agape at Mei-Ling's miraculous transformation.

'So now you see,' he said to him. 'We are instantly restored. If we are not killed, we will recover rapidly.'

After the buffalo herd had thundered by, the Brotherhood paused for a moment to catch their breath. They then emerged from where they were sheltering and again began walking together to continue their search for New Ones.

Ben caught up with Henri and Mei-Ling.

'What about those animals?' he asked them. 'Don't they need to eat either?'

'No, we don't think they do,' Henri said softly as they walked together.

'We think, like us, they exist only in a single moment of time. For them, they are always terrified of something. Always on the run.'

'Yes,' Mei-Ling added. 'They are trapped here in their moment of fear, the poor things.'

'How long do you think they've been stuck here?' Ben asked.

'It is impossible to guess,' Henri said. 'When time does not pass, it is easy to lose track of it too. They tell me I have been here for centuries, but my arrival feels recent to me. It feels like I've only been here, since the rise of the last Harvest Moon.'

As Cora walked behind, she listened as Ben spoke with Mei-Ling and Henri. She was so proud of her son and overjoyed to see him again, but she also feared for him.

On her own, Cora had managed to control her fear. She allowed herself to live in hope. She refused to give up. She did not fear for herself. But as she walked on her own behind her son, she worried about how she would manage her fear for Ben. She thought about the stampeding herd that had so nearly run them down. 'How can I protect him here? How can I keep my beautiful boy safe?' she asked herself.

Then a loud, high-pitched series of screams interrupted her thoughts.

Frank paused to listen to the shrieking shouts and then said to the rest of the group, 'That's coming from just ahead. Stay here.'

He readjusted Bird-Who-Hops on his shoulders.
'Come on, Little Birdie. Let's see what's going on.'

The others looked on uneasily as Frank and Bird-Who-Hops walked ahead toward the shouting voice.

As they disappeared around a bend in the ridge face, the shrill shouting grew louder and louder.
'Is it a New One?' Ben asked.
'Sssh,' Cora said putting her finger to her lips.

They were all taken by surprise, when Frank immediately came rushing back toward them.
'Find cover!' he ordered. 'Do it now!'

'It's a Betrayer,' Bird-Who-Hops warned them as he jumped down from Frank's shoulders. They all ran off together back to the place where they had sheltered away from the buffalo stampede.

'My baby!' a woman's voice screeched as she advanced toward them. 'Where are you? Let me gaze upon you again. My Lord is most powerful. Look! I don't need my eyes anymore and yet I can see!'

A grisly sight greeted them as the woman came into view. Ben poked his head just above the rocks behind which they were hiding and watched cautiously as the young woman began to approach. She was walking toward them with her head down as if she were looking for something on the ground. She then lifted her face to the heavens as she cried out, 'Where are you, my love? Where have they taken you?'

As the woman looked up, Ben stole a quick peek at her and then promptly shut his eyes and dropped out of sight. He squeezed his mother's hand. What he saw made him want to run away screaming. It was all he could do to stay still and silent.

Two bloody holes stood gaping where the woman's eyes should have been. Dried blood was caked around her eye sockets. It looked like she had scratched them out. Or maybe White Eyes scratched them out. Ben did not know, but it took every scrap of his courage not to shout out in fear.

'Where are those who hide with the Gift?' The eyeless woman asked. 'My Master wants to know. Call out to me. Show me where you are hiding, so I may tell my Master and he will reward me.'

The woman stopped and sniffed the air.
'Oh! How majestic is my Master?! He graces me with the virtue of his scent. He makes me as great as he! I will smell the fear of the hiders who have the Gift.'

Ben rubbed his hands over his eyes like he was trying to erase what he had seen. He thought if he looked at the woman again, he would betray the others in his fear. He did his best not to whimper as the woman walked past them and, shouting out insanely, meandered off down the valley.

Everyone was stunned. No one moved a muscle until they heard the blind woman's screams fade away.

'We were damn lucky,' Frank said as the group came out from behind their hiding spot. 'She almost found us. I nearly walked right into her.'
Everyone, including Frank himself, looked shaken.

'I never saw that Betrayer before. Another walking nightmare,' Frank said with an uneasy laugh. 'She's what we'd call in the Old Country a 'Screaming Banshee'. Bad luck and bad news.'

'For pity's sake, Frank,' Cora reprimanded him. 'Do you feel nothing for that poor woman?'
Frank shrugged. 'Pity will make us end up just like her.'

As they continued in their search for New Ones, Henri led them down a steep path. It wound down and around some rocks and brush until the path flattened out. There on their left, they noticed a series of hollows in the side of the ridge. They took a few more steps forward, when Cora suddenly froze on the spot.

'What is it, Mom?'
'Hush. Listen. Don't you hear that?'
They all gathered around Cora to try to hear what she was hearing.

'What do you hear, Cora?' Mei-Ling asked as she strained again to listen. 'Wait,' she said in a hush. 'I think I hear something too. What is that?'

Cora turned away from the others and walked over to

one of the hollows in the ridge face. She went in, bent down, and reached for something inside the hollow.

The others all looked on curiously as she picked up what she had seen. They could not see what it was, because Cora had her back turned to them. Then Cora stood back up, turned around to face them, and then they all could see.
There in her arms was a new-born baby.

'Well, you did say you wanted some new company, Frank,' Henri laughed.

Mei-Ling ran over and cooed with delight as she took the infant from Cora.
'Look at you!' she said in baby talk. 'Just look at that cute little sunhat someone put on your head! Aren't you just to die for! You are a brand new New One! Yes, you are!'

CHAPTER 16

By the time Greyhawk arrived at Chief Marty's house, the rest of the group were already assembled. As soon as he saw him walk through the door, Noah took Greyhawk aside and told him about what had happened to the wild horse herd.

'Was that the Blue Cloud thing you talked about? Is that where they went? They were stampeding and then they vanished into the sky. That's not possible, but that's what Jimmy Senior and I saw.'

Greyhawk shook his head slowly back and forth.
'I fear what you saw is only the beginning, Noah. The Legend makes reference to this. As White Eyes traps more with the Gift, the Blue Cloud will manifest itself more frequently. From what you've just told me, the rift between his world and ours is growing in size as well.'

Chief Marty walked over to where Greyhawk and Noah were speaking.
'Professor,' he said, 'we were ordered to call off the search for Ben today. The State Police can't justify the use of resources and manpower anymore, so they claim. It's now down to us to find Ben on our own. As much as I hate to admit it, you're the best chance we've got.'

'Then we better get started,' Greyhawk said as he walked away.

'Noah, Jimmy Junior told me what you and Jimmy Senior saw out there today,' Chief Marty said. 'He said his dad is still pretty shaken up about it. If it wasn't you two saying it, I would never believe it.'
'Believe it, Orin? I saw it myself and I still don't believe it.'

'Maybe my mother is right. Like she says, there are all kinds of strangeness.'
Noah smiled. 'Maybe. More than I want to admit anyway.'
'We've had a half dozen more police bulletins just this past week about people going missing. Pets and livestock too. Something wrong is going on, Noah, and I mean to put it right.'

Greyhawk asked everyone to sit down. He looked over to Carl. 'Are you ready to begin?' he asked.

Carl stood up and walked over to Greyhawk.
'If I have the Gift,' he whispered, 'do you really think it will help us find Ben and his mother?'
'That is my belief,' Greyhawk answered.
'Then I'm ready,' Carl said resolutely.

'Before I hand the Willing Stone to you, Carl, I want to share with you and everyone else what I have come to learn. It is important that you know what to expect, if indeed you do have the Gift and are transported behind the Blue Cloud.'

'Those who enter the world of White Eyes via the Stone cannot speak or hear. You will be disoriented just as Ben was. Remember that you will not really be there, but only receiving a vision of this dark domain. Nonetheless, it is perilous. White Eyes will notice your trespassing. He will reveal himself to you as he does to anyone who enters via the Stone.'

'Excuse me, Professor, but didn't you insist that this wasn't dangerous?' Mrs. Marty reminded him. 'You said it was a simple experiment. Now you say it's perilous.'
'That's right. Is it or isn't it?' Chief Marty asked.

Greyhawk reassured them that there was no risk.
'This is why I am telling Carl what he might expect. He will be in no physical danger, but White Eyes will share with Carl things he does not wish to see. He will work to frighten him and cripple him with fear. He can manipulate the image of anyone trapped in his domain. They can appear to be doing anything White Eyes desires to show Carl.'

'He's a trickster then, is he?' Carl's grandmother asked.
'Of the highest order,' Greyhawk replied.

Greyhawk directed Carl to sit back down.

'If you do have the Gift, your vision will come upon you quickly. Prepare yourself, Carl, but do not worry. If I see any signs that you are struggling, I will remove the Stone from your hand.'

Greyhawk reached into his bag and took out the Willing Stone wrapped in its soft leather casing. As at the school assembly, he placed the Stone atop its leather cover and held it out in the palm of his hand.

Chief Marty and his wife both looked anxiously at one another. Chief Marty could not help himself from again trying to stop Greyhawk's Willing Stone experiment. 'Just wait a minute, Carl. You don't need to do this. Your mother and I don't feel comfortable with you doing this.'

'I have to do it, Dad,' Carl insisted. 'I have to try to help Ben and Mrs. Cora. Please don't stop me.'
Carl looked back at Greyhawk. He took a deep breath. 'Okay, Professor. I'm ready.'

Greyhawk leaned over and whispered softly so only Carl would hear. 'Remember what I told everyone, Son. If you see your friend in your vision, touch the Stone with him and you can bring him home with you. Try to remember everything you see in your vision. It could hold a clue in reclaiming those lost there. Keep the Stone in your hands at all times. Do you understand?'
Carl nodded that he understood.

Greyhawk patted Carl on the back of his shoulder. 'Don't be afraid,' he said. 'I'll be right here with you.'

Greyhawk then held out the Willing Stone resting in his palm.
'Go ahead, Son,' he said. 'Pick it up.'

Carl took the Stone and held it in his hand. He felt how smooth it was as he ran his fingers over it. He sat there embarrassed for a moment, because everyone kept staring at him. Then suddenly he felt his fingers close involuntarily around the Willing Stone. Carl tried, but he could not loosen his grip. A wave of nausea raced through him and he doubled over from a jolt of pain in the pit of his stomach.

The room started spinning. He shut his eyes from the world whirling around him. He thought he would retch. Painful cramps contracted through him as he felt himself fall to the floor.

When Carl reopened his eyes, he saw he was no longer at home. He could not make sense out of what he was seeing or where he found himself. The world he had entered was devoid of color like some old sepia-tinted black and white movie. Everything around him kept going in and out of focus. The ground beneath him seemed to bubble up and down. He tried to walk forward, but it was as if he were seasick and could not find his legs. He struggled to stay upright and although he could not trust his balance, he began to look around at this strange, unsettling place.

He was unable to make out anything very clearly. He thought he saw a herd of horses running by, but they looked blurry and indistinct. Every time he tried to refocus his eyes, he kept seeing everything around him coming toward him and then away from him and he felt sick and nauseous.

Then he saw something that made his heart stop. Right in front of his eyes, a young woman materialized. Her eye sockets were a bloody mess. It looked like she had plucked out her eyes. She seemed to be screaming, but he could not hear what she was saying. He looked on fearfully as the blind woman ran off.
When he turned back, he was shocked dead still.

A hideous creature with dark wings stood before him. He could barely force himself to look at it. It had glowing eyes like white-hot coals. The creature looked at Carl in triumph. He unfurled his wings and grew larger. He sniffed at the air like a dog. Then, as the creature refolded his wings, he saw Ben and Cora appear directly behind it. Ben was chained to the ground. He looked like he had been beaten repeatedly and remorselessly. His face was bloody and bruised. Although Carl could hear nothing, he could see Ben crying out in pain.

He remembered what Greyhawk had told him. He tried to figure out a way to reach Ben and Cora and touch the Willing Stone together with them, but it was impossible. He could not speak. He could not hear. He could not trust the ground under his feet. How could he possibly get to Ben and Cora safely? The creature was standing in his way.

Carl stood there where he was in fear and frustration, when the creature reached out and pulled Cora into its foul arms. She appeared to be overjoyed by his sickening embrace as if she were in ecstasy and swooned in pleasure.

The creature started ripping at her clothing until she stood there naked. He then began to fondle her. They wrapped their arms around one another and kissed fervidly. As Carl watched in horror, he saw their bodies become intertwined like they were one torso with four arms and legs. They writhed together in their passion.

When they finally finished with their loathsome love-making, they both looked straight at Carl and sneered at him with contempt.
Cora's eyes had transformed to become just like the creature's eyes.
Like soulless, burning, white-hot coals.

Carl looked away in revulsion. He tried to master his fear before he turned back to look at them. But when he did look back, both Ben and his mother were gone. Only the creature stood before him. He held out the palm of his hand toward Carl and nodded at the Willing Stone. He reached out toward him and Carl stumbled back and away from his clutches to escape.

The creature glared menacingly at him. His heartless grin made Carl squirm. The creature kept pointing at Carl and the Stone. He kept staring at him with that blood-curdling smile fixed on his face. Carl had never felt so afraid in all his life.

Above the creature, six streams of black smoke descended together and landed simultaneously behind him. The smoky streams disappeared and six more winged creatures much like the first stood in their stead.

They all began pointing and grinning at Carl in eerie delight. Carl could not hear anything, but he could see that they were laughing at him. Their leader first turned to the six behind him, signaled something to them, and then quickly spun back again to fix his hideous, grinning smirk at Carl. They all kept pointing and jeering in mockery at him.

Then as one they all spread their wings and turned into what Carl thought looked like whirling pillars of smoke. The seven smoky columns slowly ascended from the ground. He watched in fear as they flew up into the colorless sky.

Carl felt his heart beating in his chest. His stomach was churning and his legs were wobbling. He thought he was going to pass out. He shut his eyes to stop himself from seeing the shifting landscape around him.

When he opened his eyes again, he imagined himself lying on the floor and surrounded by everyone at home. He kept hearing himself shouting, 'Ben! Ben!'

Carl did not know if he was dreaming or not. He feared that he was still in that awful, hellish place. His head was spinning and aching. He felt his stomach gripped in spasms.
'Wings,' he said in a daze. 'He has wings. Damn big wings.'

He heard voices shouting his name. He felt a hand gently slapping his face, but he did not know if any of it was actually happening. He did not know if he was back home or still lost in his trance.

He thought that he saw Greyhawk reach out to him with the Willing Stone's leather cover in his hand. He reclaimed the Stone from him and Carl immediately let out a heavy sigh of relief. He felt so much better once the Stone had been taken away from him, but he could not trust if what he was experiencing was real or not.

Chief and Mrs. Marty were both kneeling over Carl. 'My boy!' Mrs. Marty shouted as she held Carl close to her to comfort him.
'Carl! Carl!' Chief Marty called to him. He patted him lightly on his cheek. 'Come back, Son. Come on back.'

Suddenly, Carl shook his head and sat bolt upright.

'Where am I?' he asked uncertainly. 'Mom? Dad? Am I home? Am I still dreaming?'
'No, Son,' Chief Marty said as he put his arm around him. 'No, this is no dream. We thought we lost you for a moment there, but you are back here with us now.' Chief Marty helped Carl up from the floor and sat him on the couch.

Stacey raced over to Carl.
'Forget any sass I ever said to you. You're no daddy's boy, Carl. You are one brave hero.'
She kissed him on his forehead.
Carl smiled and sighed. He still was not entirely sure if he was dreaming or not, but if he was, it was now a pleasant dream.

Carl's grandmother brought him a glass of water. He had a few sips and felt more like himself again.
'I was there, Professor,' he finally said. 'I think I saw White Eyes.'

'What else did you see, Carl?' Noah asked. 'Did you see my Ben? Did you see his mother?'
Carl nodded. He did not want to think about what he had just seen. He wanted to forget it like a nightmare needs forgetting.

'Were they safe?' Noah asked him. 'Were they alive?'
'Yes, Mr. Crenshaw,' Carl answered weakly. 'I saw both of them there with White Eyes.'

But no matter how much prompting Noah and Stacey made, he refused to talk about it in detail. He would only say, 'I saw them.'

Greyhawk told everyone to leave Carl in peace for a few minutes.
'Give the boy time to collect himself,' he said.

He went over to Carl and sat down next to him.
'Carl, when you're ready, you must tell me everything you saw in your vision. Not now. Now, you need time to recover. Later, you can tell us what the vision showed you.'

Greyhawk then addressed the others in the room.
'Our experiment has proved itself successful. Carl possesses the Gift of the Stone as I suspected. This is exactly what I had hoped,' he said.

'It may now be possible for Carl to retrieve Ben and your wife as well, Noah. It may be possible for him to rescue others trapped there too.'

Chief Marty looked over at his son struggling for breath and sprawled out exhausted on the couch.

'This White Eyes character has seen my boy,' Chief Marty protested. 'How do we know if it's safe for Carl to go back? I can't risk losing Carl. I can't allow it. I'm sorry, Noah, but this is my son we're talking about here.'

Carl labored to get back up on his feet. He slowly went over to his father and reached out his hand to rest it on Chief Marty's shoulder for support.
'I'm going back, Dad,' he said wearily. 'You don't understand. I can't leave Ben and Mrs. Crenshaw there. Nobody should be left there in that place. No one.'

Greyhawk put the Willing Stone back into his bag.
'I must return home,' he said hurriedly. 'I have work to do, if we are to try to rescue Ben and Cora.'

As he started walking rapidly to the front door, he suddenly stopped and turned back to the others.

'When I was at the museum, they let me borrow some newly transcribed material I had not seen before. I believe it contains new source information about The Legend of the Blue Cloud. It comes from a very early reference to it. I will read through the night and learn what I can,' he explained.

'I suggest we meet again tomorrow evening. Carl will have regained his strength by then and I may have gained a valuable new insight that may prove vital in getting Ben and his mother back with us.'

After Greyhawk had gone, Carl asked his mother if Stacey could stay overnight.
'Mom, we can ride back together to the Crenshaw's right after breakfast. Please, Miss Annie, is it all right if she stays here?'
'Sure, Carl,' Annie said. 'If that's what Stacey wants.'

'Stay here, Stacey,' he whispered to her under his breath. 'I want to tell you what really happened.'
'Yeah, Mom,' Stacey quickly said. 'I'll stay over here at the Marty's and keep an eye on Carl.'

Mrs. Marty made up the bed in the spare room for Stacey. She tried to get them both to go to sleep, but Carl insisted he wanted to sit there a while longer and talk with Stacey.
'All right then, but don't stay up too late, you hear?' Mrs. Marty said with concern. 'You both need your rest with all that's going on.'

Carl told Stacey everything he had seen behind the Blue Cloud. He shared with her every gruesome detail. He felt that he could not tell his parents or Noah the disturbing things which he had witnessed there.

'How can I tell Mr. Noah what his wife was doing with that creep? He must have hypnotized her or something. And Ben battered and standing there forced to watch her with White Eyes and crying out in agony? How can I tell them that? How can I get that out of my head?'

Stacey reached out and took hold of Carl's hand. 'Carl, you have to tell that Professor what happened. All of it. Remember he said that this White Eyes freak would show you things you don't want to see and try to scare you? Maybe what he showed you means something.'
'It all seemed so real though, Stacey,' Carl said still shaken by the memory.

'I bet it did. You turned white as chalk while you held that damn Stone. But maybe it wasn't real at all. Just a big lie to shake you up. We need to tell Professor Greyhawk. He said he's gone back to his trailer to read this new stuff he found. He said he'd be up all night doing it. If we want to help Ben, you need to tell the Professor what you saw right away. It might be the clue we need to rescue Ben and Aunt Cora.'

Carl drew a deep breath and nodded. 'Okay, Stacey, we'll go over there first thing in the morning before you head back home.'

'No, not in the morning, Carl,' Stacey said with a shake of her head. 'Right now. Come on. We're going to sneak out and saddle the horses and ride over there. Right now.'

CHAPTER 17

After the Willing Stone experiment at Chief Marty's house, Greyhawk drove up and parked at his trailer. He went inside, locked the door, and sat down at his small kitchen table. He placed his bag on the tabletop, took out the Willing Stone, and laid it down next to his bag. He then took the Stone out of its leather case and held it in his hand. He ran his fingers over the Stone for a moment and then felt his hand clutch around it. He started to feel his stomach knotting. He fell to the floor as spasms of pain raced through him. He curled up in a fetal position and shut his eyes tight.

When he reopened them again, he found himself behind the Blue Cloud.

Greyhawk felt his guts heave. He tried to control the urge to vomit. The nausea, cramps, and pain overwhelmed him as he crawled up to his knees.

When he looked back up, White Eyes was standing over him.
'My Ministering Servant, Greyhawk, why have you come here by way of the Stone?'

'My Lord,' he answered. *'How is it that I can hear you? How is that I can speak here?'*
'You do not speak or hear. I speak to your mind and your thoughts come to me.'

'How great and powerful you are, My Lord Remiel!'
Greyhawk said sycophantically.

Greyhawk bowed low in homage until his forehead
touched the ground and then got back up on his knees.

'All praise and glory to My Lord Remiel! How great is My
Lord! May your reign among the living begin soon!'

He held out the Willing Stone in his hands toward
White Eyes.

'How I wish you could touch the Stone with me, so that I
may free you, My Lord. How I wish that I could rescue you
from this place.'

'Foolish servant! Have you forgotten? The Willing Stone will
not free me. I may spy upon your world, if one of the
Brotherhood intruding here touches the Stone with me. I may
lock the holder in their Willing Stone vision forever, if I
snatch the Stone from them. But the Stone itself will not
unshackle me. Only when the Last with the Gift bodily passes
through the Blue Cloud into my domain will I be freed of my
bonds,' White Eyes reminded him.

'Forgive me, Lord Remiel. I so desire your return that I did
forget.'

'Answer me. Why have you come?'

'My Lord, how glorious the day I learned of you in my
research. How great the day I found the ritual to contact you.
How honored I was to be given the task you asked of me to set
you free.'

'My Lord, my task is nearly complete. I have searched all the lands of the tribes who trapped you here as you instructed me. I have done what you have asked of me. All those with the Gift have been located. You have ensnared the one known as Cora who I told you had the Gift, when I saw her touch the Stone at the museum. I have delivered to you her son, Ben. They are here with you now.'

'And what of the one, just now, who dared touch the Stone and come before me?'
'I bring you news, My Lord. He is the Last with the Gift!'
'The one who dared spy upon me with that curséd Stone?'

'The very same, My Lord. The one known as Carl. He is the Last with the Gift. The final one on the other side who possesses the Gift of the Stone. The moment I saw that he had the Gift, I rushed away to come and inform you.'

'Then bring him to me!'
'I shall, My Lord, and then all of the Brotherhood will be in your domain. The Blue Cloud will be destroyed and you will be liberated!'

'You have served me well, Greyhawk, and shall be greatly rewarded for your service. Bring this Last with the Gift to me. Take the one known as Carl out into the countryside. Manipulate him. Tell him you have a plan to rescue his colleagues. Take him out to the valleys. I will be able to find him. He has come here with the Stone and left his mark. I now know him and his scent. I will bring the Blue Cloud entrance near to him. He will walk unaware through the Cloud and be mine.'

'Yes, My Lord Remiel. It shall be done. He will be yours. I

have misled the boy and the others, My Lord. I've lied to the boy how the Stone may be used. He believed me when I told him that he could rescue his friend during his vision. I have feigned my concern. The boy trusts me. He will be delivered to you.'

White Eyes unfurled his wings and stormed in contempt.
'Fools! They have the Gift of the Stone and do not know it. They have forgotten their ancestors and why they locked me away here. When the door is at last reopened, I will remind them! Go back! Find this Carl. Set a trap for him and I will lie in wait.'
'I shall do as you command, Most Majestic Remiel,' Greyhawk swore.

Carl found a place to hitch Daisy Mae and Zeno as Stacey walked over to Greyhawk's trailer. She looked briefly at Greyhawk's wooden wolf carving suspended over the entrance and then rapped loudly on the trailer door. But there was no response.

When Carl rejoined her, Stacey gave him a puzzled shrug.
'His lights are on,' she said. 'Why's he not letting us in?'

Stacey knocked harder on Greyhawk's door. 'Professor! Professor Greyhawk! Let us in! Carl's here with me. We need to tell you something, Professor. It's important!' But still there was no answer.

Stacey led Carl over to the window on the side of the

trailer. 'Give me a boost up, Carl,' she said. 'I want to see if he's in there or not.'

Carl lifted Stacey up on to his shoulders, so she could peer through the window.
'I see him!' she said under her breath.
'What's going on?' Carl asked struggling to hold Stacey aloft.
'Will you stand still, Carl? You're going to drop me!'
'Right,' he grunted. 'Sorry. What do you see?'

Stacey watched intently as Greyhawk writhed on the floor. She thought she heard him mumbling, 'Touch the Stone, My Lord,' but she was not sure.

'What's he doing, Stacey?' Carl asked while readjusting his hold on her.
'Quiet, Carl,' she whispered. 'Let me hear.'

She placed her ear against the window in an attempt to hear what Greyhawk was saying more clearly, but still could not make out his words.

Greyhawk remained racked in convulsions on the trailer floor.
'The one known as Carl. He is the Last with the Gift.'
He twitched in spasms as he mumbled his words softly aloud.
Stacey heard him say 'Carl' and 'Gift', but could not hear the rest.

She watched until Greyhawk got back to his feet and slumped on a chair in his kitchenette.

His face was drained of color. He looked up blearily for a moment at the window and then laid his head down on the kitchen table in exhaustion.

Stacey quickly hopped down and whispered at Carl, 'Damn! I think he saw me!'
She grabbed his arm and pulled him away from the trailer window. Carl followed her as she walked over to where the horses were tethered.
'What happened?' Carl asked. 'Why doesn't he let us in?'

'Come on, Carl,' she said. 'Let's get ourselves back before anyone notices we're missing. We'll be getting nothing out of the Professor tonight. It looks like he has a fever or something. He's sick. He was on the floor and mumbling something about the Stone, I think. He said something about you too, but I really couldn't make out what he was saying. His face looked washed out like yours did when you held that Stone.'

'Does he need help? Should we call somebody?'
'No, I don't think so,' Stacey said as she got back up on Zeno. 'He's sitting at his table now. It looks like he's feeling better. We wasted our time coming over here tonight. You tell him first thing tomorrow about what you saw when you held that damn Stone. Maybe he'll be feeling more like himself by then.'

'I think all of this is taking more out of the Professor than we know,' Carl said as they rode back together in the moonlight.

CHAPTER 18

White Eyes rose from his throne and all in his service fell quickly to their knees. He gazed down at them and then unfurled his wings triumphantly.

'Hear this, My cohort,' he announced. 'My Ministering Servant, who abides on the other side of the Cloud, is gathering all with the Gift of the Stone to me. Only the Last with the Gift remains away from my grasp and he is soon coming. All of the Brotherhood of the Gift will then be here with us. The enchantment that cast us here will be broken. Prepare yourselves to feast, My vassals! We will leave my Principality and enter the world of time and space. A rich harvest awaits us. And there we will rule without question!'

'All praise to our Lord Remiel!' One of the Grinning Dogs shouted as all those who served White Eyes bayed loudly in their pleasure.

White Eyes raised his hand for silence. 'Those who dwell beyond the Blue Cloud will be unable to perceive us as we sow fear and hopelessness among them just as we are unable to see them now locked in this vile cage. All will be again as it once was. Our liberation is close at hand!'

'All glory and praise to our Lord Remiel!' The Grinning Dogs shouted in unison.

'May all on the other side bow and kneel in fear before him!'

The Grinning Dogs began laughing maniacally. Their laughter grew more deranged and hysterical until it had completely overwhelmed them. They roared with mad laughter and boasted of their victory.

'What's that howling?' Ben asked nervously. 'Do you hear it? Is White Eyes torturing another New One?'
'Probably,' Frank said. 'That or they're celebrating some other horror.'

Mei-Ling and Bird-Who-Hops were playing with the baby.
'Bird-Who-Hops,' Mei-Ling said. 'We need to give her a name! We can't have a baby with no name!'
'That is so,' Bird-Who-Hops said. 'It is very bad luck. She must be named.'

Mei-Ling asked the others for suggestions. Only Frank was disinterested.
'This is no nursery,' he said. 'We cannot keep the wee tyke here.'
'We have no choice, Frank,' Cora replied. 'We must keep her. We can't give her back to her mother now, can we? We can't leave her out there on her own for you-know-who to find.'
Frank gave a grunt in response.

'She was found in the hollow of a rock face. We should call her Little Hollow,' Bird-Who-Hops decided.

'No,' Cora said. 'No, she's not from any tribe. I think we should call her Hope. After all, she brings hope to all of us.'

'Is that so?' Frank snorted. 'And what do you think will happen when your Hope starts bawling and wailing? What do you guess is in store for us when she does that when we're trying to hide away from some monster or lunatic?'
'She's very quiet, Frank,' Mei-Ling said while fussing over the baby.
'Quiet for now,' he replied.

'Frank is right,' Henri said. 'One of us needs to stay here with her, while the rest of us look for New Ones.'
'I'll stay with her,' Mei-Ling said. 'She likes me. I keep her calm.'
'You better had,' Frank said. 'Or we are all for the chop.'

Mei-Ling and Hope stayed in the Gathering Place as the rest of the Brotherhood set out again on their never-ending search for New Ones to rescue.

'Something big is happening, Cora,' Frank said as they walked along together. 'Something big. Haven't you noticed that there are more and more passing through the Blue Cloud all the time? More animals, more lost people, more with the Gift? Every time we go out it is more dangerous. More things to avoid.'

'And more to find, Frank,' Cora said with a smile.

They had not been out for very long, when they came across an elderly couple of tourists strolling by.

The man was wearing a baseball cap, Bermuda shorts, and a short-sleeved Hawaiian-style shirt. He had a camera and binoculars around his sunburned neck. The woman wore a gigantic floppy hat, hiking shorts, a tank top, and boots. She had a knapsack on her back. She would stop occasionally to fetch out an apple or sandwich.

The Brotherhood looked on as the couple took endless photos and walked hand in hand. They would pause together from time to time to admire some imagined view. They had no idea that they were behind the Blue Cloud.

'We know time doesn't work here and they don't,' Henri observed as he nodded in the direction of the couple. 'I wonder which is worse. Our fate or theirs. They are happy and White Eyes cares nothing about them. They do not have the Gift.'

'Their fate is far worse,' Frank replied. 'They are trapped in this moment and don't know it. It's better to know your fate than not.'
'As I said, Frank, sometimes I do wonder,' Henri sighed wistfully.

Ben overheard Henri and Frank's discussion. He thought about what they said for a moment and then walked straight over to his mother.

'Mom, I have something to tell you. There may be no time here, but I think I should let you know. You've been missing for over a year now. At least, that's how long you were gone before I came here. Maybe a lot longer now, because I don't know how long I've been here.'

Cora smiled and took Ben's hand.
'Ben, listen to me. I know it's hard, but thinking about time and its passing is a trial for all of us. Try not to think too much about it. It will only make you miserable and play into White Eyes' hands. He wants us to be miserable. It pleases him.'

They left the tourist couple and made their way down a winding path to the valley floor. But as soon as they began walking together through the valley, they had to race for shelter behind some rocks.

'There! You see what I mean?' Frank whispered to Cora as a herd of wild horses galloped frantically past where they had just been walking.
'More and more all the time,' Frank said with a shake of his head. 'We used to see the same things over and over and now there are new threats everywhere.'

'Those were fine horses, Frank,' Bird-Who-Hops said in admiration. 'I wish I could capture one and tame it. Then I could ride.'

'Tame them?' Frank laughed. 'If you could get on one of them, you'd be in that stampede forever. Don't you know that?'

Bird-Who-Hops just started to answer Frank, when the ground began to quake violently under their feet. The landscape around them lurched and buckled repeatedly and they were all tossed to the ground. They could not stand up and were thrown this way and that in the quake. Finally, the tremors eased and then passed completely. They slowly got back to their feet.

As they dusted themselves off, they looked around and saw the sky shimmering in front of them. It was like a mirror catching the light. They stared in wonder as the Blue Cloud stood before them-enormous and glittering. It ran right across the entire valley.

'Mon Dieu! Look at that!' Henri exclaimed in astonishment.
'That's a million times bigger than the one I stepped through,' Ben said to the others.

They watched as a herd of elk bounded into their world through the gigantic Blue Cloud rift. Moments later, a group of schoolchildren walked through. They were led by two of their teachers. They all looked around happily like they were on a school outing. Right behind them, two quad bikes roared through the Cloud. The young couples inside were laughing and giggling as they drunkenly zigzagged down the valley floor. Ben could see the beer cans in their hands.

One after another, more people, birds, and animals appeared before their eyes. All of them passed through the vast Blue Cloud and into White Eyes' world.

The ground then again began to shake uncontrollably. The Brotherhood all reached out desperately for something to break their fall as they lost their balance and fell heavily to the ground.

When they did manage to find their feet again, the colossal, shimmering Blue Cloud that had just formed was gone.

'Something big is happening, Cora,' Frank reminded her. 'Like I said.'

They were just about to continue their search, when high up on the ridge opposite they saw seven black plumes of smoke slowly descending.

'Get back, everyone,' Frank commanded.

Once they had found cover, Ben looked up at the ridge. The columns of smoke continued slowly to descend. For a moment, the rapidly whirling smoky pillars stood in a row hovering in the air. Ben watched as the spinning columns of smoke then touched the ground and White Eyes and his six Grinning Dogs appeared. White Eyes stood in the center with three of the Grinning Dogs on either side of him.

'Do you not see?' White Eyes asked as his voice boomed down through the valley. 'The Cloud opens ever more widely and soon will remain open forever. Why do you bother to hide from me? Can you not see that all is futile? Why do you hide, when I have so much to show you?'

Ben had mastered his fear of White Eyes just as the rest of the Brotherhood had managed to do. He had learned from them how to breathe to control his urges to panic. He now knew how to let his fears wash through him and fade away. Cora taught him how to remain calm no matter what frightful or dreadful thing came their way. Bird-Who-Hops showed him what he did to show no fear.

'I tell myself, *I am a brave from my tribe. I am not afraid. I am a brave from my tribe. They cannot see me.* I keep repeating that over and over,' he instructed him.

Ben knew that White Eyes and his followers were wickedly vicious, but he had come to know how to stop being afraid of them. But then, White Eyes showed Ben something that put his new-found courage to the test.

White Eyes and his Grinning Dogs all unfurled their wings, so that each of their wings touched those of the one next to them. It formed a wide black curtain. Like a hideous funeral pall.

'Come forth!' White Eyes shouted out at them. 'Come and see!' he jeered. 'Look at what I have for you! Look at what my servants have found! Look at what they found crying out in fear!'

He nodded to his right and the three Grinning Dogs standing there closed their wings. Ben cupped his hand over his mouth to prevent himself from shouting out in terror. There, standing alongside the Grinning Dogs, was Mei-Ling.

'It's your friend,' White Eyes smirked repulsively. 'It's your Chinese!'
'Good God, no,' Cora whispered as she held
Ben closer to her.

One of the Grinning Dogs shoved Mei-Ling to the ground and stamped on her. Even from where they were hiding, the Brotherhood could see that Mei-Ling had been repeatedly and brutally beaten.
'Help me, Frank!' she screamed. 'Oh, Frank, where are you?'

Frank stirred at the sound of Mei-Ling's cry for his help as the Grinning Dogs began mocking her plea for rescue.
'Frank! Frank! Help me, Frank!' They laughed in cruel imitation.

Frank started to get back up on his feet to go to her, but Henri pressed him back down.
'No, Frank,' he whispered. 'You know we cannot help her. No one can help her now.'

White Eyes walked over to Mei-Ling as she lay moaning on the ground. He grabbed her by her ears and lifted her in the air. She squealed and kicked at him as he held her dangling off the ground. Her cries of agony spread right through the colorless valley.
'Frank, I'm afraid!' she cried. 'He's hurting me, Frank!'
'I'm afraid, Frank!' the Dogs mocked her without pity.

Then ever so casually, White Eyes began to carry her over toward the rim of the ridge.

Mei-Ling scratched and slapped at White Eyes, but she could not free herself from his grasp. His sickening smile was pasted wide on his face as he carried her closer and closer to the ridge rim. And then without warning, he promptly threw her off the edge. He watched happily as her body hurtled down to the rocks below. She screeched in frightful shock as she fell.

'Now you know the reward for your belligerence and disrespect,' he shouted down at her.

Frank gritted his teeth to stop himself running to the spot where Mei-Ling had been thrown.
'What I wouldn't give to get my hands on that bastard,' he seethed with rage. 'I'd choke the spit out of him.'
'Calmly, Frank,' Henri said. 'Be calm.'

Ben sniffed back his tears. 'I am a brave from my tribe. I am not afraid,' he kept repeating to himself.

White Eyes then nodded to those standing to his left and the three Grinning Dogs lowered their wings. Cora let out a muffled gasp.

'Do you see? Do you still doubt my victory is assured?' White Eyes sneered.
'Look! Her fearful cries called us right to your den. Here is your baby!'

One of the Grinning Dogs grabbed Hope by her ankle and held her aloft like he was showing off a hunting trophy. The rest of the Dogs laughed insanely as she cried and cried in terror.

The Dog carried her like that to White Eyes and passed her to him as her pitiable wailing pierced the air.

'Your Chinese told us her name is Hope,' White Eyes laughed as he continued to hold her upside down by the ankle.
'This is what I think of your Hope!' he bellowed.

And just as with Mei-Ling, he carried Hope to the edge of the ridge and without a moment's hesitation flung her down to the rocks below.
Ben inhaled and exhaled repeatedly to calm his racing heart.

'There is no hope,' White Eyes crowed. 'Soon, all of your number will be here with me. Soon, we will march through the Cloud and into the world from which you came. You have no hope, but to serve me. Serve me and save yourselves. Your Brotherhood will soon be broken. You will have no protection. Hiding your fear from me will be useless and I will do with you what I will. There is no hope, but in service to me. Come out from your hiding and bow before me.'

The Grinning Dogs mindlessly chortled in their soulless emptiness. White Eyes and his servant Dogs then switched back into their dark and gloomy smoky shapes, rose slowly up in the air, and were gone.

Frank raced across to the rocks where Mei-Ling and Hope had been thrown. The others chased behind him as quickly as they could.

When Frank reached the bodies, he knelt down over them and began to slap his face and beat his chest in his despairing misery.

He looked at the others still running toward him and barked, 'Stay away! This you don't want to see.' Frank was so overwhelmed with grief that it was enough to make the rocks around him cry out.

He covered his eyes with his hand, lowered his head into his chest, and wept.

CHAPTER 19

Early the next morning, Carl saddled Daisy Mae and rode with Stacey on board behind him back to Noah's house. There was not a cloud in the sky and the air was dead still. The predicted forecasts for heavy rain and thunderstorms had yet to come to pass.

'You ride over and see that Professor right after we get back to Uncle Noah's. You tell him every bit of what you saw,' Stacey kept badgering him as they rode together. 'You don't leave out one single, solitary thing. You hear me?'
'Okay, Stacey,' he said. 'That's what I plan to do.'
'And don't tell him we were there last night!'

As Carl rode alone over to the trailer park, he thought about everything he had seen after he touched the Willing Stone. Even though he did not really want to think about it, he wanted all the details clear in his mind. He decided to tell Greyhawk everything he experienced in his Willing Stone vision before they all met together that evening. He did not want everyone to know what horrors he saw. He thought though that it might mean something to Greyhawk and help rescue Ben and Cora.

Greyhawk welcomed him inside. 'What is it, Carl? Why have you come to see me?'

Carl thought to heed Stacey's advice. He did not tell Greyhawk that they had spied on him the night before or that they saw he was ill.

'I need to tell you what happened in my vision last night,' he said.
As difficult as it was, Carl then told Greyhawk every detail that he could remember even if the memory made him squirm inside.

'Professor, I can't tell the others what I saw there. Ben and his mom tortured and bewitched. What does it all mean, Professor?'

Greyhawk looked at Carl with compassion.
'What you saw may not be true at all, Son. I warned you about this before you touched the Stone. He will show you things that you do not wish to see. The one we call White Eyes feeds on fear. He lies and creates lies to undermine and confuse. Your vision showed that you do have the Gift of the Stone and we may be able to use your Gift to reclaim your friend and his mother.'
'But it all seemed so real!' Carl said shaking his head.

Greyhawk nodded at some books on a chair.
'I went through that new material the museum was good enough to lend me. I read through the night and found some new information that might help us.'

'Did you find out anything that could get Ben and his mom back to us?' Carl asked hopefully.

'I will share what I learned with everyone this evening. But as you're here, perhaps you can help me gain some more information before we meet. I was just about to go out to the area where Noah and Mr. Groves saw the Blue Cloud form. It would be a great help if you would come with me.'

'How can I help?' Carl asked. 'I don't understand.'

'There was a passage in the new material that warned that the Blue Cloud rifts would grow in size and number as White Eyes' power grows. I want to take you out there with me to see if that is so.'

'So what do you want me to do, Professor?'

'You are able to see the Blue Cloud formation. I cannot. I want to check the area where they saw the wild horses disappear. I want you to tell me if the Blue Cloud is still there or not.'

'You said yourself it doesn't stay in one spot. It moves,' Carl reminded Greyhawk.

'True, but we must see for ourselves if it is in fact still there. I do not wish to pass through it, if it is.'

Greyhawk opened the door to his rusty Chevy Pickup and Carl got in.

As they drove along together, Greyhawk said, 'I want to measure the Blue Cloud rift to see if it is indeed growing larger. Noah and his friend claim they saw many horses racing through. Its size must have been considerable. We may be able to determine the exact size of the rift by locating the hoofprints the horses left behind.'

When they arrived at the area where Noah and Mr. Groves had used their metal detectors, Greyhawk pulled over to the side of the road.

'Noah said it happened just below that hill over there. Come on. We'll walk over and see what we can find.'

They had not walked very far, when Carl stopped and pointed to the ground.
'Professor, the horses passed right through here.'

He knelt down to look at the tracks the horses had made. 'Sure were a lot of them,' he thought to himself as he studied their pattern. He then looked up and pointed to his left.
'Professor, they were running that way.'

They followed the tracks until they all stopped along the same line.
'Do you sense the Blue Cloud is still there, Son?'
'No, Professor. I don't see anything.'

Greyhawk let out a little puff of air in relief. 'Very well then,' he said. 'I will now try to measure its distance.'

He began to pace the long line of the horses' disappearance. He stepped away from Carl and called out at every ten paces. He continued doing so until he shouted, 'They stop way over here!'

Carl could not believe it. Greyhawk must have been more than a hundred yards away.
'Wow!' he said aloud. 'That was one big ripple.'

He stood there watching as Greyhawk slowly walked back toward him. As he approached him, something caught Carl's eye. He blinked in its direction a couple of times, but decided he had not seen anything. But then, as he turned back to look at Greyhawk again, he sensed that there was something there just out of his eye line.

'What is that?' he asked himself.

Once he got back to Carl, Greyhawk said, 'This is very serious. The Blue Cloud rift here is quite substantial. It is a very bad sign. We are running out of time to save your friend.'

'The Cloud that Ben went through was only a couple of yards long,' Carl informed him.

Greyhawk shook his head with concern.

'That means that White Eyes' power is growing significantly. Others may fall into his world through the Blue Cloud and be lost.'

'So what can we do about it?' Carl asked.

'This evening I will explain what must be done.'

Then Carl saw it.

It was not his mind playing tricks on him. Just a few yards away from where they were standing, the Blue Cloud had formed.

'Professor,' he said quietly as he pointed.

'The Blue Cloud is just over there.'

'The Cloud is there? You can see it? How I wish I could!' Greyhawk said enviously.

'Stacey can't see them either,' Carl said as he kept staring at the Blue Cloud. 'Like you said, not everyone can. You need the Gift. But it's there all right.'

Greyhawk went over to Carl and grasped his arm. 'Show me, please,' he said. 'Show me exactly where it is. Tell me what you see.'

Carl led him forward only a few paces or so. 'There, Professor,' he said as he stopped short. 'It's right there. You can't see that? You can't see it twinkling?'

Greyhawk took a step toward the spot Carl indicated and waved out his hand in front of him. 'Careful, Professor!' Carl warned him. 'You'll walk right through it!' 'I can't see anything,' he answered. 'It's right here? Are you sure?'

Greyhawk took another step forward and Carl ran to him instinctively to pull him back. 'Professor!' he shouted. 'You'll fall through!'

He grabbed Greyhawk's elbow and tried to tug him back and away from the Blue Cloud. As he did so, Greyhawk quickly spun Carl around. He stood behind him with his right forearm tight under his throat.

'What are you doing?' Carl gasped as he thrashed around to escape Greyhawk's stranglehold.

'There, Professor. It's right there,' Greyhawk mocked.

'Yes, I know, Carl. I have the Gift too. I can see it too. I know.'

'What are you talking about?' Carl asked uneasily. 'What do you mean you have the Gift too?'

'Only one with the Gift can remove the Stone from the hand of another with the Gift. Did I neglect to tell you that? Why do you think I never touched the Stone with my own hands? Why do you think I always used its cover to hold it or reclaim it from someone else? Had I not, I would be transported myself.'

'Get your hands off of me!' Carl shouted as he squirmed to get away.

'Don't you know that I saw your little lady friend spying on me last night? Were you there with her too? What did you see? What did you hear? Tell me!'

'We didn't see anything, Professor. We just thought you weren't feeling very well.'

Greyhawk frog-marched Carl closer to the edge of the Blue Cloud.

'Please!' Carl screamed. 'Don't push me through!' He yelled out for help at the top of his lungs.

'But don't you want to be with your friend?' Greyhawk asked. 'Soon, you will be with him. In just a moment, there will be so much more that you will come to know! And my Master will be well pleased with me!'

Carl felt Greyhawk begin to shove him forward. He closed his eyes in terror. The memory of his Willing Stone vision came rushing back to him. Just to think about those chilling, staring white eyes filled him with fright. He tried to kick at Greyhawk and struggled with all his might to break free, but Greyhawk was too strong for him.

He cried out again desperately for help. He flailed about in fear and flung himself from side to side to break Greyhawk's grasp, but there was no escaping him. He shut his eyes tight and held his breath as Greyhawk was about to push him through the Blue Cloud, when a rifle shot rang out.

In that instant, it was almost as if time had stood still or gone into slow motion.

Carl felt Greyhawk slowly loosen his grip and moan. The gunshot spun him away from Carl and he began to stumble and fall. He grabbed out as he fell to push Carl through the Blue Cloud, but he could not reach him and screamed in pain as he hit the ground hard.

Carl jumped back and scrambled away from the Blue Cloud horizon. He sat down and put his hand to his heart. It was beating so fast. He gasped for air. His head was spinning and his hands were trembling uncontrollably.

He was in shock. He was confused. He was not certain, but he thought he heard people running and shouting from behind him.

He glanced over at Greyhawk. He lay on the ground as he winced and groaned in pain. Blood was everywhere.

'My Lord,' Greyhawk moaned softly.

Carl could see blood still gushing from the wound. When he looked more carefully, he saw that Greyhawk had been shot straight through the side of his left shoulder.

'Carl! Carl! You all right?' A voice called out.
Carl looked away from Greyhawk and turned to the voice shouting behind him.
It was Jimmy Junior.

'Me and your dad, we tailed you and that Professor. Your dad said Stacey told Noah what she saw at the trailer park and then Noah called him. He had suspicions and when he heard you were riding over to see the Professor, we got in the cruiser and followed you. Good thing we did,' he said all in a rush.
'Did he hurt you, Carl? You sure you're all right?'

'Yeah, Jimmy Junior. I think so. Thanks. Thank you.'

As he lay there in agony, it flashed through Greyhawk's mind to crawl through the Blue Cloud himself and escape. He grimaced as he tried to move, but then stopped.
He thought to himself, 'How can I cross to my Master's world without the boy?'

Chief Marty arrived red-faced and breathing hard.
'Carl, my Carl,' he said as he threw his arms around his son. He looked up and asked, 'Is he injured, Jimmy Junior?'

'No, I'm fine, Dad,' Carl said still trying to catch his breath.
'I told Jimmy Junior to keep watching Greyhawk through his riflescope. I told him to take his best shot, if he attacked you.'
'I had him in my sights all the while,' Jimmy Junior added.

'Noah said you went over with Stacey to see Greyhawk last night,' Chief Marty explained. 'What Noah told me she saw didn't sound right to me.'

Carl was just about to tell his father what Greyhawk had said to him, when he suddenly remembered the danger they all faced.

'Get back! Everyone get back!' he screamed.
He shuffled up to his feet and clutched at their sleeves to try and pull them away from the Blue Cloud horizon.
'What is it, Carl?' Chief Marty asked.

As Carl kept trying to drag them back, he pleaded with his father and Jimmy Junior to move toward him.
'Back away!' he implored them.

Jimmy Junior looked over at Chief Marty.
'What are we meant to be backing away from?' he asked with a perplexed look on his face.

'It's there!' Carl shouted. 'The Blue Cloud's right there! Stay back! It's right in front of us. I know you can't see it, but it's there!'

Neither Chief Marty nor Jimmy Junior could see anything, but Carl's fearful coaxing convinced them both to back away from what they could not see.

Jimmy Junior walked over to Greyhawk still writhing on the ground. He handcuffed Greyhawk's hand to his own and helped him to his feet.
'You got yourself some explaining to do, Mister,' he said.

He held Greyhawk by his good arm and marched him back toward the police cruiser. Chief Marty walked alongside. Carl started to follow them and then stopped. He turned back to look at the still shimmering Blue Cloud. He was almost too afraid to look and when he did, he turned quickly around and followed the others back to the car.

CHAPTER
20

Greyhawk was rushed to the hospital. They stemmed his bleeding shoulder, cleaned the wound, braced it, and put his arm in a sling. After his medical attention, the police took him to a holding cell to await his arraignment.

Chief Marty and Jimmy Junior had a personal interest in the matter and were removed from any police involvement in the case. The State Police took over the investigation. After they interviewed Carl, Greyhawk was charged with his assault and in connection with the disappearance of both Cora and Ben Crenshaw.

The State Police searched Greyhawk's trailer and found a canvas satchel. It contained the Willing Stone and his laptop computer. They also discovered a small leatherbound diary. It was hidden in a secret compartment in the carved wolf totem over the entrance to his trailer.

Greyhawk sat uneasily in his cell. His injury made him squirm uncomfortably and he had to reposition himself several times to find some relief from his pain.

He sat there trembling with fear. He was not afraid of the law. He feared something beyond the law.
'I failed you, Lord Remiel,' he lamented softly aloud.

'Why did I delay? I should have thrown the boy through the Blue Cloud the moment it appeared. It would be done!'

He stood up and paced. 'How can I contact you, My Lord? How can I let you know that I have failed you?'

He shook in nervous anxiety that White Eyes would show him no mercy, once he discovered that he had failed in his great task.

Two policemen arrived and opened Greyhawk's cell. They led him to the station's interview room. A detective was already there waiting and greeted Greyhawk. He was heavyset and wore an ill-fitting sports jacket that was far too tight for him.
He pointed to a chair and told Greyhawk to sit down.

'I'm Detective Spence,' he said. 'You've been read your rights?'
Greyhawk nodded that he had.
'And you say you do not wish to have a lawyer present?'
'I need no lawyer,' Greyhawk answered softly. 'Ask what you will.'

Detective Spence sat quietly for a moment looking at Greyhawk before he began to question him. He then showed Greyhawk the items they discovered at his trailer.

He pointed to the Willing Stone in front of him.

'What's this, Professor?' he asked. 'What's this used for? We have several witnesses who claim it's dangerous. What can you tell us about that?'
But Greyhawk said nothing. He just stared down at the table.

Detective Spence took the Willing Stone out of its soft leather case. He began to toss the Stone up and down into the palm of his hand. Greyhawk quickly looked back up at him.
'You see, Professor? This stone does grab your attention after all.'

When Greyhawk saw that Detective Spence did not possess the Gift of the Stone, he dropped his head and again began staring down at the tabletop.

'But why, Professor? What is it about this stone? How can it be dangerous? It feels like any other stone to me.'

Greyhawk shrugged and looked away as if he were bored. Detective Spence then put the Willing Stone aside. It lay there atop its leather case on the table.

'All right then, Professor. Let me ask you about this diary found at your premises.'
He showed it to Greyhawk and opened its pages.

'Is this yours? Is this your writing? We can find out ourselves, of course, but why don't you save us all the time?'
Greyhawk looked up briefly at what he had written, but said nothing.

'I'm going to read some of this to you, Professor Greyhawk. Let me know if it sounds familiar.'

For so long, the Blue Cloud barrier between our worlds was shut tight. Through your power and majesty, you contacted me, when I performed the ancient rituals of my ancestors. You showed me how to open the Blue Cloud doorway again. How great you are! You have given me my task to serve you, Lord Remiel. I will deliver all with the Gift of the Stone to you as you commanded me.

'Who's Lord Remiel, Professor?'

Greyhawk looked up and glared briefly at the detective. He wanted to blurt out, 'Someone whose name you are not worthy to utter,' but he controlled himself. He just looked blankly and said nothing in response.

'And what do you make of this?' Detective Spence asked.

From my research, I learned how to reach your world. The door between us will soon be open. The lock created by the rites of my ancestors will be picked. You will be free to rule again in all your glory among the world of the living. I have found the boy with the Gift at the school assembly. He was transported via the Stone. I will trap him, my Lord, and send him to you.

'The school assembly?' Detective Spence asked feigning confusion. 'Isn't that where you met Ben Crenshaw?' But again Greyhawk said not one word.

159

Detective Spence paged through the diary again. A smile crossed his face, when he found the quote he wanted.
'And what about this diary entry here, Professor Greyhawk?'

I have delivered the boy to him. He will be most pleased with me.

'Who will be pleased? What boy did you deliver?'
Greyhawk said nothing. He sat there unmoved and stared straight ahead.

'Okay. You have no comment about that either? Then perhaps you might have something to share about this.'

I have found the Last with the Gift. I will tell my Lord Remiel of his victory.

'Victory? What victory is that, Professor? Who's the Last with the Gift?'
But Greyhawk refused to speak.

Detective Spence continued thumbing through the diary and looking for more damning quotes, when Greyhawk unexpectedly lunged across the table and grabbed the Willing Stone.

Detective Spence jumped to his feet.
'What do you think you're doing, Professor? That's evidence!'

Greyhawk quickly placed the Stone in the palm of his

hand and wrapped his fingers around it as Detective Spence rushed around to Greyhawk's side of the table. By the time he got there, Greyhawk was already reeling in pain and rocking on the floor.

'Call for an ambulance!' he shouted down the corridor from the interview room door.

When Greyhawk opened his eyes, he found himself rolled into a fetal position. He could see the Willing Stone in his hand. The spasms of pain piercing through him made him want to cry out.

He groaned and looked up and saw that he was behind the Blue Cloud. Slowly, he got back on his feet. He kept opening and shutting his eyes to gain focus in the swirling world around him.
He then began to call out the thoughts in his mind.

'Lord Remiel! I have come! My Lord! I must speak with thee! Speak to my mind and let my mind speak to yours as before!'

He looked around for a moment and then, descending from above, he saw a black spinning plume of smoke. When the smoky column touched down, it disappeared and White Eyes was standing before him.
Greyhawk fell to his knees.

'I have failed you, My Lord. The police stopped me from delivering the Last with the Gift to you. I am in their custody. They have foolishly allowed me to touch the Stone and come to inform you.'

White Eyes stared down at him coldly. He went over to Greyhawk and lifted him back to his feet.

'Yes, my Ministering Servant, Greyhawk. The boy has escaped for now, but he will be brought here soon enough. The one known as Carl will not know that anytime he goes out into the valleys or walks along the plains, I will be waiting for him. He will come through the Blue Cloud and all with the Gift will then be collected. My deliverance is still close at hand.'

'How great you are, My Lord,' Greyhawk replied. *'I will be unable to help you now. The police deny me my liberty. How merciful you are, Lord Remiel, for not being displeased with me.'*

White Eyes stood before Greyhawk. He placed his hands on either side of his head.

'But you have displeased me Greyhawk and for that you must be punished. Do you understand? Failure is not tolerated nor will it be.'

Greyhawk nodded in fear as White Eyes pressed his hands hard against both sides of his head.

Immediately, he shook in agony. He felt pain shoot through him like he had never felt pain before. Every nerve was on fire, but he could not shout out. He could not turn his eyes away from White Eyes' stare. He felt like he would pass out, but every time his consciousness began to slip away, White Eyes slapped him roughly across the face and he stood awake again.

He could make no sound. He could find no relief from the agony that gripped him. White Eyes then loosened his hold on him and Greyhawk fell to the ground. He quaked in his pain and misery.

'Hear me!' White Eyes howled. 'You will go back to your police. You will tell them nothing about me or my plans. Instead, lie to them. Pretend you are sorry for what you have done. Act as if you hope to make amends. Lead them astray. Make them think you are complying with their demands.'
'I shall, My Lord!' Greyhawk said still racked in fear and pain.

'And I will show you mercy, Greyhawk. Once the Last with the Gift is here, I will free you from your prison just as I will be freed from mine.'
'Thank you, My Lord Remiel! You are most merciful indeed!'

Greyhawk shut his eyes as another wave of bowel-curdling spasms tore through him.

When Greyhawk reopened his eyes, he found himself back in the real world. He blinked in confusion and looked around. He was not at all sure where he was. He still felt the after-effects of White Eyes' torturing. He breathed heavily and began to feel the pain slowly dissipate.

'Professor? Professor Greyhawk? Can you hear me?' a voice called out to him.
'You are in the hospital. Can you understand me? Professor?'

163

Greyhawk turned his head to the voice and saw a doctor standing by his bedside.
'You fell unconscious and were taken here, Professor.'

'How long have I been here?' Greyhawk asked groggily. He looked around his bed and saw an IV tube had been put in his arm.

'You've been in and out of consciousness for over two hours. You screamed out in pain when you momentarily came around, but then fell unconscious again. We need to go through your medical history, when you feel up to it. I want to know if you have any preexisting conditions which might explain your collapse.'

'Where is the Stone?' Greyhawk croaked.

'Yes, that is another puzzling thing. When you were brought in, you were holding a stone in your hand. No matter what we tried, we could not loosen your grip. In fact, the stone remained in your hand until you regained consciousness just a few moments ago. Do you suffer from carpopedal spasms, Professor Greyhawk? Parkinson's disease perhaps? That may explain why your hand was shut tight in rigor around the stone. Have you ever had epileptic fits before? It may account for the spasms you experienced in your seizure.'

Greyhawk looked down and saw the Willing Stone lying next to him. The doctor reached over, picked up the Stone, and put it in his pocket.

'The police asked me to return this to them. They claim it may be evidence against you.'
'Tell the police I am ready to cooperate,' Greyhawk rasped in exhaustion.

Greyhawk stayed overnight at the hospital. He tossed and turned all night and could not fall asleep. The next morning he was taken back to his cell. He told the two policemen transporting him that he had information he wanted to share.

'Tell them I want to talk. Tell them I know where Ben Crenshaw is.'
'Tell them yourself,' the driver said dismissively.
'I'm sure they'll be happy to listen.'

CHAPTER 21

Frank sat away from the others in the Gathering Place. No one made a sound. Nothing was said. The only noise to break the silence was the occasional sniffle of tears being held in check. Everyone was devastated by the brutal killing of Mei-Ling and Hope.

Cora sat there stunned and numb. She had just lost both her best friend and the baby she hoped to protect. She stared out into space and blinked back her tears. Everyone was in mourning. None more so than Frank.

He could not get the horror of what had happened to Mei-Ling and Hope out of his mind. He kept seeing their deaths replay in vivid detail over and over again.

'I've grown too soft,' he muttered darkly to himself. 'I should have stopped them from bringing that baby back here. Hope! There is no hope here, so why should I pretend any different?'

He was not even afforded the comfort of burying their bodies. After their murders, the Brotherhood had to drag Frank away less his rage and grief called the Grinning Dogs back down upon them. Mei-Ling and Hope still lay out on the rocks where they were thrown.

Henri tried several times to speak with Frank, but to no avail. Frank would not be comforted. He would not allow himself to be consoled. He just looked away and grunted, 'Stay away from me. Leave me alone.' He was heartbroken and sat there feeding on his misery. He refused to make eye contact with anyone and stared down at the ground.

'This wound won't magically disappear,' he thought to himself bitterly. 'This scar will never fade away.'

Frank's sorrow drained all of his energy. He sat there alone moping and lost in his thoughts, when he was roughly shaken from his brooding.

Immediately above them, the Brotherhood heard a loud cracking noise. It made Ben jump. He looked quickly around.
'What was that?' he asked nervously.
But no one knew.

They then heard the cracking sound again. It kept coming in waves and growing louder each time it came. They pressed their hands over their ears to try to block out the sickening din. It became so loud that it grew insufferable to hear it.

'Now what in the name of all that's unholy is that?' Frank said rousing himself. He stood back up and sighed.
'Stay here,' he grumbled at the others. 'I better see what's going on.'

Frank walked across the rocky floor of the Gathering Place, crawled up the rocks, and squeezed himself through the boulder canopy above him. He climbed out and found a spot to shelter and view the surrounding area.

He looked around and saw nothing, but still the cracking sounds rang out like cannon fire.
Then he looked up.

Suspended above the valley floor was the Blue Cloud. It was none like he had ever witnessed before. He watched as it expanded to an enormous size and then with a deafening, thunderous crash collapsed back down to the size of a pea. He looked on astonished as the Blue Cloud kept growing larger and then receded with another head-splitting, crashing bang.

He threw his hands over his ears and flinched every time the intolerable boom blasted out. He watched in discomfort and confusion as the Blue Cloud waxed and waned repeatedly.

The sound of the Blue Cloud collapsing was as loud as if the Great Rift that formed the Snake River Plains all those millennia ago had suddenly reawakened from its slumber.

Frank kept looking out from his vantage point at the Blue Cloud. He stared in consternation as the Cloud continued to balloon out across the valley and then collapse with an unbearably loud, shattering pop.

'So this is the end of this cesspit,' he said to himself. 'This ugly squaw of a place is tearing itself apart.'

Frank looked across the valley and observed Mei-Ling and Hope still lying on the rocks where they had been pitched.

He swallowed and let out a long, sad sigh. Then he climbed out from behind the place where he was sheltering and made his way across the valley floor.

After each collapse of the Blue Cloud, the ground shook and Frank fell to the ground, but he would not be stopped. He forced himself back up on his feet and kept making his way toward Mei-Ling and Hope.

When he reached the spot where they were slain, he began to select some rocks around where they lay. He carefully placed them over their bodies.

'This world's going to damnation, Mei-Ling,' he said as he lovingly placed the final rock over her. 'And now our world will too. That son of a coyote plans to fly this coop. But I give you my word, you will be avenged before he does.'

He kissed his fingers and then placed them atop Mei-Ling's make-shift tombstone.
'You've escaped this Gehenna at last, My lovely lady,' he said. 'Rest in peace.'

Frank climbed back down into the Gathering Place. He looked at the others to get their attention.
'It's the Blue Cloud. Huge like the one we saw before that bastard, White Eyes, and his poodles showed up,' he explained.

'It's unstable. It grew as big as the sky in front of my eyes and then makes that god-awful racket when it collapses again.'

Just as Frank finished speaking, the ground beneath them began shaking violently and they were all thrown off their feet. When they stood up again, another wave of tremors greeted them. They held on to one another to prevent themselves from being flung around like fallen leaves in a gust of wind.

Bird-Who-Hops pointed to the canopy ceiling above them. 'Up there,' he said. 'Look.'

They glanced up to where he was pointing. Rock dust and bits of gravel had begun to fall from the canopy. Another devastating jolt slammed them all heavily to the ground and the canopy started to crumble away. Fist-sized fragments of rock began dropping all around them. Then, after a particularly loud ear-splitting boom, the canopy gave way completely. They scurried out of the way as several massive boulders plunged speedily down on where they were standing.
'Run!' Bird-Who-Hops warned them. 'Quickly!'

They scattered to the walls of the Gathering Place and watched in horror as the ceiling above them collapsed on their hideaway. Cora and Ben stood together pressed against a wall as the rocks rained down.

'What is it, Mom?' Ben asked trying his utmost not to be afraid. 'Is it White Eyes?'
I don't know,' Cora said.

'This place is coming down on our ears,' Henri shouted over to Frank as the ceiling continued to collapse. 'It's like this out there too?'

Frank ignored Henri. Instead, he barked at everyone to follow him. 'Come on! Move your fanny. Let's climb out of here while we still can.'

Just as the Brotherhood began following behind Frank, the ground beneath them again began to shake uncontrollably. They grabbed on to one another to stop themselves from falling heavily onto the rocky floor.

Frank growled at them to keep going.
'Don't stop! Come on! Get a move on!' he ordered.

He led the way as he began climbing up on the newly fallen rocks to try to find a route to the top.
'This way!' he called back to the others. 'Follow me!'

Frank feverishly shoved away the rocks in front of him as he clambered up toward the surface. He only paused, when he heard a desperate cry for help behind him. He quickly looked back and saw Ben hanging on to an overhanging ledge and about to fall to the rocks below. He reached down and grabbed his hand.
'Come along, Lad. Find your feet. Keep going. Don't look down. Look up. Look up at me. Keep moving.'

They all scrambled up the treacherous, fallen rock debris. After each new tremor, the rock and rubble would slip away from under their feet or roll down on them as they crawled their way up out of the pit.

When Frank finally reached the ground above them, he stayed there and offered out his hand to pull the others free.

After they all safely reached the surface, they looked back down on what was their Gathering Place. The canopy was gone and the only reminder of it was the pile of stone fragments and broken boulders below.

Henri spotted a rocky outcrop where they could find cover. Frank and the others trailed along behind him. When they reached the outcrop, they slumped on the ground in exhaustion.

The Brotherhood had all suffered some cuts, bumps, and bruises, but seemed to have escaped in one piece. They sat there together gasping for air.
'We'll rest here for a moment,' Henri advised, 'while our scrapes fade away.'

After they caught their breath, Frank got back to his feet and pointed above them.
'There,' he said. 'There it is.'
'Zut alors!' Henri said awestruck.

They looked up in fearful wonder as the Blue Cloud above them expanded and then with a teeth-clenching, crunch shrank again. The ground quaked as the Blue Cloud fluctuated in size. They stayed low and held on to the rocks around them, so they were not thrown to the ground.

'Maybe you're right, Frank. Maybe something big is

happening after all,' Cora said as the ground shook around them.

'This is what that white-eyed jackal was gloating about,' Frank replied. 'His prison is falling apart and the door that locks him in with it.'

Ben cringed every time the crashing, shattering roar blasted out. The ground would not stop shaking. The Blue Cloud above them kept growing and collapsing in on itself repeatedly. Ben could not peel his eyes away from it and sat there mesmerized even if he was gripped in fear by it.

'I am a brave from my tribe. I am not afraid,' he repeated softly to himself.

The Blue Cloud dwindled back down again to the size of a button and let out an explosion of sound. A bone-jarring tremor raced right behind it and tore a path through the center of the valley floor.

A loud thunderous voice then began crying out all around them. It was as deafening as when the Blue Cloud collapsed in on itself.

'Soon!' the booming voice taunted. 'Soon we will come to your world and you will come with us. Then you will know your fate. I will use you for my pleasure. I will have my revenge. I will show those on the other side my glory and majesty and they will kneel before me in their fear!'

They then all heard maniacal laughter of a kind that made their blood freeze.

CHAPTER
22

Greyhawk waited for the buzzer to sound and then the door opened. The guard led him down the small cell block corridor. They stopped at his cell as the guard opened the cell door and shooed him in.
'In you get,' the guard said wearily.

He waited for Greyhawk to enter his cell. He shut the door, locked it behind him, and walked away. Greyhawk said nothing and sat on the cell's single bed.

That night a powerful thunderstorm struck the area. Greyhawk sat and listened to the loud thunderclaps. He could not see, because his cell had no windows, but he knew the storm was severe. The lights in the cell block corridor kept flickering on and off all night.

He could not sleep with the noise of the raging storm and stayed up thinking about what he would say tomorrow when he was interrogated again.

He kept shouting for the prison guard. When the guard finally arrived to see what Greyhawk wanted, he told the guard that he wanted to cooperate and had some information about Ben Crenshaw's disappearance.

'Tell Detective Spence tomorrow,' the guard yawned. 'Now stop hollering and get some sleep!'

Carl sat with his grandmother and listened to the storm raging outside.

'Grandma, it's just like the one that night before Greyhawk came to our school,' Carl said.

'It's a sign,' Carl's grandmother replied as she sipped her tea. 'You can bet your bottom dollar something is coming. Believe you me.'

Chief Marty came back in after checking on Daisy Mae and Zeno. He kept the door open as he flung off the water on his hat and coat.

'They've been promising these squalls all week,' he said. 'It's wild and wet out there. I've never seen weather as unsettled as this. Zeno's all right, but I can't get Daisy Mae to calm down. She's always been fidgety and she sure as shooting isn't fond of thunder.'

'I'll tend to her, Dad,' Carl offered.

'No, you stay put. You just stay warm inside.'

Carl waited until his father had hung up his wet coat and sat down.

'Dad, did you hear any news about Greyhawk?' he asked hopefully.

Chief Marty let out a little laugh and shook his head.

'Jimmy Junior's State Police buddy told him Professor Greyhawk now claims he wants to talk. He said they had to send him to the hospital, because he had some fit or something, but he said he's all right now. Funny thing is, until now, he wouldn't say a damn thing,' he said suspiciously.

'Now he has a total change of heart and wants to tell them everything he knows. That just doesn't sound right to me. Jimmy Junior's friend said they called that Detective Spence back in. He's coming over to interview the Professor again tomorrow.'

'Did he say anything about Ben?' Carl asked.
'No, like I say, he hasn't said a word yet, but now he promises he has information about Ben and wants to come clean.'
Chief Marty put an arm around Carl before he added, 'Don't you worry yourself about it, Carl. You leave it to the police and the grown-ups to deal with Greyhawk.'

Carl had not stopped thinking about what happened the day he went with Greyhawk and was nearly shoved through the Blue Cloud. He wondered what it all meant. Greyhawk had the Gift of the Stone just as he and Ben did. Why did he lie? Who is this 'Master' he talked about? Why did he want to push him through the Cloud? He felt some relief that Greyhawk was finally going to talk. Maybe then things would start to make some sense.

Sometimes though he felt like no one was taking him seriously. When the State Police arrived to interview him soon after Greyhawk's arrest, Carl told them about the Willing Stone and the Blue Cloud, but he did not think they really believed him. Even when his father informed them that he had seen Carl affected when he touched the Stone, they just looked puzzled.
'I guess they took it like I used to do,' Carl thought. 'Indian mumbo jumbo.'

Stacey tried calling Carl twice after she heard about Greyhawk's attack. The first time, Carl's grandmother answered and said to call back and then promptly hung up the phone on her. The next time she rang, Mrs. Marty answered. She asked Stacey to call back in a day or so. She wanted Carl to recover first from his trauma. 'He needs some time alone, Stacey. I don't want it all dragged up again just now.'

Stacey was so relieved that she had told Noah about what she saw that night at Greyhawk's trailer.
'If I hadn't,' she thought, 'Carl's dad never would have followed them out there. Carl would've disappeared through the Blue Cloud and be lost just like Ben.'
She shuddered to think of it.

Annie called them all to dinner. They ate in silence. The only sound came from the raging storm outside. Stacey was too upset to talk. She was desperate to go and see Carl, but her mother would not let her.
'Things are too fresh at the moment,' Annie said. 'You can go over there soon.'

She hoped so. The school holidays were nearly over and she would have to go back to Boise without knowing what really happened.

Noah sat at the table and fiddled with his food.
He kept trying to understand why Greyhawk attacked Carl. He could not fathom why he would do such a thing. Chief Marty shared what little he knew about the investigation, but nothing had been discovered yet to explain why Greyhawk did what he did.

'Why did he lie to us?' Noah kept asking himself. He was kicking himself for trusting Greyhawk. He worried now that no one could save Ben and Cora. He had let himself hope and now he felt hopeless.

Detective Spence arrived at the police station early the next morning. He asked the guards to bring Greyhawk back to the station's interview room.

'So you're ready to talk now, Professor? Isn't that what you told the guards? You want to talk? You told them you know something about the whereabouts of Ben Crenshaw? Isn't that so?'
Greyhawk looked up at Detective Spence and nodded.

'All right then. Let's get started. Tell me what you know about Ben Crenshaw.'
'He's fallen through the Blue Cloud,' Greyhawk said matter-of-factly.
'Blue Cloud? What's that? What's a Blue Cloud?'
'It's another dimension created by my ancestors.'

Detective Spence raised his eyebrows and smiled. 'Another dimension? I see. And Ben Crenshaw is in this other dimension right now, is he?'
'Yes, but I know how to get him out,' Greyhawk asserted. 'That's why I tried to get Carl to cooperate.'

'So you didn't attack Carl Marty? You were hoping he'd cooperate?'
'Yes, I told him to go through the Blue Cloud himself and bring back his friend, Ben, and his mother too.'

Detective Spence scanned his interview notes and the police report on his laptop until he finally found what he needed.

'Professor, Carl Marty claims you turned on him and choked him. Is that untrue?'
'He was afraid. I was only trying to assist him to save his friend. He misinterpreted my actions.'

'Okay, let's say I believe you, Professor Greyhawk. Ben Crenshaw is in this Blue Cloud dimension. How do you suggest we retrieve him?'

Greyhawk grew agitated. The detective was speaking to him like he was a fool.
'I told you already! You must bring Carl to me. Let me explain this to him. We need to find the Blue Cloud again like we did on the plain that day I was shot.'

'And why do you need Carl Marty for this?'
'Because he has the Gift of the Stone.'

Detective Spence stroked his chin for a moment.
'What sort of game is this guy playing?' he thought to himself.

'Professor Greyhawk, are you sure you've fully recovered from your fit yesterday? You're feeling better now? Because what you're saying is hard for me to believe. I've lived in these parts all my life and I never came across any Blue Clouds and neither did anyone else I know.'

'Bring me, Carl,' Greyhawk demanded. 'Let me go out with him to find the Blue Cloud. Then you'll see. Then you'll believe me.'

'Because he has this stone gift?'

'Precisely,' Greyhawk answered. 'It is a truth of my tribe.'

Detective Spence continued to ask Greyhawk about Ben and the attack on Carl, but all he would talk about was the Blue Cloud and the danger it posed.

'You must bring Carl to me,' he kept urging insistently. 'For everyone's sake.'

Detective Spence ended the interview. He called for the guard and Greyhawk was taken back to his cell.

He remained in the interview room while he typed his report of Greyhawk's interrogation on the laptop.

'I believe Professor Greyhawk is planning some defense by reason of diminished responsibility,' he concluded.

He decided to contact the forensic psychology consultant up in Boise to interview Greyhawk. He thought he would let her decide whether Greyhawk was concocting some fairytale to excuse his actions or if he really was disturbed.

Stacey saddled Bess and rode over to Carl's house. She had to return to Boise in a couple of days and she was determined to speak with him before she left. She did not tell Noah or Annie that she was going over there. She just said she was going out for a ride.

When she arrived, she tied off Bess as she gathered her thoughts before she went to the door.

'I'm seeing Carl and no one is going to stop me,' she said to herself.

She then strode up to the door and knocked. She was relieved when she saw it was Carl who answered.

'Come on,' she whispered to him. 'Tell them you're going out riding or something. I want to know everything that happened.'

'Okay,' Carl said. 'Give me a minute.'

He shut the door and went back inside. When he returned, he led Stacey over to the stable.

Carl got up on Daisy Mae as Stacey hopped back on Bess and they rode out together.

'I didn't tell them you were here,' he said. 'They're all treating me like I'm made of glass.'

As they rode along, Carl told Stacey all that had happened the day he went out to measure the Blue Cloud with Greyhawk.

'He just turned on me,' he said to her. 'He was going to push me through the Blue Cloud. He kept going on about his 'Master'. His voice changed too. It was like he was in a trance or something.'

'His master? Who's his master?'

'I don't know. I've been thinking about that too.'

'Maybe he's in cahoots with that White Eyes,' Stacey suggested.

'But why? Why would anyone serve that thing? You should've seen him, Stacey. White Eyes is one evil dude.'

'Well, maybe we can find out,' she said.

Stacey promptly turned Bess around and started heading in the opposite direction.

'Where you going?' Carl called out after her.

'Follow me,' she shouted back at him. 'We're going to get ourselves some answers.'

Stacey kept riding on until they arrived at the trailer park. When they reached Greyhawk's trailer, they saw there was yellow police tape marked 'Do Not Cross' around the building.

'We're going in there,' she said.

'We can't cross a police line, Stacey,' Carl said while shaking his head.

'It's against the law.'

After they tethered the horses, Stacey said, 'We're going in there, Carl, and we are going to find something the police missed. Uncle Noah told me they found the Stone and some other stuff in there, but they don't know what to look for and we do.'

'Well, what are we looking for?' Carl asked her.

'We'll know when we find it.'

As Stacey walked up to the trailer door, she saw Greyhawk's wooden wolf carving lying broken on the ground. She tore the yellow tape away, but the door was locked.

'Come on, Carl,' she said as she led him over to the trailer window. 'I'm going to crawl through the window. And don't tell me your dad won't like it! We're way past that by now, aren't we?'

Carl lifted Stacey up, so she could reach the window. She found the window was unlocked and slid it open. It was a tight squeeze, but she wormed her way through.
'Go to the door, Carl, and I'll let you in.'

They looked around the trailer in shock. Furniture had been knocked over on the floor and papers and rubbish had been flung everywhere. Cabinet drawers were left open and Greyhawk's clothing and other personal items had been pawed through, tossed aside, and lay where they fell. Broken bits of plates and dishes and shards of glass lay scattered on the linoleum flooring in the kitchen.
'It's like a tornado tore through this place!' Stacey said. 'I guess the police don't clean up their own mess.'

Carl sat on the floor and started going through the books and papers lying around him, while Stacey began rummaging rapidly through Greyhawk's belongings. They carried on hunting for clues in silence, but could find nothing which might explain what Greyhawk was really planning. Stacey grew more and more frustrated as she looked.

'There's nothing here! It's all junk, junk, junk!' she said in exasperation. 'I guess I was wrong. I was sure we'd find something the cops missed.'

183

Just then Stacey heard a car approaching the trailer. 'Quiet, Carl,' she whispered. 'Someone's coming.' They both paused to listen until they heard the car drive by without stopping.

'Come on, Carl,' Stacey said. 'We better get ourselves out of here before somebody finds us.' She started to make her way to the trailer door.

Carl remained seated on the trailer floor and continued to look through more of the books and magazines strewn around him, when something caught his eye.

'Hey, Carl!' Stacey shouted. 'You coming or what?' 'Whoa!' Carl shouted back. 'Hang on, Stacey! Help me look through this.'

Stacey walked quickly over to him. 'Did you find something? What did you find?' she asked excitedly.

'These books are all marked the Property of the Shoshone-Bannock Museum,' Carl said as he kept looking through them. 'Here's one called *The Legend of the Blue Cloud*. I think this is the new stuff the Professor found when he was up there to borrow the Stone again. When I came over here to tell him about my vision, he said he found something in them. He said it was new information he was going to share when we all met, but he didn't say what it was.'

Stacey looked around and began rifling through the kitchen cabinets. She found some plastic shopping bags and grabbed a handful.

'Take them all,' she said. 'Take everything you found. Put them in here. We need to go. We'll read through all of it later. You see? I told you we'd know what we were looking for when we found it!'

They stuffed the books and magazines Carl discovered into two of the larger plastic bags and made their way quietly out the door.

They left the trailer park and rode out across the plain toward Carl's house. When they were out in the open, they put Bess and Daisy Mae into a trot to get back quickly before Carl's parents started worrying why he had been out for so long. They were making steady progress as they rode side by side.

'We'll split up just before we get back to your place,' Stacey suggested. 'Then you can just tell them that you went out riding to clear your head.'
'What about the books?' Carl asked. 'What do we do with them?'

Stacey thought carefully for a moment. She decided that Carl could not possibly read all the books by himself and look for clues to rescue Ben and Cora at the same time.
'We'll each take half of them and see if we can find something useful. If you see something important, call me. They still won't let me speak with you.'

It began to shower. It was spitting down at first and the raindrops pinged off them and the horses. The sky then grew much darker and the rain intensified.

They looked up at the black rain clouds and started riding faster to get home before the storm grew worse.

They had only just begun to pick up their pace, when a burst of lightning forked down to the ground. A second or two later, a crash of thunder rang out.
'Come on, Carl,' Stacey urged. 'We better get a move on. This storm is right on top of us.'

They galloped their horses in the pouring rain. Stacey took the lead and Carl pushed Daisy Mae to keep up. They continued their gallop as the thunderstorm grew more fearsome and pelted them with rain. At each thunderclap, Daisy Mae would buck and flash her tail. Carl struggled to keep her moving forward.
'Don't fret, Daisy,' he said as he stroked her along her neck.

'Come on, Carl!' Stacey shouted behind.
'Hold up! She won't keep up this gallop,' Carl shouted back.
He finally stopped and dismounted. Stacey swung Bess around to where Carl was standing.

'I got to walk her in this, Stacey,' Carl explained. 'Thunder spooks her. If we keep riding, she's going to throw me.'

Stacey got off Bess and then she and Carl led their horses by the reins as they started walking home through the driving rain.

The thunderstorm drenched them until they were both

sopping wet. Daisy Mae kept snorting in fear, pricking up her ears, and stamping her hooves every time the thunder came. Carl had to keep reassuring her to calm her down. He was stroking her along her neck to try to settle her, when he stopped dead in his tracks.

The sheet of rain in front of him slowly began to transform. It wrinkled and glimmered. The rainwater within it started to bubble up as if it were boiling.

'What's up with her now? Is she refusing?' Stacey asked wiping the rain from her face. 'I swear your Daisy Mae is like a mule sometimes.'
'No, it's not her,' Carl said.
He pointed ahead in the direction they were walking.

'What is it? What you pointing at?'
'We can't go this way,' he said cautiously.
'Why not? It's the quickest way back,' she said as she continued walking Bess forward.
'Stacey! Stop!' he ordered.

Carl looked over to his left and then to his right to be certain he was seeing what he thought stood before him.
'The Blue Cloud's right there,' he said as he nodded at the rain in front of them.

'Okay then. We'll just go around it,' Stacey said with a shrug of her shoulders.
'No, we can't. I can't see the end of it. It stretches clear across the plain.'

'Really? Are you sure, Carl?' Stacey asked with a nervous laugh. 'I see nothing. It just looks like wet rain to me. I would have walked right through it.'
'You just stay behind me, Stacey,' he said.

'But how will we get back? Do you know another way?'
'There is no other way. Not while that thing's there. We need to go back to town. I'll call home and tell them I'm waiting out the storm.'

They decided to take shelter at Groves Gas Station and started walking the horses back there.
'We can tether Bess and Daisy Mae in his garage and use the phone to call home,' Carl suggested.

By the time they arrived, they were sodden through and through and their shoes squelched as they walked. Mr. Groves helped them tie up the horses in the garage and then invited them inside his office.
'Get yourselves out of this wet mess,' he said with a smile.

They went into Mr. Groves' office and used his phone to call home. They both told everyone they were waiting out the storm and nothing else.

'Come on, Carl,' Stacey said. 'While we're riding this out, let's have a look at what we found at the trailer.'

They took off their soaking shoes and sat on the office floor near the radiator, while Mr. Groves sat behind his desk doing some paperwork. Then they took out the bags with the books and scattered them on the floor.

Carl looked around at the pile of books and periodicals surrounding them and sighed.

'I didn't realize we took so many. Where do we start?' he asked.

'Right here,' Stacey replied already leafing through one of the books.

'Have yourself a look at this!'

She showed Carl the book he had found in Greyhawk's trailer entitled *The Legend of the Blue Cloud*.

'Just look who wrote it,' Stacey said as she passed the book to him.

Carl read the author's name aloud.

Professor Edwin Greyhawk.

They sat together and skimmed through the book. They read in silence looking for some clue in the Legend that might help them. They read about the Blue Cloud and how it was created to trap White Eyes. They found a passage about the Gift of the Stone and how someone with the Gift can have a vision about White Eyes' dark world. Carl pointed out a section to Stacey which discussed how Native American totems can protect against dark spirits, but they could not find anything that would help them to enter that dark world and bring Ben or anyone else trapped there back home.

They were just about to give up on *The Legend of the Blue Cloud*, when Stacey noticed a multi-folded piece of of paper wedged firmly in its inner spine.

'What's this?' she asked as she shook it out from the binding. She picked up the paper and unfolded it. It was typewritten. She read it to herself for a minute and then shouted out loud, 'Listen to this!'

Since the publication of this book, I have discovered some important new information about The Legend of the Blue Cloud. According to this new source material obtained through recent transcriptions of tribal oral storytelling passed down from generation to generation, White Eyes will break his bonds once he has collected all with the Gift of the Stone behind the Blue Cloud.

None with the Gift can be retrieved once collected, unless entrance is gained through the Blue Cloud itself by one of the Brotherhood with the Willing Stone in their possession. Only the one who enters through the Blue Cloud with the Willing Stone can free the others with the Gift imprisoned there. They must touch the Willing Stone together with those trapped with the Gift. The Blue Cloud window will then form and they can walk back through it into this time and space. Once all with the Gift have been released, the Blue Cloud passageway will be closed again forever.

Stacey let out a dismissive little snort and shook her head. 'Gosh, why do you reckon the Professor neglected to mention that when we were all meeting at your place? Because he's a double-dealing, double-talker! That's why! I knew he was up to no good. I knew it!'

'What's this Brotherhood thing you read about?' Carl asked.
'It's in the book. I saw something about that,' she said.

Stacey picked up Greyhawk's book and started to leaf through it rapidly.

'I know it's in here somewhere... Here it is!'

She traced the words with her finger and read the passage aloud.

Those with the Gift, who are not in league with White Eyes, form a kind of collective. One with the Gift can recognize, on some level, another with the Gift. This is known as The Brotherhood of the Gift. They share a bond with one another often unknowingly. Many become close friends or partners. They are bound together one to another often by familial or tribal connections.

'Now we know what we have to do!' Carl shouted happily. 'We'll find the Blue Cloud and I'll go through it with the Stone. I'll get Ben and his mother and anyone else trapped there with that monster. No way am I in league with White Eyes.'

'But how do we do that?' Stacey asked. 'We don't have the Stone. How are we going to get it?'

'I know where it is,' Mr. Groves said.

Stacey and Carl both nearly jumped out of their skins. They were so engrossed in their reading that they had totally forgotten Mr. Groves was there.

'You know where it is?' Carl asked trying to be sure he had heard correctly.

'Sure I do,' Mr. Groves said casually. 'Jimmy Junior's meant to fetch some psychologist from up in Boise. The police want to see if that Professor is nuts or not.'

'One of his State Trooper pals has to take his son to the dentist and asked my Jimmy to pick up the psychologist and then return the Stone to that museum in Pocatello for him. He told him the Stone has nothing to do with the case. That Detective Spence said it's no longer considered evidence, so Jimmy Junior said.'

'Jimmy Junior has the Stone?' Stacey asked unable to believe their luck.
'No,' Mr. Groves answered. 'He went out hunting at first light with a few of his buddies. Bet they're all soaked to the bone by now!'
'So he doesn't have it?' Carl asked disappointedly.
'No, he left it here. He's sure to be back soon to collect it and then he's heading up to Boise.'

Stacey looked at Carl, coughed, and gave a wry smile at Mr. Groves' literal-mindedness.
'Can we see it, Mr. Groves?' Carl asked.

'I don't see why not. You two been reading about that Blue Cloud thing. Noah and I saw those horses clean vanish into nothingness. If you can use that Stone, Carl, and get rid of that Blue Cloud, I say good riddance to it.'

CHAPTER
23

Mad Tom ran down the valley and called out wildly in every direction in his flowery and grandiloquent manner.

'Fair is foul and foul is fair! Something wicked this way comes! Double, double toil and trouble; Fire burn and cauldron bubble!'

Ben and the others stayed hidden away from him and laid low behind the rocky outcrop Henri had discovered after the collapse of the Gathering Place.

They had not moved from that spot, since their former sanctuary was destroyed in the quakes. But they found their new refuge offered them little comfort. The Blue Cloud still repeatedly grew and shrank accompanied by earth-trembling sonic booms that reverberated down the barren valley.

Frank tore at some of his clothing, ripped it off, wrapped it around his ears, and tied it off with a knot. 'The rest of you protect your hearing too,' he suggested under his breath. 'It doesn't help much, but it's better than nothing.'

They all followed suit and began plugging their ears while keeping one eye out for Mad Tom's antics.

Ben tore off a sleeve from his shirt and gave it to Bird-Who-Hops and Henri. Their clothes were made of animal skins or sagebrush bark and fur and would not tear easily.

'It is better, Frank,' Henri said in a whisper. 'I can just about hear myself think again.'

Mad Tom kept skipping childishly and quoting lines from plays he must have performed before he was trapped behind the Blue Cloud. He fell to the ground, when the tremors were very severe, but paid no notice. He simply got back to his feet, continued skipping, and shouting maniacally.

'Now is the winter of our discontent!'

The others kept a careful watch on him and when he turned and ran in their direction, they dropped down out of view behind the rocky outcrop they now called home.

As they watched Mad Tom in his lunacy, a deep rumbling rose up from beneath the surface of the valley. The ground around them shuddered strangely until without warning the valley floor split wide open. Huge jagged rocks shot up from the ground. They sprung up and up like a mountain range forming right in front of their eyes. Mad Tom froze briefly with a crazed look on his face as the new rock formation lifted him high up into the air. He giggled in merriment like he was on an amusement park ride.

Ben wrestled with himself to keep his fear in check. He tried his best to master it, but the relentless chaos playing out in front of him overwhelmed his efforts. He slapped his hand over his mouth, so he would not scream in terror. Cora saw her son grappling to contain himself and threw her arms around him. She beckoned the others over to join with her. As the surrounding landscape continued to transform instantaneously, they all gathered together low on the ground with their arms around one another in one tight-knit huddle of support.

After Mad Tom had finally skipped away, another deep and low rumbling was followed by yet another seismic shift. Part of the ridge bluff opposite them collapsed and tumbled loudly to the valley floor. Rocks began bouncing rapidly across toward them and smashed above their heads.

They were pinned to the ground as the broken rocks from the rockslide kept flying in their direction as if they were launched from a catapult.

'We won't survive this,' Frank said to the others. 'We better find ourselves somewhere safe. Pronto.'

He hopped back up to his feet and looked out at the mayhem and pandemonium that confronted him. He ducked rapidly out of the way as a rock shard flew right at him. When he stood up again, another quake slammed him back to the ground. Finally, he managed to stay upright and started running as he waved at the rest of the Brotherhood to follow him.

'This way!' he shouted above the discordant commotion around them. 'Follow me! Come on! Move!'

The rocks from the collapsing ridge whizzed nonstop across the valley floor. As Ben ran behind Frank, a jagged rock fragment whistled just over their heads. They had to veer around boulders that suddenly rolled across their path. It was as if the sky were hailing rocks and stones.

The Brotherhood raced behind Frank as he led them down a steep path. He took them toward the hollows in the ridge where they found the abandoned baby, Hope. When they arrived there, they split into two groups. The hollows were neither wide nor deep enough to accommodate all of them together. Ben and Cora sheltered in one of the hollows and Bird-Who-Hops, Frank, and Henri in an adjoining hollow nearby.

As the rock storm continued unabated, Frank came out from his hollow, so everyone could hear him.
'We'll stay here. We'll be protected from those falling rocks. Maybe we will. Get back as far as you can.'

He rejoined Bird-Who-Hops and Henri and they looked on together as the world where they were trapped was being torn apart.

CHAPTER
24

Mr. Groves took the Willing Stone out from a drawer in his desk. It was in its leather pouch. He handed it to Carl.

'You two do what you have to do with that Stone thing,' he said. 'I'll be sure to tell Jimmy Junior you have it.'

When the thunderstorm at last subsided, Stacey and Carl thanked Mr. Groves and then went out to his garage and climbed back aboard Bess and Daisy Mae.

They rode back out across the plain to where they had seen the Blue Cloud, but it was no longer there.
'We'll try to find it again tomorrow,' Carl said.
'I have to go home tomorrow evening,' Stacey protested. 'Why don't we look for it now?'

'No, we'll look for it first thing in the morning,' Carl insisted. 'I want my dad there, when I go through the Cloud. We need to read all these books more carefully anyway. We may have missed something important we need to know. You get your mom and your Uncle Noah to go through the books and I'll get my dad, mom, and grandma to do it too. The more we know, the better chance we have to save Ben and your Aunt Cora.'

They rode side by side back toward Carl's house.
Just before they got there, Stacey pulled up Bess.

'I'll head back to Uncle Noah's from here. That way your folks won't know we were out together. You be sure to be ready early tomorrow. I ain't missing this. I want to be there in person when you bring them back.'

Stacey brought Bess alongside Carl and Daisy Mae and stopped. She looked at Carl, reached over to him, grabbed the front of his shirt to pull him nearer to her, and kissed him.

'You call me, if you find something in your books. You hear?'
And she rode off.

Carl sat there stunned with a silly grin on his face as he watched Stacey ride away. He followed her with his eyes until she was just a silhouette against the horizon. Then he shook his head to clear his mind, smiled again, and started to make his way back home. But after only a few strides, his blissful ecstasy suddenly abandoned him.

He pulled Daisy Mae up short and stopped. The enormity of what he hoped to do suddenly struck him. He thought again about White Eyes and the horrors he saw. He wondered what would greet him, if they could find the Blue Cloud and he did try to rescue Ben and Cora.

Maybe what Greyhawk had written about the Legend was another of his lies and he would end up trapped there himself in that sinister place.

Maybe Ben and his mother were already dead or no longer themselves. What if they now served White Eyes and he would be tortured for trying to save them?

He gulped hard and then shook his head.
'No, I have to try. I mustn't be afraid. That's what White Eyes wants. I won't give it to him. I won't be afraid.'
He made a clicking noise with his tongue to get Daisy Mae moving again and headed back home.

Greyhawk sat in his cell thinking. He thought about what White Eyes had said to him during his vision after he grabbed the Willing Stone in the interview room. It gave him some solace. White Eyes had no doubt that Carl would be trapped behind the Blue Cloud.

'It doesn't matter that I failed him,' he thought. 'His victory is assured. He will come here to this world and release me. I showed him the Last with the Gift. He knows who it is and he will reward me for it.'

He closed his eyes and eventually drifted off to sleep. It was the first time he had slept properly, since the day he was shot.

Stacey ran inside the house, slammed the door, and shouted for Annie and Noah.
'We have it, Mom! We have the Stone! We found Greyhawk's books, Uncle Noah! We know how to save Ben! And Aunt Cora too!'

'Slow down,' Annie said. 'Who's 'we'? Were you out with Carl? Didn't I ask you to leave him be?'

'Sorry, Mom, but I had to know what was going on. It's a good thing I did too. Now we know exactly what we have to do!'

'Start from the beginning, Stacey,' Noah said trying to calm her down. 'What did you find out exactly? How do you know that we can rescue Ben and your Aunt Cora?'

'It's all in the books we found in Professor Greyhawk's trailer,' she replied.

'You broke into his trailer, Young lady?' Annie asked in shock.

'I climbed through the window and look what we found!'

Stacey dumped out the books from the plastic shopping bag onto the kitchen table and showed them the material they had taken from Greyhawk's trailer.

'Carl has some of the other ones. One of the books explains how people behind the Blue Cloud can be returned here. Carl has that one, but we all need to go through this other stuff to see what else we can find out.'

Noah and Annie looked at one another. They did not know what to say about any of this.

'Please!' Stacey begged them. 'Just believe me. Carl has the Stone. He's going to go through the Blue Cloud and find Ben and Aunt Cora. He's doing it first thing

tomorrow morning, but we have to look for other clues first.'
'Carl has the Stone?' Annie asked.

Stacey gave her mother a look and slowly shook her head back and forth. She let out a long exasperated sigh and tried again to explain everything that had happened while she was out riding with Carl.
'Now do you see?' she pleaded. 'Now will you help?'

Carl settled Daisy Mae in the stable. He took a deep breath before going back inside the house.

'Carl, dry yourself off,' his grandmother said when she saw him. 'Come and get yourself warm. You'll catch your death.'

Chief Marty came in from the kitchen. When he saw Carl was home, he shouted back behind him, 'Marian, Carl's back.'
Mrs. Marty dropped what she was doing and rushed out as quickly as she could.

'Carl! Are you all right?' she asked. 'You had me worried silly! That was a terrible storm while you were out. How did Daisy Mae cope with the thunder? She didn't throw you, did she?'
'No, Mom. I'm fine. Don't worry.'

Carl asked everyone to sit down. He decided that he was going to tell them everything, except for the part about Stacey being with him. He even took the blame for breaking into Greyhawk's trailer. He told them about the books he found and that he discovered how they could bring Ben and Cora back home.

Chief Marty began lecturing Carl about crossing the police line.
'You know better, Young man. That trailer was taped for a reason.'
'I had to go in there, Dad,' Carl explained. 'Professor Greyhawk told me that he had some new material from the museum with information that could help us. I had to find out what it was.'

Just as Stacey had done, Carl showed them all the books he had with him.
'This one is written by the Professor himself,' he said. 'It's called *The Legend of the Blue Cloud*. I went through it, while I was waiting out the storm with Mr. Groves. It tells us how we can save Ben and Mrs. Crenshaw too.'

Carl gave one of the books to each of them.
'Look for any clues about getting someone out from behind the Blue Cloud,' he said. 'Grandma, you're good at seeing if something is a sign or not. We need to know as much as we can before I try to rescue them.'

'What do you mean?' Mrs. Marty asked uncertainly.

Carl showed her the Willing Stone in its leather case.
'Mr. Groves let me borrow this. I'm going to use it again tomorrow morning and get Ben and anyone else I can out of that awful place.'

Mr. and Mrs. Marty quickly looked at one another.
'No,' Mrs. Marty said. 'No, Carl. It's too dangerous.
Didn't you hear your father tell Noah it wasn't safe
after you used that Stone the first time? We can't risk
losing you too.'

'Mom, I'm going to bring back Ben and Mrs. Cora too,'
Carl said calmly. 'I have to try, but I need your help to
do it.'
'Of course, we're going to help you,' Carl's
grandmother interrupted.

'Orin, Marian, we're going to help. We're going to do
just like Carl asked. Let me get my specs. I got some
reading to do and so do all of us. Now be a dear,
Marian, and make me some tea.'

CHAPTER
25

After the Brotherhood had weathered the rockslide, they decided unanimously to call the ridge face hollows their new home.

'We may not all be together,' Henri said. 'But we are still together.'

If no Betrayers were around, they could take the short walk between their two hollows to meet. They could still venture forth together to look for New Ones. Cora suggested, 'We can take any New Ones we find to the other hollows in the ridge nearby.'

And so it was agreed. The hollows would be their new haven and sanctuary from the tremors and chaos caused by the Blue Cloud's fitful fluctuations.

It was growing late. The Martys had been sitting there reading in silence for hours. Only the raging tempest outside vied for their attention. The windows rattled and shook in the wind. The driving rain striking the roof kept up a staccato beat.

No one said a word, until Carl's grandmother spotted something. It proved to be the only really important new information about attempting to rescue someone trapped behind the Blue Cloud. It was not good news. She read it aloud so the rest would know.

Several myths about the Blue Cloud mention what will happen when White Eyes attracts more with the Gift to his world. The Blue Cloud will grow more unstable. It will appear and disappear rapidly. It will swell in size and then collapse back in on itself.
If one with the Gift enters through the Blue Cloud with the Willing Stone in hand in an attempt to rescue others with the Gift trapped there, White Eyes will be aware of it. He will do everything in his power to destroy the intruder before he can seek out others with the Gift marooned there and set them free.

Just then the phone rang. Chief Marty went over to answer.
It was Noah.

'Orin, Stacey told us what happened when she was out with Carl. She claims they know how to rescue Ben and Cora. We've been reading the stuff they found at Greyhawk's trailer, but we couldn't find much that was useful. Stacey read something about a ritual to contact this White Eyes character, but nothing about getting Ben and Cora back with us. She said Carl had some of the Professor's books too. Did you find out anything?'

Chief Marty glanced over at Carl and smiled.
'That's right, Noah. Carl told us the same thing. He neglected to mention though that he was out with Stacey. My mother just found something important she read in Professor Greyhawk's book. From what she discovered, a rescue attempt sounds very dangerous. I'd like to say it also sounds ridiculous, but I've learned better now. Despite the risk, Carl insists that he wants to try to bring your Ben and Cora back home.'

'What do you think we should do?' Noah asked.

'There's no stopping Carl over this. Believe me, we tried, but he won't listen. He's determined to go out tomorrow and find that Blue Cloud thing and walk through it whether we support him or not. Marian and I aren't happy about it, but he's hell bent on doing it. He wants us all there with him while he looks for the Cloud. I'm suggesting we all meet over here early tomorrow morning. Let me call Jimmy Junior and see if he's back from Boise. I want him with us when we set off. We'll ride out together. I'll see if one of Jimmy Junior's buddies will lend us an extra horse or two.' They said their goodbyes and hung up.

Chief Marty looked at Carl. 'Did you hear what your grandma just read? If all this craziness is true, you'll be walking into a world of trouble with that White Eyes on your tail. I want you to think about that.'

A thought then came to him.
'Hang on. Why should you have to do this? Give me that Stone. Maybe I have this Gift thing too and can do this myself.'

Carl gave the Willing Stone to his father. He removed it from its leather case, ran his fingers over it, and squeezed it into his fist. But nothing at all happened.

Mrs. Marty tried her luck with the Stone too and even Carl's grandmother insisted on giving it a go.
'If I have Carl's Gift, I'm going to give that White Eyes character a piece of my mind!' Carl's grandmother said.

But the result was the same. Chief Marty shook his head with chagrin.
'Sorry, Carl, but it looks like you're the only batter on the team.'

Early the following morning, the cell block guard stood outside Greyhawk's cell. He waited while he finished his breakfast and then led him back to the police station interview room.

'Wait here,' he said tonelessly. 'Sit down and someone will be in to talk with you directly.'
The guard then shut the door and left.

Greyhawk looked around the plain room. There was a table and two chairs and nothing else except for a table microphone to record whatever might be discussed. The off-white painted walls were bare. It was drab and featureless.

As he waited, a self-satisfied smirk crossed his face.
'My Lord Remiel will soon release me from this place. I'll keep telling them what they think they want to hear. Just as my Master said I should.'

The door to the interview room opened. A pleasantly plump woman entered. She was dressed in a grey pantsuit, flat shoes, and a multi-colored scarf.

'Professor Edwin Greyhawk? I am Mrs. Perot, a forensic psychology consultant for the police. May I sit down?' she asked politely.

'I have read the transcript of the notes from your previous interviews,' she began. 'There are a few questions which I hope you might answer for me. You know, just to clear a few things up in my mind. Would you indulge me, Professor?' she asked kindly. Greyhawk nodded and then rubbed his still aching shoulder.

'Are you uncomfortable?' Mrs. Perot asked with concern. 'Shall I get you some water? Are you in too much pain to continue?'

'No,' Greyhawk replied. 'What do you want to know? I'm more than happy to cooperate.'
'Thank you, Professor.'

Mrs. Perot opened her laptop. After clicking on a file, she said aloud, 'Here it is.'

'Professor Greyhawk, would you tell me more about this Blue Cloud you mentioned to Detective Spence? Have you seen such a Cloud yourself?'
'No, only those with the Gift can see one.'

'Yes, the Gift. That is something else I was hoping you might shed some light on. You told the detective that Carl Marty has this Gift, isn't that so?'

'Yes,' Greyhawk said. 'He has the Gift. He is the only one who can rescue those lost behind the Blue Cloud like his friend, Ben. I tried my best to explain that to him.'

Mrs. Perot excused herself as she typed on her laptop.

'Forgive me, Professor. As you were saying, Ben Crenshaw is behind this Blue Cloud and you were trying to help Carl Marty pass through this Cloud and find him?'

'Yes, I was only trying to help. I'm sorry if the boy thought I was attacking him. I was only hoping to assist him in retrieving his friend.'
'I see,' she said as she looked back down at her notes.

'And what of these statements in your diary?' she asked. 'You've written that you 'delivered the boy to him' and in several instances you mention a 'Lord Remiel' whom you serve. Would you help me understand what you meant by that please?'

Greyhawk gritted his teeth for a moment when Mrs. Perot mentioned White Eyes' name. He then said calmly, 'It's all material for an article I am writing about Native American dream myths.'
'So you do not imagine that you serve this Lord Remiel?' she asked.

Again, Greyhawk struggled to contain himself when she spoke White Eyes' name, but he forced a smile and said casually, 'Of course not. He is simply a part of the dream myth. However the Blue Cloud phenomenon is true enough. Several people in the area have seen one. I am not alone in that. To acknowledge that there are such things is part of my tribal belief system.'

Mrs. Perot paused. She looked directly at Greyhawk. 'So you yourself had nothing to do with Ben

Crenshaw's disappearance? He is missing, because he went through this Cloud?'

'Yes, that's true. I personally had nothing to do with it. It's the Blue Cloud that is to blame. I went to his school and showed the kids the Willing Stone. Young Ben picked it up and had a funny reaction. That's my only involvement.'

Mrs. Perot looked straight at Greyhawk again.
'And you did not attack Carl Marty?'

'No, I did not. He does not understand my faith and he was frightened about what he did not understand. He misinterpreted my motivations.'

'You told Detective Spence that he must bring Carl Marty to see you, so he could rescue Ben Crenshaw. Isn't that would you said?'

'Carl has the Gift. If we want Ben returned, Carl must go through the Blue Cloud to do it. This is the teaching of my people. It is the only way.'

Mrs. Perot nodded and smiled.
'I think that's enough for now. I don't wish overly to tax you with your injury and recent hospital stay. Perhaps we can speak further about this later. Thank you, Professor Greyhawk. That was very helpful. I believe I have a far better understanding now. Thank you for clarifying all of this.'

Mrs. Perot summoned the guard and Greyhawk was

led back to his cell. She remained in the interview room to type her notes of her discussion with him.

My preliminary view is that Professor Greyhawk may be suffering from a type of religious mania. I am not yet certain if he is responsible for his actions or not. He may well be. He does state strongly that this Blue Cloud to which he repeatedly refers is real to his mind. I am convinced that is true and his religious convictions may have influenced his grasp on reality. He may not appreciate that his actions with Carl Marty were aggressive. I recommend he be referred to a mental health facility where he can be evaluated further.

As the guard opened his cell door, Greyhawk entered quietly and sat on his bed. He heard the door slam shut behind him and the guard walk away. He smiled to himself and mumbled softly, 'My Lord Remiel, you are safe. I have fooled them. When you come to free me, may you punish these blasphemers first.'

CHAPTER
26

The first thing the following morning, Stacey and Annie rode Bess and Willy over to Chief Marty's house. Noah drove up not long after them. A few minutes later, Jimmy Junior pulled up with a horse trailer hitched to his pickup. He led two horses over to Noah and Chief Marty and passed them the reins.
'My friend said neither of them spook easy,' he informed them.

Mrs. Marty made everyone breakfast, but there was little conversation. No one knew what to say. They all sat and ate lost in their own thoughts. Everyone's mind was on Carl's quest. They ate rapidly and then went back outside, climbed up on their horses, and awaited further instruction.

Before they set off, Chief Marty pulled his horse around and announced to everyone, 'Marian and I want you all to know that we're not comfortable with any of this. We just hope everyone understands what we're asking of our boy.'

They all looked to Carl for an indication on which way they should head.

'I think we should go back to the Magic Valley where we lost Ben,' he suggested. 'If the Blue Cloud isn't there, we can try again where Stacey and I saw it out on the plain yesterday during the storm.'

They left together in one group with Carl and Daisy Mae in the lead. When they reached the valley, Carl looked for the steep and narrow path where Ben had led them before he disappeared. Once he found it, he waved his hand to signal the others. They all had to ride uphill in single file before the path flattened out and widened again.

'This way,' Carl called out to the others riding behind him. 'We took this trail to our left back down to the valley floor.'
He put Daisy Mae into a canter and the others followed suit as he led them down the hill path.

'It was right around here, Carl,' Stacey yelled from behind. 'I remember we stopped to admire the view.'

When they reached the valley floor, dark clouds soon began to form overhead. The wind died down, the sky became intensely dark, and everything grew very quiet. A fearful flash of lightning followed by a crack of thunder shattered the silence and rain began to fall. It started coming down hard and soaked them mercilessly. Bolts of lightning shot through the sky to the ground with peals of thunder not long behind. Daisy Mae began to rear and buck in panic. Carl struggled to keep her moving forward.

Chief Marty rode up to Carl. 'It isn't safe to be out in the open in this.' He then turned back to the others. 'Let's get some cover over there.'
He led them toward the vertical rock face of the valley ridge.

The thunderstorm grew more severe. They rode together to the rock face as the driving rain bucketed down on them without pity and the lightning strikes kept hitting the valley floor. Loud claps of thunder followed quickly behind each bolt of lightning. When they reached the face of the ridge, they all dismounted.

'We'll have to wait this out until it eases off,' Chief Marty told the others.

Both Willy and Daisy Mae kept snorting and flashing their tails and their panic made the others horses jumpy too.

Carl held Daisy Mae by her reins and spoke soothingly to her to stop her fretting.
'Easy, Girl. It's okay. That's my Daisy.'

As Carl was trying to settle her, Daisy Mae abruptly jerked her head away as another thunderclap rang out. She pulled Carl around in her panic. He held on to her reins firmly to keep her still.
And then he saw it.

Only a few yards away from where they were waiting, the Blue Cloud appeared. Just like the Cloud that Carl had seen when he and Stacey rode toward home after breaking into Greyhawk's trailer, the veil of rain in front of him bubbled up and sparkled. It stretched out clear across the valley basin. Carl kept staring at it. He tilted his head from one side to the other to be sure that he was seeing the rippling in the rain.

Stacey noticed Carl staring out into the storm.
'Do you see something?' she asked. 'What do you see? Is it the Cloud?'
Carl looked at her and nodded.
'We found it,' he said.
Willy began to snort and stamp again as if in agreement.

Carl walked Daisy Mae over to his father.
'It's there, Dad,' he said pointing in the Blue Cloud's direction. 'It's gigantic. A thousand times bigger than the one Ben went through.'

He then looked at the others and said, 'I know you can't see it, but that Cloud thing is just over there. Keep back where you are. Don't let your horses pull you toward it.'

Carl reached into his jacket pocket. He took out the Willing Stone protected in its case and held it in his hand. He stared down at it for an instant and then started stepping toward the Blue Cloud, when Jimmy Junior stopped him.
'Hang on, Carl,' he said.

Jimmy Junior was not wearing his uniform. Carl could not remember a time when he had ever seen Jimmy Junior without his police uniform. He was wearing jeans held up by a wide leather belt adorned with a large, silver buffalo head buckle, snakeskin boots, a long-sleeved, pearl-buttoned checkered shirt, and a Kansas City Chiefs NFL bobble hat on his head.

Carl struggled to keep a straight face. Maybe it just was the butterflies in his stomach over what he was about to do, but for some reason Jimmy Junior's civilian look struck him as kind of funny.

'Be sure to bring that Stone thing back with you, Carl,' Jimmy Junior requested. 'I need to return it to the museum after I drive the police psychologist back to Boise. I have to keep it safe until then. I promised my friend in the State Police. He's supposed to take care of it, but he has to take his kid back to the dentist.'

'Sure, Jimmy Junior. I'll give it right back to you as soon as I see you again.' As Carl put the Stone back in his pocket, Jimmy Junior slapped him on his back.
'Good luck,' he said.

Stacey ran up to Carl and squeezed him with a hug.
'I'm waiting right here until you get back with Ben and Aunt Cora,' she swore.
She turned to Annie. 'Mom, we can't go home until Carl gets back. I couldn't stand it!'
She went back over to Carl and hugged him again.
'You come back,' she said. 'I'll be waiting for you.'

Mrs. Marty's eyes filled with tears. She said almost in anger, 'You will not go through that Cloud, Carl Marty. You are coming home with me and your father right now!'
'I can't, Mom,' Carl replied. 'I have to do this. I have to go. Don't you see?'
'No, I don't see! You don't have to go!' she cried.
'Please don't do this!'

Chief Marty went over to his wife to comfort her. His eyes were also teary.

'Get in and get out, Son,' he said trying to control himself.

Noah walked over to Carl and began shaking his hand. He would not let go of his grip.

'No matter what happens, I'll never forget what you're trying to do here. Be safe and come back. You just come back. You just…' His voice trailed off and he swiped the back of his hand across his eyes.

Carl was not sure if Noah was wiping the rain away or if he too was close to tears.

Carl patted the Willing Stone in his jacket pocket. He breathed in deeply and exhaled. He turned away from the others and took a couple of steps forward. The rain kept sheeting down punctuated by flashes of lightning and rolls of thunder as he approached the Blue Cloud.

He heard his mother crying behind him. He paused for a second and then took another step forward…and he was gone.

Jimmy Junior looked over to Noah. 'That's what Pop said happened to those horses you saw. It's disturbing strange.'

CHAPTER
27

Carl felt as though he had just walked into someone else's bad dream or the setting of some old black and white horror movie.

Within seconds, he was shocked to discover that all of his clothes were bone dry again. He shook his head and touched his face to convince himself that he was awake and that what he was seeing was real.

All the color had been bled out of the joyless landscape into which he had wandered. Everything around him looked dreary, gloomy, and lifeless. He quickly turned back in the direction of the others. For a moment or two he could still see them, but they looked fuzzy and out of focus. He could still hear his mother crying and even Willy's snorts of protest. He could still see the rain teeming down on them. And then, in an instant, the world he had left behind faded away entirely.

Carl took a few steps into the bleak and unwelcoming realm he had entered. He did not feel nauseous like he did when he visited there during his vision with the Willing Stone. Then everything was out of focus, but now he could see well enough. He turned around in a full circle to try to get his bearings. He saw a rockslide off to his left and kept hearing an odd, recurring popping noise off in the distance.

He found it difficult to stay upright. The ground shifted and shook beneath his feet. A particularly violent tremor sent him crashing to the ground. He got back up unsteadily and braced himself against some rocks.

A sudden, loud rumbling sound distracted him. When he looked to where the sound emanated, he shook his head hard in disbelief. He was unable to process what he was seeing. A herd of hundreds of bison were stampeding just off to his right. The ground vibrated with their force. As he watched the animals racing in panic, he saw two backpackers walking right toward the rampaging herd. Somehow, they seemed oblivious to the peril that confronted them.

Carl shouted over to warn them. 'Look out! Get out of the way!'
But they would not or could not listen. He watched in horror as the wildly panicked herd bore down on them. He winced and looked away. He heard the bison storm past him and then looked up. He started to run over to the backpackers to help them, but they just continued their hike as if nothing had happened.

'How are they still alive?' Carl asked himself as he shook his head again. 'Why weren't they trampled to death?'

He made his way over to the couple and tried to talk to them, but they ignored him like he was not there. He stood there flummoxed briefly as they walked away happily.

Then he remembered why he had come.
'I have to find Ben and his mom,' he reminded himself.
'That's why I'm here.'

He started walking forward again. He looked to his left and right and began to call out loudly as he went along.

'Ben! It's Carl! I've come to bring you home! Mrs. Crenshaw? Can you hear me? It's Carl Marty!'
But he heard no response.

He continued walking in his search for any trace of Ben or Cora, but the dreary valley seemed deserted. He saw flocks of birds flying frantically as he went along, but could see no people. He had just stopped to try to figure out what to do, when suddenly from behind him he heard a human voice giggling and shouting.

'When beggars die, there are no comets seen. The heavens themselves blaze forth the death of princes.'

Carl turned around to see who it was. Skipping toward him was a young man dressed in a frilly shirt. He was wearing stockings and short trousers just below his knees. He wore old-fashioned buckled shoes and a hat like Carl once saw in a pirate movie.

The strange fellow kept skipping toward him, gesturing dramatically, and declaiming in a loud voice.

'Woe, destruction, ruin, and death. The worst is death and death will have its day.'

Carl waited for him. 'Maybe he knows where Ben is,' he thought hopefully.

When the bizarrely dressed man reached Carl, he blinked at him for a second, smiled, and then began screaming out in every direction.
'Master! I have found him! The Last with the Gift!'

He turned back to Carl and stared at him with a wild look in his eye.
'My Master will be pleased with me! He will reward me!' He raised his eyes to the sky as he raved.
'Master! Master! He is here! Come claim your victory!'

The peculiar young man bowed deeply to Carl and skipped blissfully away. He kept yelling as he made his way from Carl.
'He is here, My Lord Remiel! He is here!'

The police guard opened the corridor door and walked into the cell block. He ambled over to Greyhawk's cell.
'You're going over to St. Luke's on a treatment referral. Stand back from the cell door.'

The guard led Greyhawk out of the block and took him outside. There was a police van waiting.

'Wait here,' he said as he lazily strolled over to open the back door of the van. He turned back to Greyhawk.
'Get in,' he said without emotion.

Greyhawk started walking slowly toward the van and then abruptly stopped. Something caught his eye. He thought he saw something rippling in the air just a few feet away from him. He tilted his head and looked curiously at it.

'Time's a wastin'!' the guard said impatiently. 'C'mon!'

Greyhawk suddenly erupted in shouts of joy.

'My master has trapped the Last with the Gift! My Lord Remiel is calling me!'

'What the hell?' the guard sighed. He started walking over to Greyhawk. 'I got no time for this!' he said gruffly.

The guard reached out to grab Greyhawk, but he darted away from him as he called out in thanksgiving, 'How great you are, My Lord Remiel! You have come to set me free!'

Greyhawk then raced through the Blue Cloud and, in a blink, vanished from sight.

CHAPTER
28

Mad Tom prostrated himself before White Eyes' throne.
'My Lord Remiel!' he said obsequiously. 'Sir, I love you
more than words can wield the matter; Dearer than eye
sight, space, and liberty!'
He then lifted his eyes momentarily.
'Master! I have seen him!' he said. 'The Last with the
Gift has arrived!'

White Eyes rose and looked down on the fawning Mad
Tom groveling on the floor.
'I have heard your cries, My useful servant,' he said. 'I
know the Last with the Gift has entered here. You have
done well.'
'Your victory is at hand, My Lord!'
'And soon you shall have your reward,' White Eyes
said with a joyless smile.
'All praise to Lord Remiel!'

White Eyes then turned and faced the Grinning Dogs
awaiting his command.
'As I have promised you, our triumph is now assured.
The Blue Cloud bond is broken. Can you not taste our
sweet revenge? It will soon be on our lips. Are you not
pleased?'

'My Lord,' one of the Grinning Dogs said as he bowed.
'Shall we all walk through now into the world of time
and space? Why do we delay?'

White Eyes bristled up in anger.

'Silence, Ungrateful cur! Know your place!' he snarled. 'No, we shall not walk through now! The Last with the Gift has dared to enter through the Cloud with the Willing Stone in his possession. I will first take my revenge upon him for my pleasure. Go! Find this upstart! Find him and I will destroy him exquisitely.'

'Yes, My Lord!' The Grinning Dog replied.

'Go! He must not be allowed to find the others of his kin, his Brotherhood, who hide their fear from me. Find this intruder before he finds them and they touch the Stone together and escape me!'

'We shall do as you command, Lord Remiel,' another of the Grinning Dogs said.

'Search for him! Bring him here to me!' White Eyes demanded furiously.

The Grinning Dogs began to mutate into their strange, jet black, smoky forms.

'Fly off! Find him!'

And they all flew off together away from White Eyes' Court and out into his bleak kingdom.

White Eyes went over to Mad Tom still lying prostrate on the floor.

'And you,' he said. 'Go! Look for this Last One again. Point him out to my servants.'

Mad Tom stood back up and bowed theatrically.

'I am at your service, My Lord!'

Carl continued to hunt for Ben and Cora, but wherever he wandered, he kept arriving back at the same spot where he started. He could not make head nor tail of it. He seemed to have lost all sense of direction. He was sure he was walking forward and then found that he had made no progress at all.

'How can I find anyone when I can't find where I am myself?' he asked himself in frustration. He tried to make his way back to where he first arrived, but nothing looked familiar.

'Why can't I retrace my steps?' He felt panic coming on him for a moment, but then took a deep breath and told himself not to be afraid.

He called out repeatedly for Ben and his mother as he tried to find his way, but there never was any response. He began to worry whether this was all a foolish mistake and that Greyhawk had tricked him into coming to this unfathomable place.

'What if Ben isn't here at all? What if I am here on my own?' he fretted to himself.

He started to walk down a steep path, but found it hard to stay on his feet. He kept hearing a strange cracking boom coming from afar and each time it came, the ground would shift and throw him off balance. He went over and braced himself against the vertical wall of the ridge and tried to make his way forward with the palm of one hand on the rock face for support.

As he walked carefully trying to prevent himself from falling, something from above caught his eye. He looked up and stared as six dark smoky forms crisscrossed the colorless sky like black jet contrails. He watched as the smoky shapes repeatedly went in one direction and then another. He wanted to step out and away from the side of the ridge to get a better look, but he could not move away from the ridge wall without toppling over in the shifting landscape.

'I wonder what they are?' he thought.
Then he froze. He remembered the disturbing black pillars of smoke that appeared in his nightmare vision of this place. He remembered what his grandmother had read to him.
'White Eyes is looking for me.'

He pushed back against the ridge wall to try to hide away from the smoky and macabre creatures looking for him. He stood there breathing softly and trying to master his fear, when he heard something coming down the valley. Blood-curdling whoops kept growing louder and louder. His jaw dropped when he saw what was coming his way.

Riding hard across the valley floor was a cavalry troop. He could even hear their bugles calling. He watched as they rode forward together in a mighty gallop. The valley floor bowed and twisted beneath their charging horses after every tremor, but did not seem to affect their progress. He gaped at them as they rode by as if the valley floor were level and undisturbed.
'Why aren't they falling off their horses?' he wondered.

He looked up and saw the eerie black plumes fly off and away from where he was hoping to hide himself. He paused and closed his eyes in relief and then resumed his search for Ben and Cora with his hand pressed firmly against the ridge wall.

Eventually, the ridge bent away sharply to his left and he carried on making his way forward in its direction. As he did so, he saw someone in the distance walking down the valley. He stopped briefly and watched as the stranger made his way toward him. As the man kept walking, Carl saw him fall down and struggle to get back up only to fall over again after each shuddering far off boom shifted the ground under his feet.

'When he gets here, I'll ask him if he's seen Ben,' Carl reasoned to himself.

He waited there quietly with his back against the wall face as the stranger slowly walked closer toward him. He still could not make out who it was.
'It's not that oddball with the pirate hat,' he determined. 'I'd hear him spouting his poetry by now.'

As he looked on, something in a cloud of dust appeared behind the approaching figure. He strained his eyes to see what it was, when suddenly dozens of feral horses burst through the dust cloud and galloped uncontrollably right at the stranger. Carl started to shout out a warning, but the stranger saw them himself and leapt quickly to his side and out of their way.

Carl watched as the horses continued racing forward in

mad panic as if trying to escape some danger. The ground beneath their hooves lurched up and down without warning every time the odd noise rang out in the distance. And yet they galloped past him, just like the cavalry troop had done, as if the valley floor were flat and even.

He shook his head again in bewilderment.

'At least this person seems real enough,' Carl thought to himself. 'I can finally ask someone what's going on in this place. I just hope they know something.'

But when the mysterious stranger came into view, Carl pushed back hard against the flat ridge wall, so he would not be seen.

'My Lord Remiel! Where are you?' the man called out as he fell to the valley floor with every few steps. 'Let me see you and praise you, My Lord! You have rescued me and set me free! Let me find you on the day of your great victory! It's your Ministering Servant, Greyhawk!'

Carl dropped to the ground and laid down flat as quietly as he could. He heard Greyhawk repeatedly calling out for White Eyes as he continued making his unsteady headway down the valley floor. He trembled at the thought that Greyhawk might see him. He breathed slowly and tried not to be afraid. He stayed there flat on the ground at the wall's edge until Greyhawk had passed him by. He heard Greyhawk's shouts grow fainter until he could not hear them anymore.

He dusted himself off as he got back up on his feet. 'What's he doing here?' he asked himself in alarm.

He tapped his jacket pocket to be sure that he still had the Willing Stone with him and had not lost it in the commotion. He shut his eyes and prayed in the hope that Greyhawk had not noticed him.

He was considering what he should do next, when a powerful tremor shook him violently and threw him face down on the ground. He got back up with a groan and held on to the ridge wall to steady himself. He then heard a distant rumbling from above. When he looked up, he saw rocks had started to break free from the top of the ridge above him. They began to rain down on where he was standing. He dashed away from the wall face and looked around for some place of safety. He dodged out of the way as the falling rocks bounced over and around him.

But then as the ground beneath his feet gave way yet again, he lost his balance and tumbled over. As he lay helpless on the ground, a large slab of rock plummeted down directly at him. He shut his eyes and awaited his fate.

Then from nowhere, he felt a large hand grab him by the arm and drag him away like a rag doll from the rocks heading right for him.

'Come on! Get up!' a rough and deep voice ordered. 'Find your feet! Follow me!'

Carl scrambled to stand back up as the rocks continued to pepper down from above. He looked at the giant of a man who had grabbed him and began to follow behind. He did not know who he was, but felt he had no choice but to trust him.

'Come on, Lad!' the man repeated as he kept leading Carl out of harm's way.

CHAPTER
29

The phone rang and Noah walked over to pick it up.
'Uncle Noah? It's me. Have you heard any news yet?'
Stacey asked hopefully.
'No, Stacey. I'm sorry. There's nothing new to tell you.'

Three days had now passed, since that stormy moment
when Carl had walked through the Blue Cloud.
Everyone who went out riding with him that morning
waited for hours in the pouring rain for him to return.
But there was no sign of him. They all stood looking
out at the vacant valley around them and hoped.

Jimmy Junior was the first to leave.
'I have to drive Mrs. Perot back up to Boise, Orin. I
better stop off at the museum too, while I'm up there,
and tell them what's going on. They'll be expecting me
to get their Stone back to them.'
He went over to Noah. 'Ride my friend's horse back to
your place, will you? I'll collect him later.'

Annie finally convinced Stacey that they had to leave as
well.
'You have school tomorrow morning. Uncle Noah will
call us as soon as he hears any news.'

At first, Stacey protested and stubbornly refused to
budge, but finally she relented. She walked over to
Noah and hugged him.

'Please, Uncle Noah,' she pleaded. 'Call Mom, the moment you hear something, won't you?'

She left Noah and began calling out to the empty vista in front of her.
'You come back, Carl! You hear me? That's an order!'
Annie put an arm around her shoulders to try to console her.

Noah walked his horse over to Chief Marty.
'Orin, I better go back with Annie and Stacey. There's no point waiting out here. Maybe that Cloud thing shifted somewhere else by now.'
'Maybe so,' Chief Marty replied. 'You go ahead and leave. I'll stay and wait with Marian a while longer before we head back.'
'I bet Carl's waiting at home with his grandmother right now,' Noah said optimistically.
'Yeah, maybe.'

After the others had gone, Chief Marty and his wife stared hopefully at the spot where Carl vanished for another hour or so. When they at last reluctantly accepted that it was pointless to wait any longer, they remounted Daisy Mae and Zeno and rode back home.

After his escape, the police put out a statewide bulletin to find and detain Greyhawk. The guard, who was with him when he went through the Blue Cloud, claimed he had run off somehow. After Greyhawk disappeared, the guard looked around briefly befuddled and then ran back into the station to raise the alarm.

When he made his official report to the desk sergeant, he said, 'He squirmed right through my fingers. I never saw anyone run that fast. He was right there with me and then, poof, he was gone in a flash!'

The desk sergeant gave the guard a look. 'And he did all this with his arm in a sling? Okay, so who are we looking for?' he asked. 'Professor Greyhawk or The Flash?'

A manhunt began to find their missing prisoner. The State and local police were all on the lookout for Greyhawk. The police helicopter was also put on the hunt. But there were no sightings of him. No one they spoke to had seen him. No one had heard from him. It was as if the earth had swallowed him whole. Jimmy Junior's friend in the State Police told him that Greyhawk had somehow slipped away.
'It's like he's fallen off the grid, Jimmy Junior,' he said. 'We don't got a sniff on where he's holed up.'

The following weekend, Stacey arrived alone on the bus from Boise. Noah picked her up. As he was driving her home, she said, 'I'm coming back every single weekend, Uncle Noah, until Carl gets back with Ben and Aunt Cora. And if he gets back during the week, I'm coming straight back then too.'

Noah got Stacey settled and told her again that there was nothing new to report. She was so disappointed. She asked if they could ride back out to the spot where they last saw Carl. She could not accept that there was nothing she could do. Her helplessness made her feel miserable. She thought she would feel better, if she could do something, anything, which might help.

'I'll keep calling out for him, Uncle Noah. Maybe he'll hear us. Maybe he's having trouble finding his way back home.'
Noah knew exactly how she was feeling. 'We'll go back out there together tomorrow morning,' he promised her.

Anytime the phone would ring, Mrs. Marty raced over to answer it. She was desperate for any news about her son. Chief Marty was so concerned about her that he asked well-wishers not to call.

'It's hard on her. I know you mean well,' he told them. 'But please don't call or stop by to ask about any news. Marian's not slept a wink, since Carl left us. I'm worried about her. If we hear anything, I'll be sure to let you know.'

Chief Marty decided that he needed to be strong and protect his wife. But while she suffered with worry about her son, Chief Marty allowed himself to descend into bitterness and anger. He said nothing aloud, but inside he blamed Noah for his son's disappearance. He had convinced himself that Noah should have insisted that Carl stay away from the Blue Cloud.

To his mind, Noah acted selfishly and only cared about his own loss.

'I hope it makes him feel better,' he thought to himself filled with resentment. 'Now we've both lost our boys.'

At work the following morning, Jimmy Junior broke the news to Chief Marty about Greyhawk's escape from custody.

'I just heard about it myself, Orin. They're keeping us both in the dark on the investigation, but my buddy in the State Police has been telling me what's been going on. They're all out looking for him, but they can't get a bead on him. My friend said Professor Greyhawk was with the jail guard and then he wasn't. Like he vanished into thin air. The guard's claiming he ran off, but with all the hocus-pocus going on around here lately, I'm not so sure. Since the Professor got away, they ain't seen hide nor hair of him. Where do you reckon he went?'

Chief Marty felt a chill run down his spine. He turned away from the deskwork he was completing.
'You want to know what I think?' he asked.
'I think that bastard went through that Cloud thing somehow and is after my boy.'

'I'm thinking the same thing, Orin. The whole thing makes no sense. How'd he get away like that? It's just not humanly possible. I tried telling my trooper friend about that Cloud thing, but he just thought I was yanking his chain.'
Then he asked, 'Chief, you want me to tell Noah about this too?'

Chief Marty glared at Jimmy Junior.

'What the hell does it have to do with Noah?' he snapped at him.

Jimmy Junior looked around in surprised shock for a moment.

'I don't know, Orin,' he said sheepishly. 'I just thought you'd want him to know.'

'No, it's nothing to do with him. It's a police matter. You keep this between us, you hear? It's my boy he's after. Not Noah's.'

'Sure, Chief. If that's the way you want it,' Jimmy Junior replied.

'It is,' he said as he turned back to his work.

But Chief Marty was too upset to concentrate for long. He smashed his fist down hard on his desktop.

'Damn it all!' he shouted. 'Carl's gone and I can't do anything about it! Now Greyhawk's gone missing too. That's it! We're not sitting idly by anymore, Jimmy Junior. I've had enough. First, we're going to find out if we're right about Greyhawk. Maybe he didn't slip through that Cloud. The State Police don't want us involved, fine, but there's no reason we can't keep an eye out for him ourselves. I'll call the University where he teaches. Maybe they've heard something from him.'

Noah let Stacey put the tack on Bess. He watched as she made an enormous fuss over her. It made him smile for the first time in days.

He got Willy ready for their ride out to the Magic Valley. He did not hold out much hope that they would come across Carl, but he was happy for the company and for something to do other than worry. No one was telling him what was going on and that made him more concerned than he already was. He had not heard anything from Chief Marty, since the moment they split up and headed home after Carl had walked through the Blue Cloud. He did not want to call him himself either. He felt guilty that Carl had risked his own safety to try to find Ben and Cora. He thought his voice would be the last thing Chief Marty would want to hear.

'I should have stopped him,' he kept tormenting himself. 'I should have tried harder. I should have insisted Carl stayed here.'

He felt he had let his hope get the better of him and now he had jeopardized Carl too.

CHAPTER
30

'My Lord Remiel! Can you not hear me? It is your loyal servant!' Greyhawk cried out relentlessly.

He wandered through the bleak, achromic valley and looked for any sign of White Eyes. He fell over again and again as the ground repeatedly shifted in the tremors and used his good arm to brace himself to get back up on his feet.

'My Lord! It's your Ministering Servant!'

Something from above startled Greyhawk. He looked up and saw six dark and misty streaks cutting through the sky. As he stared up at them, one of the streaks split away from the others and headed toward the ground. Greyhawk followed it with his eyes until it landed right in front of him.

A black-winged creature appeared where the whirling smoky streak had touched down.
'Why do you call out for my Lord? Why do you speak his name?'

Greyhawk fell to his knees.
'I am his loyal servant, Greyhawk. My Lord Remiel has rescued me through the Blue Cloud from the clutches of my captors.'

'Get to your feet,' the Grinning Dog said with disdain. 'I am not to be worshipped. Come, Greyhawk, loyal servant,' he sneered. 'I will deliver you to your Lord.'

He grabbed Greyhawk roughly by his injured shoulder and twisted it. He spat at him and said, 'Are you the Last with the Gift? Have you come to retrieve your Brotherhood from my Master? Do you dare mock My Lord Remiel by speaking his name?'
'I am his servant. He knows me!' Greyhawk sputtered in pain.
'We shall see,' the Grinning Dog said. 'We shall see if you are worthy to call yourself his servant.'

He pulled Greyhawk toward him and tucked him under his wing. They then flew off together to White Eyes' Court.

The Colossus who saved Carl kept urging him to move quickly and follow him.
'Move it, Lad! Come along! Keep going!'

The rocks continued plunging down from the top of the ridge to the valley floor below every time there was another quake. As they ran together, they dodged and shimmied away from the falling rocks that smashed and shattered around them.

Carl ran and swiveled for all he was worth. He ran with one eye to the sky raining stones down on him and his other eye on the huge fellow running ahead of him. Just as he turned his head to look where his savior was leading him, a huge V-shaped chunk of rock slammed on to the valley floor right in front of him. He only just managed to swerve out of the way before running right into it.

'Come on, Lad! Stop your dawdling!' the gigantic man barked back at him.

Carl sprinted ahead until he was running side by side with the man leading him to safety.
'Who are you?' Carl asked breathlessly.
'That's not important now. We need to get away from this rockslide. That's what's important. Keep up! Keep moving!'

His rescuer led Carl on and away from the rocks raining down on the valley floor until he found a shallow recess in the side of the ridge.

'Get in. Hurry. Shove back as far as you can. It'll give us some protection. We'll wait out this avalanche here,' the man said. 'Later, maybe we can get to where the others are hiding.'

'Others?' Carl asked. 'There are others here like us?'
'A few,' he answered. 'We saw the Grinning Dogs flying through the sky and figured they were out looking for a New One. I suspect that's you. You have the Gift of the Stone, don't you?'

Carl was just about to ask what a New One was, but thought better of it. He hoped the man might know Ben and Cora and where they were hiding.

Instead he said, 'Yes, I have the Gift. Just like my friend, Ben. I'm looking for him and his mother, Cora. Do you know where they are?'

The Giant looked Carl up and down. 'Maybe I do,' he said without committing himself. 'I'm Frank.'
He stuck out his big paw for Carl to shake.

'Here's the first rule in this place. You must show no fear. If you do, both of us will be caught in a bear trap. And be quiet. If you must speak, do it softly. Otherwise you'll call our doom to us. You're here now. You can't be a child anymore. You understand?'

'Yes, I do. Yes, Frank. I won't be afraid. I'll be quiet. I'm Carl. I'm here to rescue Ben and his mom, if I can find them.'
'You know Ben and Cora, is that right?'

Carl nodded. 'That's why I came through the Blue Cloud. So I can bring them both back home.'

Frank started to laugh. 'And how do you imagine you're going to do that, Lad? You're trapped here now just like the rest of us!'
'Not if the Professor's book is right. It says I can bring them back.'

'Professor? Professor who?' Frank asked wondering if Carl was right in the head.
'Professor Greyhawk. He's the one who gave the Willing Stone to Ben at our school. Then Ben walked through the Blue Cloud, when we were out riding.'

'All of us thought Greyhawk was trying to help Ben get back home, but now I think he's been working for White Eyes and lying to us the whole time.'

Carl continued talking rapidly in his enthusiasm. He was so relieved to have met someone who might know something useful that he could not slow down.

Frank looked again at Carl and tried to size him up. He still was not sure if Carl was a lunatic or not. He was not sure if he could trust him. He then asked to be sure he understood.
'You know about White Eyes?'

'I saw him in my vision, when Professor Greyhawk handed me the Willing Stone to see if I had the Gift or not. But then he turned out to be a liar and tried to push me through the Blue Cloud.'

'So that's how you came to be here? This Professor Greyhawk pushed you through the Cloud?'

'No, Dad stopped him and then he was arrested. My dad's in the police. But Greyhawk must have escaped somehow, because I just saw him here. He didn't see me though. At least I think he didn't.'

Frank nodded like he understood, although he was not sure if he did.
'This Greyhawk you talk about. He serves White Eyes and now he's here through the Cloud?'

Carl stopped to catch his breath. He was speaking so

quickly that he started gasping for air. He gulped in another deep breath before he continued.

'Yes, but we read his book. He wrote a book about the Blue Cloud. And then Mr. Groves had the Stone and gave it to me. Ben's family and my family, we all went out riding together to find the Blue Cloud again and I walked through.'

Frank put his huge hands on Carl's shoulders.
'Listen to me carefully, Carl. You passed through the Cloud with the Willing Stone? Are you saying you have the Stone with you right now?'

Carl took the Willing Stone out of his jacket pocket and showed it to Frank.
'Yes, I do, Sir. You see, it's right here.'

CHAPTER
31

The moment he arrived at work, Chief Marty phoned the State University. He was hoping that they might have some information about Greyhawk and where he could be hiding. He still feared Greyhawk had passed through the Blue Cloud somehow and was after his son, but he wanted to check if there might be a more natural explanation for his disappearance.

He was shocked by what he discovered.

'No, I'm afraid we haven't heard from Professor Greyhawk for quite some time now,' a pleasant woman in administration said.
'A few years ago, he became obsessed with Native American sagas of this area. He began to miss his lectures and grew incommunicative and distracted. One day he went into the lecture hall and started shouting at the students that they were all doomed and some dark spirit would make them all pay for their arrogance. He babbled something about finding everyone with some 'Gift' and delivering them to his 'Master'. Some of the students were very upset. I am afraid Professor Greyhawk suffered a debilitating breakdown and was hospitalized. We hoped he might recover and return to his teaching work, but after he was released we never heard from him again.'

Chief Marty thanked her and put down the phone.

After he finished explaining to Jimmy Junior what the university administrator had to say, he added, 'I've a good mind to contact Carl's school. They let that charlatan come speak to the students without checking his credentials.'

'Well, what that woman at the university said makes perfect sense to me, Orin. That Professor's a crackpot. That explains a lot, if you ask me.'

'It doesn't explain where he is,' Chief Marty replied. 'I still haven't told Marian he escaped. What could I say? I think he's after Carl? She's barely holding up as it is.'

'So what are we going to do?' Jimmy Junior asked. 'First, I'm going to call the Shoshone-Bannock Museum. Let's hear what they have to say.'

Chief Marty looked up the number, called, and then asked to speak with the museum curator. He told him that Greyhawk had been arrested and then escaped from custody. He asked the curator if he had heard anything from Greyhawk.

'I certainly do not know the whereabouts of Professor Greyhawk,' the curator said testily. 'We've been looking for him too. I have contacted the local police. He has stolen several valuable artifacts from us and some extremely rare literature as well. One of our staff saw him in the museum several weeks ago. The following morning, we noticed that some rare books and transcriptions of Native American tribal stories and legends were missing.'

Chief Marty asked the curator about the Willing Stone Greyhawk had in his possession.

'Yes, that too,' he answered. 'We believe he has stolen that among other valuable exhibits. The Shoshone and Bannock peoples are very proud of their heritage. Professor Greyhawk has undermined it for his own purposes. The man is a scoundrel and cannot be trusted. Please, if you locate Professor Greyhawk, do let us know.'

He put down the phone and shook his head with a bewildered smile on his face.
'What is it, Orin?' Jimmy Junior asked. 'What did they say?'

When Chief Marty told him what the museum curator had said, Jimmy Junior began shifting around uneasily. 'Orin, I never stopped by the museum after I dropped Mrs. Perot back home. I didn't know what to say to them. I should've told them about that Stone. If I had, maybe we'd have known about his tricks a lot sooner.'

'It's not your fault,' Chief Marty said. 'He played us all like we were half-wit fools.'

There was no sign at all of Greyhawk, but since he was a fugitive from justice, the police were still on the lookout for him. Jimmy Junior's police friend kept him informed. He told him that they would keep searching for him, but assumed he had crossed the state line. 'No news, Jimmy Junior,' he told him. 'They think he's out of our jurisdiction by now.'

Chief Marty was not sure what to do. He had to accept that Greyhawk was nowhere to be found, because he had slipped through the Blue Cloud and could not be found. He drummed his fingers briefly on his desk, picked up the phone, and dialed.

'Marian,' he began. 'I found out something just now and you should know.'

He then told his wife everything he had come to learn about Geyhawk. He told her about his escape from custody. He shared what he had discovered during his conversations with the university administrator and the museum curator. He told her about his fear that Greyhawk had passed through the Blue Cloud and was after their son.

'I didn't want to tell you, Marian, because I can't be sure, but that's what I think is going on.'

'What did Noah say when you told him?' she asked. Chief Marty let out a little nervous laugh. 'What's it got to do with him?'

There was a long silence from the other end of the line. When Mrs. Marty did finally respond, Chief Marty was surprised by her reaction.

'Orin, you stop what you're doing right now. You go tell Noah about this. If you have time to call me, you have time to call Noah. I know you're holding a grudge against him. I can sense it.'

'This bad feeling you have about Noah has to stop. Right now. There's no point blaming Noah. He's not responsible. He has a right to know what's happening too. His boy is missing just like ours. You tell him right now. Holding a grudge isn't going to bring Carl back home. We all need to stick together. Now more than ever.'

CHAPTER
32

The Grinning Dog flew with Greyhawk still under his wing into White Eyes' Court. When he landed, he flung Greyhawk toward White Eyes sitting on his stone throne. Greyhawk squealed in pain as he fell awkwardly on his wounded shoulder.

'My Lord, I heard this one shouting out your name in your domain. He claims to be in your service. I have never seen him here and bring him to you to do with him as you wish.'

Greyhawk was lying flat on his face after he was tossed unceremoniously to the floor. White Eyes rose from his throne.
'Show yourself! Show me who you are!'

Greyhawk struggled back on to his knees, rubbed at his shoulder, and said weakly, 'It is Greyhawk, My Lord Remiel. I have come through the Blue Cloud you put before me. I am here, My Lord, at your service. Your Ministering Servant, Greyhawk, is here.'

'This is not the Defiler who entered here with the Stone,' White Eyes told the Grinning Dog.
'Go! Fly off again and keep looking for him.'

'Yes, Lord Remiel. I will find the one with the Stone as you command.'

The Grinning Dog then transformed back into his wispy and smoky pillar state and flew away.

'Arise, Greyhawk,' White Eyes said imperiously. 'I have called you here at the moment of our final victory. The one known as Carl is here among us. The Last with the Gift is here in my realm.'

Greyhawk scrambled back to his feet.
'I had no doubt, Sire! I knew you would trap him and set me free!'

Greyhawk lifted and waved his good arm to the heavens.
'Oh glorious day! All the world is now yours to command! May you punish those who imprisoned me and profaned your name!'

'All will be as it should be, Greyhawk. We will find the Last with the Gift. You will see what I shall do with one who dares enter here with the Stone. Once I have squeezed every drop of fear out of him, we will march triumphantly through the opened Cloud.'

'He must be stopped, My Lord!' Greyhawk replied. 'He must not find those already here with the Gift! I will help you, Master. I know the boy. I know him just as you do. I will find him for you and do you final service before your reign begins in the lands beyond the Cloud.'

Greyhawk bowed worshipfully. He started to walk out into the collapsing world of White Eyes' prison, when

White Eyes stopped him.
'Come here,' he said. 'Let me tend to you.'

Greyhawk turned around and tentatively made his way over to White Eyes. He did not know what he meant by 'tend'.
'Kneel down,' White Eyes ordered.

Greyhawk trembled anxiously as he got down on his knees. He shut his eyes, when White Eyes reached down, pulled his sling out of the way, and exposed the wound. White Eyes then touched his thumb to his lips and put his thumb directly into the wound. Immediately, Greyhawk doubled over and shrieked and wailed in agony. Then White Eyes removed his thumb from the wound and stepped back.

A feeling like an electric shock fizzled through Greyhawk. He quivered in fear for a moment and then abruptly knelt upright again and lifted his head. He sniffled back his whimpering, blinked, and looked down at his shoulder. He kept staring at it not believing what he was seeing. It was as if he had never been shot. There was no sign of the wound whatsoever.

Greyhawk lowered his head to the floor in homage.
'My Lord Remiel! You have healed me! How great and magnificent is my Lord!'

'Stand, Greyhawk. We shall hunt together and claim our prize.'
'You honor me, My Lord!'
'All who do me service will be rewarded.'

White Eyes held Greyhawk close to him, transmuted into his misty, black and smoky form, and they flew off together in their search for Carl.

Bird-Who-Hops and Henri awaited Frank's return to the hollow in the ridge where they first found the baby, Hope, and now called home. As he waited with Henri, Bird-Who-Hops fretted that he could not convince Frank to let him join in his search for the New One.

'We should not have let him leave here alone. The Dogs were in the sky and we know what they were seeking. There must be a New One out there somewhere. I could have helped Frank look and kept watch on what the Dogs were doing.'

'Be patient, Bird-Who-Hops,' Henri replied. 'Frank cannot be stopped once he makes up his mind. There was nothing to be done. He will return and he will bring the New One with him. You will see.'

In the ridge hollow nearby, Ben stood there looking out from their shelter and then turned back to Cora.
'Mom, are we just going to wait here? Frank's out there on his own. Shouldn't we go out and look for him? He said he'd return before we knew it, but there's no sign of him. What if the Grinning Dogs have captured him?'

'Then there is nothing we could do to help him. Frank was right. With the tremors and all the upheaval out there, it was safer for him to go on his own to look for the New One. We'd only hold him back.'

And just as Henri had said to Bird-Who-Hops, Cora added, 'Be patient.'

When the rockslide at last relented, Frank looked up to the sky. He could see the trails of the Grinning Dogs swooping through the air.

'We're staying here,' he said to Carl. 'They're hunting for you. You're too valuable to lose now. When I see they've cleared away, prepare yourself to run. Like a jack rabbit. We must get you to the others with the Gift before the Dogs return.'

Frank kept his focus firmly on the sky. He was looking for the chance to make a dash with Carl back to the others waiting at their hollows in the ridge. He reckoned that once the sky was clear of the smoky black plumes streaking above, they could flee before the Grinning Dogs reappeared in their hunt for Carl.

Frank thought about Mei-Ling and Hope.
'I could do nothing to protect them,' he said to himself. 'But this one, I will protect. He's brought the Stone with him and can take us home. This one I will keep safe from the clutches of that beady-eyed bastard and his mongrels. And you will be avenged, Mei-Ling. And you too, Baby Hope.'

Carl stood beside Frank in the cramped refuge they had found to escape the rockslide. He looked out on the turbulent terrain in front of him. The ground would split open and then reseal after each sonic boom from the collapsing Blue Cloud. It would buckle and twist around on itself and then relent. It was as if the landscape had become a seascape with constant waves of motion.

As he watched the chaos in front of him, Carl saw two mountain bikers come into view. The ground was so unstable that the cyclists appeared to be defying gravity. He shook his head in wonder as they rode along sometimes perpendicularly to the valley floor. And yet the pair of them paid no notice. They smiled and laughed as they rode by like they were cycling on a flat track.

Carl glanced at Frank to see what he thought of the surreal spectacle in front of them. He wanted to ask him how what he was seeing was possible, but Frank would not take his eyes from the sky. They stood there together waiting in silence-Frank's eyes to the sky and Carl's on the shattering landscape in front of them.

They were both lost in their thoughts, when suddenly a woman's shrill screams pierced the air. Carl jumped back in shock. He could not see who was shouting, because the ridge's recessed edge blocked his view. Frank broke his focus from the sky and said softly, 'Be still. Be silent. Show no fear.'
Carl nodded and prepared himself for yet another ghastly fright.

'My baby! Where have you gone?' Carl heard the woman shriek in desperation.
'What have they done with you? Where have they

taken you, my love?'

The screaming woman continued crying out for her lost child until she came into view. She stopped and stood directly in front of where Carl and Frank were standing.

When he saw her, Carl was struck rigid and held his breath. Bloody streaks ran down from where her eyes once were. It was the eyeless woman he had seen in his Willing Stone vision. The sight of her blood-soaked eye sockets made him twitch. Frank placed his hand on Carl's shoulder to keep him calm.

'Master Remiel!' she cried out as she lifted her bloodied face to the heavens. 'They've taken my little girl! Won't you tell me where she is?'

She waited a moment for a response and then turned and walked away from Carl and Frank. She wandered off down the valley floor. The bewitched young woman stumbled and fell to the ground with each new tremor. Carl watched as she got back up on her feet and put her hands in front of her to help her find her way.

'Do you know who that woman is, Frank?' Carl asked when she was finally out of sight.

'A Betrayer,' he answered. 'If she'd sensed our fear or heard us shouting, she would have called out to White Eyes and told him where we were. He tortures and drives to distraction anyone with the Gift he captures and enslaves them into betraying others with the Gift.'

'I think I met a Betrayer right after I got here,' Carl said. 'He wore old-fashioned clothes and skipped around reciting poetry. He started calling out to White Eyes as soon as he saw me.'

'Mad Tom,' Frank said. 'That's what I call him anyway.'

'And what about that woman with no eyes looking for her baby, Frank? Does White Eyes have her baby?'

Frank looked at Carl momentarily, but said nothing. He turned his attention back to monitoring the sky.

A terrible thought struck Carl. What if White Eyes already had his hands on Ben and Cora? What if he did something to them like he did to that strange young man and poor tortured woman?

He asked half-afraid to know, 'Are Ben and his mom like Mad Tom and that blind woman?'

Frank patted him on the shoulder. 'No, Lad,' he said. 'They are still with us. You'll see for yourself soon enough.'

Frank looked back up and saw the sky was now clear. He craned his neck to look more thoroughly and could not see any pitch black smoky vapor trails anywhere.

He looked at Carl and said plainly and seriously, 'You get yourself ready to follow me and run until you can't run anymore. Look at nothing and no one on the way. You just follow me. You hear?'

Carl nodded and took a deep breath.

'Okay, then,' Frank said. 'Let's go!'

They ran out of their shallow ridge alcove and Frank immediately swerved to his left with Carl running right behind him. They tried sticking as close to the ridge as they could, because the footing was better there. But still, even with the ground more certain, they would often stumble and fall as the valley floor shifted with each new deafening blast.

They kept up a lung-busting pace when the ground would allow. Frank abruptly veered off to his right and led Carl down a steep path. When the path evened out, it presented an open view across the entire valley. Carl almost stopped running, when he saw the incredible sight before him. The Blue Cloud stretched out right across the horizon. It shimmered in its enormity making the sky buckle around it. He tried to keep up with Frank's unrelenting pace as the Blue Cloud ahead of them collapsed in on itself with a mighty cracking roar. Carl ran on with his hands over his ears to try to block out the excruciating noise.

Frank came to a stop and Carl caught up with him. They were both breathing hard.

'Did you see that, Frank? Did you see it?' Carl asked breathlessly.
'That's been going on for a while now. Something big is happening,' he said. 'We'll rest here against this ledge. I don't think any Betrayers will see us here, if there are any of the bastards around.'

They stood together both fighting to regain their breath.

Carl felt dizzy from his exertions and bent over and rested his hands on his knees.

'How much farther, Frank?' He gasped in exhaustion.

Frank nodded over to his right.

'You see that path over there? We take it straight up. It gets steeper the higher we climb it. Then it'll flatten out like a tabletop. There's another path at the top that takes us back downhill. The rest are waiting just toward the bottom.'

When Carl straightened back up to see the path Frank indicated, he also noticed something in the sky. He nudged him and said, 'Look. Up there. What's that?'

A single black and smoky stream cut through the air and then began slowly descending to the valley floor.

Frank put his arm across Carl's chest and pushed him back against the ledge. 'Keep back,' he ordered.

The dark, misty plume was just above the ground, when Carl saw it change into a hideous black-winged creature and touch down. He was clutching someone with him. Carl began to tremble at the sight. It was the terrifying creature of his Willing Stone vision.

'Is that White Eyes?' he asked uneasily.

Frank put his hand on top of Carl's head and pushed him down.

'Stay low, Carl,' he whispered very softly as he stooped down next to him. 'Don't be afraid.'

Carl could no longer see White Eyes or his companion from where he and Frank were hiding, but he almost panicked and screamed from what he heard.
'I saw him, My Lord! He was running behind someone. It was the boy! I'm sure of it!'

'That's the Professor, Frank,' Carl whispered hoarsely. Frank nodded and put his finger to his lips to stop Carl from speaking.

White Eyes screeched at the top of his voice.
'The one known as Carl! Have you come to save your friends?'

The sound of White Eyes' voice rang out as loudly as the crash of the Blue Cloud collapsing. Carl covered his ears, but could not block out White Eyes' mind-numbing threats.

'You will be my final act here in this place! I will shake the fear from your marrow! Your squeals of pain will make my servants dance! There is no escape! There is no mercy! I will show you agony beyond your imagination! And then I will lead my entourage into the world from which you came and do the same there!'

'All glory and majesty to the great Lord Remiel!' Greyhawk called out in response.

CHAPTER
33

The early morning sun had just broken through the clouds as Stacey and Noah set off to reach the spot in the Magic Valley where Carl had disappeared through the Blue Cloud.

Noah felt the ride might lift both their spirits. He could see Stacey had become weighed down by her concern for Carl. He feared she blamed herself for encouraging Carl to try and rescue Ben and Cora. He noticed the toll on her.
'She's too young to be carrying that sort of worry,' he thought to himself as he rode along behind her.

When they arrived at the place where they last saw Carl, they both dismounted. They held their horses by their reins and looked out into the empty valley.

'I don't think that Cloud thing is still there, Uncle Noah. Willy seems to have a nose for it and plays up when the Cloud's nearby.'

Noah said nothing in reply and stood there silently taking in the magnificent valley view.
'But it could still be around here somewhere,' she added. 'Maybe Willy will let us know if he senses it.'

As she stood beside Noah, Stacey rubbed Bess lovingly down her neck. The morning sun made the valley glow.

'It's so beautiful here,' she sighed. 'It really does take my breath away.'

'It's the same for me, Stacey. No matter how many times I see it.'

After admiring their surroundings for a few minutes, Stacey passed Bess's reins to Noah and walked out toward the middle of the valley. She cupped her hands around her mouth and began calling out in every direction.

'Carl! Ben! Aunt Cora! Can you hear me? It's me, Stacey, and Uncle Noah! If you can see me, if you can hear me, we will never give up hope that you'll come back to us! If you can hear me, follow my voice and come home!'

Stacey and Noah stayed out in the Magic Valley all morning long. They remounted their horses and began to ride out into the valley. Stacey was convinced that Willy would notice the Blue Cloud, if it was there, and they might be able to call out through it and lead Ben and the others home. She cried out occasionally as they rode through the valley together.

'Carl! Ben! Aunt Cora! Here we are!' But Willy never reacted as if the Blue Cloud were nearby.

After a couple hours of riding in the morning sun without any luck or direction, they decided to ride back to the spot where Carl went missing.

'We can rest the horses there and give them some shelter,' Noah suggested.

As they were making their back, they noticed two horsemen heading down the path that led to the place where Carl had walked through the Blue Cloud. One of the riders started waving his hand and yelling, but they could not make out what he was saying.
'Who are they, Uncle Noah?' Stacey asked.

When they reached their destination, they were surprised who was there to greet them.

'There they are!' a familiar voice said.
'Noah! We've been looking all over for you,' another familiar voice added.
It was Jimmy Junior and Chief Marty.

After they dismounted and shaded their horses, Chief Marty walked over to Noah. He looked down, rubbed his boot on the ground nervously, and cleared his throat before he spoke.

'Not that I know much about what's going on, Noah, but what I do know I should've told you,' he began. 'Marian said something and it hit me hard to be honest. It's why we came straight out to find you. This isn't just about Carl. You lost your boy too and your wife. I should've called you before and told you what little I do know. I'm sorry now I didn't. I tried calling you just now and when you didn't answer, we headed over to your place. When we stopped for gas, Jimmy Senior said he saw you and Stacey riding out this way.'

'I wanted to call you plenty of times myself, Orin. I just wasn't sure you wanted to hear my voice after what happened. I should've told Carl not to try. I should have insisted that he stayed here.'

'No, it's not your fault,' Chief Marty said. 'It's what Carl wanted to do. It was his choice.'
'You found out something about Carl?' Stacey asked hopefully.

Chief Marty and Jimmy Junior told them about Greyhawk's escape outside the police station.

'He vanished from custody, so they're claiming,' Jimmy Junior said.
'I've checked myself and no one knows where the Professor is,' Chief Marty added. 'The State Troopers can't find him. They're acting like he skipped over the state line.'
'What do you and Jimmy Junior think?' Noah asked.

'We're thinking he went through that Cloud thing somehow and he's after Carl wherever he is. That's my best guess. The lying dog is after my boy.'

'I never trusted that Professor from day one!' Stacey said incensed with fury.
'He's been after Carl this whole, entire time! Professor Double-talk! Professor Two-face!'

And almost as if in reply, a thumping blast rocked through the valley.

They stood there stunned for a moment and looked around in confusion. Willy began to stamp and snort and Daisy Mae joined in kicking and whinnying in panic.

'Whoa, Boy, easy now,' Noah coaxed Willy to try to settle him.
'Go easy. That's my girl,' Chief Marty said as he rubbed Daisy Mae below her ears to calm her.

'What in the world was that?' Stacey asked. 'My ears are still ringing!'

Everyone looked around and across the valley to try to discover from where the eardrum-bursting blast had come.

'That was the loudest thing I ever heard!' Stacey said. She shook her head hard from side to side to try to clear her hearing.
'What do you think it was?'

'I'll give you my guess for free,' Jimmy Junior said. 'I bet it's the weather. That's what I reckon. We've been having all kinds of weird rain, thunder, and lightning for weeks now. Been kind of spooky around here lately, if you ask me.'

CHAPTER
34

'Go, Greyhawk. Find the one you saw running. Find the boy and bring him to me!' Carl heard White Eyes shout.

Frank kept his arm around Carl to keep him calm, but he was straining to control his own fears too. White Eyes and the Grinning Dogs could only sense those with the Gift, if they showed fear or made any loud sounds. Greyhawk presented a new problem altogether. White Eyes had not driven him mad. He was in his service willingly. He could see and hear the same as anyone with the Gift. He could find Carl just like Frank and the others could find a New One. Hiding from Greyhawk would offer no protection like it did when another Betrayer crossed their path.

'I will find him, My Lord,' they heard Greyhawk say. 'He can hide from you no longer. He is nearby and you will have your pleasure with him.'

Frank squeezed his arm tighter around Carl and held him close to him. He looked at him and mouthed, 'No fear'.

They listened intently as Greyhawk began to head up the path toward the ledge where they had taken refuge. Carl never tried to be so quiet in all his life. He could hear his heart pounding and worried that Greyhawk or White Eyes might hear it too. He breathed as silently as he could.

Carl and Frank concentrated on every sound he made as Greyhawk came nearer and nearer to their hiding spot. They sat there still and silent with their ears tuned to Greyhawk's progress, when the sound of his footsteps suddenly stopped. He called out to White Eyes while standing on a boulder to the side of the path.

'I do not see him anywhere in the valley below, My Lord. He must have taken this route where I stand.' Greyhawk then climbed down from the boulder and continued taking the path toward the ledge.

Frank thought carefully about what he should do. He could not let Greyhawk simply stumble across them, shout out, and allow White Eyes to do his devilry.

An idea came to him. He nodded to himself to get ready and then pushed Carl gently back against the ledge and looked at him. He held out the palms of his hands to indicate to Carl that he should stay where he was. He smiled at him and then began to crawl away toward the advancing Greyhawk.

Frank snaked himself forward until he came to a point where there was some brush and loose rocks to the side of the path. He rolled toward the spread of rocks that lined the trail and waited. It offered little cover, but he thought if he stayed low he might be able to take Greyhawk by surprise when he approached.

He listened for each and every step as Greyhawk made his way to where he was lying. He forced himself not to worry that Carl might cry out as Greyhawk made his way toward him. He put every shred of his concentration on what he now must do.

'The lad came through the Cloud with the Stone. He's the only one who can use it to bring us home. He must find the others. I don't matter. He does.'

He trained his eyes on the path. He could hear Greyhawk walking nearer and nearer to his location. As the sound of his approach grew louder, he coiled himself ready to spring out.

Finally, he saw Greyhawk stride into view. He decided to wait until he got as close as possible to him before he attacked.

When Greyhawk came across Frank lying in wait, he blinked at him in surprise and stopped. As he stood there perplexed, Frank sprung out like a mountain lion. He threw one arm around Greyhawk and wrestled him to the ground. He put his free hand over his mouth, so Greyhawk could not call out to White Eyes.

Greyhawk tried to squirm out of his grasp, but Frank kept his hand firmly over his mouth and put his other hand around his throat. The more Greyhawk struggled, the harder Frank choked him.

Carl could hear muffled sounds coming from the direction where Greyhawk had been walking. He wanted to call out to Frank, but knew he must not.

Frank continued pressing his hand down hard over Greyhawk's throat as he reached over with his other hand to pick up a rock on the ground beside him. As he stretched over to grab the rock, his hand pinning Greyhawk loosened and Greyhawk croaked aloud, 'My Lord!' in a stifled burble.

Frank tightened his grip again and then repeatedly smashed the rock against Greyhawk's head.

Carl heard Greyhawk briefly cry out, heard some dull thudding sounds, and then there was silence. He stayed hunched down low and waited. He held his breath almost afraid to look. When he saw Frank on his belly slowly making his way back toward him, he was so relieved that it was all he could do to keep quiet.

Frank crawled back beside Carl and then stooped down again next to him at the ledge. They stayed there and tried not to breathe. Everything was still. Everything was silent. Like a moment frozen in time.

Then the sound of White Eyes' thundering voice roared around them.
'I heard your cry, Greyhawk. Did you find my prize? Tell me what you see. Where is the boy?'
But there was no reply.

Carl's mind was racing. He prayed White Eyes would fly away. He wanted to get up and run. He felt sick from his efforts to control his fear.

He shut his eyes tight and tried to remain calm. He focused his mind on happy things. He thought about Stacey and when she kissed him after they had weathered the storm together at Mr. Groves' garage. He remembered the time when he went out riding with Ben to the Shoshone Falls. He pictured himself on the day his father brought Daisy Mae home for the first time. But when he reopened his eyes, he could not control himself.

There, hovering directly over him, was White Eyes. He fluttered his dark and venous wings in all his awful glory. His piercing, soulless, white-marble eyes gleamed as he howled.
'Where are you, Greyhawk? I know you are nearby. Show yourself! Why do you not answer me?'

The shock of suddenly seeing White Eyes floating just above him shook Carl to his core. He screamed out in horror.
Immediately, White Eyes touched down to the ground.

'There you are! I can sense you at last!' White Eyes squealed in dreadful delight.
'It is you! The one known as Carl! The Last with the Gift! I have found you! Come! Let us play!'

Carl could not contain his terror. He wanted to stand up and run away, but his fear froze him and he could not move. His eyes darted wildly as he looked around for a way to escape.

Again, he screamed in fright and panic.

Frank immediately reached over and grabbed Carl by his jacket and pulled him up to his feet.

'Run, Carl!' he said in a hush. 'You remember where I told you the others were? Run there! Now!'

Carl was so frightened that his body would not obey him. Frank shoved Carl away from him to get him moving.

'Run, Carl! Don't look behind you! Run for your life!'

'I sense your fear! Why do you run away? You will not escape me! I now know your scent,' White Eyes gloated as Carl raced ahead to the steep uphill path that Frank had pointed out to him earlier.

'Where will you go, Boy? Where will you hide?'

White Eyes stood there directly across from the ledge where Frank and Carl had been hiding. He unfurled his wings again and lifted his nose to the sky.

'Such a sweet scent!' he said as he prepared to lift off the ground to find Carl. But just as he began to rise into the air and transition into his wispy and smoky form, Frank charged out and tackled him.

They both fell to the ground in a tumble.

'You ugly, hateful bastard!' Frank snarled as he grappled with him. 'How I've longed to get my fingers around your vile throat!' he hollered.

He began to throttle White Eyes.

'This is for Mei-Ling, you murdering son of a pig!' he

shouted. 'This is for Hope, who you killed without pity, you flint-hearted abomination!'

As Frank kept choking White Eyes, he felt a sudden sharp pain shoot through him. Another searing wave of pain hit him followed by yet another. Each jolt of agony was more excruciating than the one before. Frank began to stumble back and loosen his stranglehold on White Eyes. He screamed and fell to his knees in agony. He looked down at his hands. The skin was melting from the bones.

White Eyes stood back up and preened his wings. He looked down at Frank as he squirmed on the ground and shouted out in pain.

'Giant Man,' he sneered savagely. 'You have been my guest here for so long. So many times you have denied me my pleasure with those with the Gift. But now your stay is over!'

Frank gritted his teeth and grunted back hoarsely. 'You'll never drive me mad, you bat-winged bastard.'

'No?' White Eyes challenged. 'Are you certain, my mortal lodger? Then let us see just how strong you really are, shall we?'

White Eyes reached down and slapped the palms of his hands on either side of Frank's head. Instantly, Frank howled out again in hideous pain.

'Yes, Big Man!' White Eyes exulted in cold-hearted joy.

'Yes! Let me breathe in your fear at long last. Give me the taste of your terror!'

When White Eyes finally released his hold, Frank rolled on the ground and gasped for breath.
'You're a coward,' he groaned. 'I piss on you and your tricks. You're too afraid to fight me like a man.'
'But I am not a man,' White Eyes replied. 'I am far more than that.'

White Eyes leaned back and opened his mouth. A horrendous squeal tore through the air.
'My Dogs will come for you now,' he whispered sadistically into Frank's ear. 'And we will have so much fun with you!'

Frank whispered back defiantly.
'You'll never get out of here, you underbelly of a cockroach. The lad will see to that.'

White Eyes suddenly stepped back in surprise as if he had forgotten something important.
'Yes! The boy! Of course! The boy!'

He fixed an empty stare into Frank's eyes. 'How foolish of me! I forget myself!' he said with false modesty.
'Let me find the boy now. And both of you can watch the other plumb the depths of pain!'

Frank looked back down at his hands. They were now just bones dripping with melted flesh. He tried to stand up and continue his fight with White Eyes, but fell back on his knees and gasped for breath.

White Eyes once again squeezed his hands around Frank's head. Straightaway, Frank cried out in unspeakable pain. Then his eyes grew wide with fear, as he saw his melted fingers magically transform into wriggling, green-eyed snakes. With their fangs drawn, they kept striking at his face. White Eyes danced a little jig of joy at his evil conjuring.

The sounds of Frank's tortured screaming filled the air. It echoed down the valley in waves sharing its pain with anyone who heard it.

Bird-Who-Hops poked his head out of the hollow and listened to the unnerving squeals of terror. The howling agony washed over him putting his courage to the test. He turned in shock and looked at Henri.
'That's Frank shouting out! He's nearby!'

Bird-Who-Hops' instinct took over and he started to rush toward Frank's anguished cries. Henri blocked his way, threw his arms around him, and pushed him back into the hollow.

'Let me go!' Bird-Who-Hops hissed in fury. 'Let me go to him!'
'There's nothing to be done,' Henri said as he tried to calm him down. 'White Eyes has him. Frank is lost to us. He cannot be saved.'

Bird-Who-Hops stopped struggling. He turned away from Henri as the horror-filled screams continued unabated.

He forced himself to accept the truth that he hoped beyond hope was not true.

'I am a brave from my tribe. I am not afraid,' he whispered to himself.

He turned back to Henri and said, 'Frank was the bravest of all the braves.'

Cora and Ben held on to one another in the adjoining hollow. Cora put her hands over his son's ears in a vain attempt to stop him from hearing the awful cries outside.

'We must not be afraid,' she murmured quietly as she tried to master her own fear.

'But that's Frank!' Ben said. 'Can't you tell? That's Frank screaming.'

Cora thought about the many times she had told Frank not to give up hope. Now the tortured shouting of her surly friend called her own hope into question.

White Eyes looked up to the sky as Frank writhed on the ground in his unceasing suffering. The ghastly black smoke columns of the Grinning Dogs appeared overhead. They quickly landed simultaneously around where White Eyes stood.

'You have summoned us, My Lord?' one of the Dogs asked.

'I have found the one who dared enter my domain with the Stone,' White Eyes proclaimed.

'I go to claim him now. Take this one groveling on the ground. Take this pathetic hero. Take him into the sky and do with him what you will. His fear disgusts me. I've grown tired of it.'

'My Lord Remiel, do you not wish to turn this wretch into one of your servants?' another Grinning Dog asked.

'No, I have no need for more servants. All with the Gift are already here. I know the scent of the Last with the Gift. I will disembowel him for daring to hope that he could deny us our destiny. Then I will open the Cloud and we will destroy the rest of them at our leisure.'

The Grinning Dogs howled in their depraved jubilation. They jeered at Frank in his misery. They took turns kicking at him. They grabbed him by the throat, spat at him, and mocked his wide-eyed terror. On a signal from White Eyes, they then all switched back into their smoky plume state.

'Show him the world he has called home for so long. Give him a bird's eye view!' White Eyes commanded them.
The Grinning Dogs flew back into the sky with Frank in tow.

Carl continued making his way up the steep and arduous path that Frank had told him to follow. The path became so precipitous that he could no longer run up it. He could only trudge upward one slow step at a time. He slogged his way up the hill until he had to stop completely. A massive boulder was embedded right across the path and blocked his way. He looked around it until he found a foothold and then climbed onto it. He had to use both his arms and legs as he wearily hauled himself over it. He kept going, despite his exhaustion, not only to get away from White Eyes, but to find the others with the Gift who Frank said were hiding toward the bottom of the hill he was climbing. As he continued forcing himself uphill, he kept hearing Frank's howls of pain and White Eyes' voice calling out to him. It was as if the voice were inside his head.

'Where do you run, Boy? Where do you seek to flee? Do you look for your Brotherhood? Do you hope to take the Stone to them? Do you not wish to see what I do to your protector? Foolish child! I now know your scent. You cannot hide from me. Surrender to your fate and I will show you mercy!'

Bird-Who-Hops and Henri stood together looking out of their hollow just as Ben and Cora were doing from the hollow beside them. They saw the six Grinning Dogs descend and land nearby. Very soon after their arrival, Frank's screams quickly faded away. They looked at one another equally confused and bewildered. They then saw the six pillars of smoke rise again to the sky.

Cackling laughter rained down as the black jet streams of the Grinning Dogs looped through the air. The flying plumes then began to interlace to form one enormous, dark and smoky ring spinning above.

The swirling circle began to rotate slowly at first, but soon gained momentum and revolved faster and faster. The black whirlwind they created began to transform into a kind of vortex. Like a sinister and sooty cyclone. As it grew in size and spun furiously, the hideous cackling coming from within it grew louder. It sounded like the malicious taunting of demented children.

The whirling mass of black smoke dominated the sky like an approaching tornado. The spinning vortex floated freely through the sky until it suddenly stopped on the spot and began to hover in the air. It hung there in place whirring menacingly directly above the Brotherhood in their rock face hollows. They stood there staring at it in wonder. The empty, cold-blooded laughter from above grew to a fever pitch and then something dropped from the tail end of the funnel-shaped whirlwind.

The Brotherhood peered in confusion at the object as it hurtled rapidly toward the ground.

They tracked the falling object with their eyes. At first, they could not make out what it was. But as it dropped closer to the ground, they turned their heads away in horror as Frank's body smashed into the rocks right in front of them.

After the Grinning Dogs had formed their black ring of death in the sky and thrown Frank to the rocks below, they split apart and again began to descend to the ground. Moments later, the sound of their blood-curdling, soulless laughter rang out from not far away.

Henri had to use all of his strength to prevent Bird-Who-Hops from running out to try and help Frank. He slapped and kicked at Henri to get free of his hold on him.

'Let me go to him!' he begged. 'Get off me! Let me go!' 'No one can help him now,' Henri told him sorrowfully. 'Our dear friend is gone.'

Bird-Who-Hops fell silent. He gave up on his attempts to get away. In despair, he looked up at Henri and his eyes began to well up in tears. He put his head against Henri's chest and wept. Henri held him close to console him while fighting back his own tears. In all their time together, it was the only time he had ever seen Bird-Who-Hops cry.

Ben and Cora held one another and quivered in their sorrow.
'Don't be afraid,' Cora said with tears pouring from her eyes. 'Don't be afraid,' she said over and over again as much for herself as for her son.

They then heard White Eyes' voice call out.
'I come for you! Why do you run away? Did you not enjoy what my servants have done to your giant? You are the Last with the Gift, Boy. Fear me and serve me and I promise you I will do you no harm.'

'What does he mean, Mom? What boy?' Ben asked. 'Has he found us? We weren't afraid. How did he sense we were here? Did he hear us? Who's the Last with the Gift?'

When Carl at last reached the top of the steep and rocky hill, it flattened out into a wide featureless plateau just as Frank had said.

He was desperate to stop and rest. His legs and arms ached painfully and he was gasping for air, but he knew he could not delay a single moment. White Eyes kept calling out to him or whispering to him inside his head. He saw the black forms of the Grinning Dogs ascend back into the sky and knew they were searching for him. He wandered across the plateau looking for the path that would lead him back down to the valley, but he could see no sign of it.

'Where's the way down?' he asked himself. He started running down the plateau and swiveled his head right and left looking for the path downhill that Frank told him would take him to Ben and Cora, but he could not find it.

He stopped and whispered to himself in frustration. 'Where the devil is it?'

He started to question if he had taken the right path after all. He was just on the verge of panic, when he spied a spill of rocks to the edge of the plateau in front of him. When he went over to look, he saw the pathway winding its way down through the sprawl of rocks. He let out a relieved sigh.

The way down was steep. It was rocky. It looked dangerous. He swallowed some more air, set himself ready, and then started to make his way downhill.

As he went along, he scanned the area for any signs of the others Frank promised were there hiding.

Carl could no longer hear Frank's screams of torture. He did not know if that was a good sign or not. He just knew that he had to keep going.

He continued making his way downhill. He found it was far easier to go down the hill than he imagined. It was certainly easier than the struggle going up it.

The downhill path was flanked by a high ridge to his left and rock-strewn and boulder-covered terrain to his right. He could see the wide, colorless valley just beyond the rocks.

As he kept walking down the slope, he glanced over the rocks to the valley and saw the vast Blue Cloud that he had seen before when running with Frank. It loomed ominously just above the valley floor. Carl paused and looked at it in wonder for a moment. He was just beginning to walk down the path again, when the Blue Cloud collapsed in on itself. A booming crashing sound was followed by heavy tremors which shook the ground. He fell over in a heap. He scrambled to get back up on his feet and kept heading downward.

Carl battled with himself to control his fear as he hiked down the hill. The Blue Cloud continued to grow and collapse, White Eyes kept whispering to him in his head, and the harrowing black smoky plumes kept circling in the sky above him. He felt as if he were being hunted like a wild animal.

But he knew full well that he must not succumb to his fears. He knew that if he indulged his fear, it would call White Eyes right to him. He tried not to let panic get the better of him. To steady his nerves he repeated softly to himself, 'I must keep going. I must not be afraid. I must find the others.'

The footing on the downhill path started becoming rockier and more treacherous. He had to leap from side to side to keep going forward and avoid falling over the jagged rocks jutting out from the path. The Blue Cloud continued to expand and then crash in on itself as he descended. He learned to stop when he saw the Blue Cloud collapse, so the monstrous noise and tremors that followed did not make him fall down again.

He continued to look for anywhere along the path where other people could possibly be hiding, but he could see nothing except the flat ridge face on his left and the wide open valley floor to his right.

'Where could they be? There's nowhere to hide!' Again, he began to let doubts creep in that he had taken the right path.

The downhill track dog-legged sharply to his right and immediately grew steeper. He had to stop running entirely and step over the rocks one by one. The loose shale on the path made his footing dangerously slippery. He looked up and saw the pillars of smoke had stopped circling and began to float in place just above the Blue Cloud. He convinced himself that they had seen him.

He was so exhausted. He was unsure if he had gone in the right direction. He had to fight back thoughts of what would happen to him, if White Eyes or his Grinning Dogs got their hands on him. He was losing confidence that even if he did find Ben and his mother that he could take them out of this place.

'I believed what was in Greyhawk's book, but what if he was lying?' he worried. 'Maybe it was another of his tricks and I can't rescue them with the Stone.'

He gritted his teeth and shook his head. 'No, I must keep going. I can't give up. There's no hope in that.' He put his hand against his jacket pocket, felt the Willing Stone, and soldiered on.

He stepped carefully over the many rocks embedded in the path. It seemed to grow steeper and more hazardous with every step he took. But he no longer looked at the Grinning Dogs in the sky. He refused to listen to White Eyes' mocking catcalls in his head. He continued making his way downhill one painful step after another until the path at last started to level out. He took a deep breath and stopped.

'Frank said the others were hiding near the bottom of this hill,' he reminded himself. He looked around, but could see nowhere where anyone could hide.

He was just about to start running again, when he spied something up ahead. He cautiously began making his way down to it.

Something was stretched out on the scree of rocks and broken boulders to the right of the path. He kept moving slowly toward it.

'Maybe that's where they all are,' he reckoned. 'Maybe there's some hiding place under there.'

But as he got close enough to see what was sprawled across the rubble, he froze. He turned his head quickly away. Lying there was Frank's broken, lifeless body shattered on the jumble of rocks.

His eyes filled with tears. It was all too much to bear. Just like it was when he saw White Eyes hovering above him as they were hiding back at the ledge, he wanted to shout out again in terror. He tried so hard to master his fear that he felt his heart would stop. He thought he would go mad, if he tried to contain himself any longer. He took another deep breath and forced himself to carry on looking.

He had just started to move away from Frank's body to begin his search for the others again, when he felt a hand on his shoulder.

'Come,' a voice whispered. And then a second voice said, 'It's safe. Come with us.'

Carl jumped away like he was scalded and quickly turned around to confront the voices whispering to him. There stood a small Native American boy. He was wearing clothing made of twined sagebrush bark and rabbit fur. Standing next to him was a man dressed in buckskin and wearing a fur hat.

'Who are you?' Carl stuttered.
'Come with us. It isn't safe out here,' the man in the fur hat said.

The boy grabbed Carl's sleeve and started tugging at him.
'You come now!' he ordered.

CHAPTER
35

The Blue Cloud continued to swell and shrink. The insufferable bang that accompanied it punctuated each fluctuation. The tremors that followed would shake the ground with such force that loose rocks rolled across the valley floor like tumbleweeds. There was no peace to be found. There was no respite from the Blue Cloud's instability. It shook White Eyes' domain to the core as it relentlessly tore his prison apart.

The young boy continued tugging at Carl's sleeve and pulling him forward toward the face of the ridge. 'Come! You come with us,' he kept insisting.

As he trailed behind the boy, Carl noticed a series of hollows along the ridge face. When they got to the ridge, the man and the boy went into one of the hollows and Carl followed them in.

'I am Henri and my young friend is Bird-Who-Hops. You must not be afraid. Do you understand me? No matter what happens, you must show no fear.'
'And be as quiet as a rabbit hiding in its warren,' Bird-Who-Hops added.

'I know,' Carl said. 'Frank told me.'
'You were with Frank?' Bird-Who-Hops asked. 'You are the New One who Frank went out to find?'

285

'I suppose I am. He found me. Frank saved me, but White Eyes…'
Carl looked down to try to control his emotions. He paused for a moment to collect himself.

'Are you the others with the Gift? Frank told me you were here. He told me where you were hiding. He helped me get away from White Eyes before…'
Carl paused again as the words caught in his throat. He looked at Henri and Bird-Who-Hops and took a deep breath before he finally blurted out, 'Frank helped me escape before White Eyes killed him.'

Bird-Who-Hops stared menacingly at Carl. He glared at him with a false smile on his face.
'White Eyes killed him, you say? I think not. I think you speak with a double tongue. He did not kill him. You killed my friend,' Bird-Who-Hops spit back at him.
'You did! You were afraid and your fear killed my friend! I blame you! You!'
Beside himself with rage, Bird-Who-Hops charged at Carl and started clawing at his face.
'You! You killed Frank!' he sputtered in fury.

Henri raced over to pull him away.
'Bird-Who-Hops,' he said as he fended off his attack.
'He is a New One. Everyone new to this place shows fear. Do you want to make him afraid again? What will happen then?'

Bird-Who-Hops shrugged off Henri's hold on him. He backed away from Carl and sat down.
He glowered at Carl bitterly.

'You are a yellow feather,' he said with his face red in anger. 'My people say-Bihi Siamp! You are a coward.' He turned his back on Carl and refused to look at him.

Henri took Carl aside. 'Tell me who you are.'
'I'm Carl Marty, Sir. Ben Crenshaw's friend. I'm looking for him.'
Carl then told him why he was there.

'I've come to rescue him. Do you know where Ben and his mother are? I want to bring them home. Maybe I can take you away from here too.'

'How? By getting us killed as well?' Bird-Who-Hops asked sarcastically.
'No,' Carl replied. 'With this.'
Carl took the Willing Stone out of his pocket and showed it to them.

'We can all leave,' he said. 'I think so anyway. It was in a book I read. It said, if we touch the Stone together, we can walk through the Blue Cloud and go home.'

Bird-Who-Hops got back to his feet and rushed over to Carl to see the Willing Stone in his hand. He looked up at Henri.
'That's the Stone! I have seen it before. In my village, a medicine man once came and showed it to me. It's the Willing Stone! He's brought it here through the Cloud! He can take us home!'

Henri was unable to believe what he was hearing. He asked Carl to be sure that he understood correctly.

'Your book says we can be released from this place with the Willing Stone?'

'Yes,' Carl said. 'But first I need to find Ben and his mother. Her name is Cora Crenshaw. Do you know them? Frank said they were still alive. I was hoping to find them here. Do you know where they are?'
'Come,' Henri replied. 'I will take you to them.'

'They're here?' Carl asked in shock. He was so happy that he forgot for a moment about White Eyes and his henchman looking for him. They went outside together and Henri led them away to his left.
'They're right over there,' he said softy while pointing ahead at a nearby hollow in the ridge face.

Carl could not contain himself. He started sprinting to the neighboring hollow as quickly as his legs would carry him. As he ran, he shouted at the top of his voice.

'Ben! Ben! It's me. It's Carl! Mrs. Crenshaw! It's Carl Marty! I'm here to take you home!'
Bird-Who-Hops raced quickly after him.
'It's Carl, Ben! It's me!' Carl continued to shout.

Bird-Who-Hops caught up with Carl and grabbed him. 'Quiet!' he said under his breath. 'Or you will bring the Dogs here. We told you they can hear...'

Bird-Who-Hops then abruptly stopped speaking and looked up to the sky.
'It is too late,' he said. 'They are coming.'

Swooping above them, six dark columns of smoke began to descend rapidly to the spot where they were standing. Another smoky trail appeared just above the other six smoky plumes and it too began to come back down to earth.

'Get back,' Henri said urgently. 'Quickly now. We must not be found in the open. They have heard us. Hurry.' They made a rapid retreat back to their hollow.

'You are like the fool of my tribe. Jabbering with no sense of danger coming,' Bird-Who-Hops whispered at Carl impatiently. 'You will show no fear or the Stone will be worthless to us.'

'Did you hear someone shouting?' Ben asked his mother. 'Are the others in trouble?'
Cora pointed to the black pillars in the sky coming down toward them.
'Get back, Ben,' she whispered.

The Brotherhood moved as far back in their hollow sanctuaries as they would allow. They stood there in silence not moving a muscle and almost too afraid to breathe, when they heard a bellowing voice.

'Boy! Did you call out for me? Where are you hiding? Send me the scent of your fear again, so I may find you. We know you are nearby. We will wait here until your fear betrays you to us.'

The chilling, childish laughter of the Grinning Dogs resounded like a perverse chorus through the valley.

White Eyes and his Grinning Dogs stood together around Frank's broken corpse. One of the Grinning Dogs began to tear at his body like a vulture. He tore off one of Frank's arms at the shoulder and flung it at the ridge face. They then all began to rip his body to shreds.

'Do you see now what we do with those who dare oppose us?' White Eyes crowed.

He went over and knelt down over the mutilated body. He placed his hands on either side of Frank's head and, in one swift jerk, pulled it off. He stood back up and held it with one hand.
'Here!' White Eyes cried triumphantly. 'Here is your brother! Here is your savior!'

He waved the head from side to side and then threw it. It bounced and then landed just outside the hollow where Carl and the others were hiding. The Grinning Dogs roared their approval and laughed in their odious pleasure.

The Brotherhood pulled their heads away in revulsion. Henri threw his arms around Carl to stop him from screaming in terror. Bird-Who-Hops closed his eyes and mumbled to himself to control his own fear.
'I am a brave of my tribe...'

'No?' White Eyes asked. 'You refuse to fear me still? You still resist me? You still cling to your foolish hope? You still long for deliverance? Then let me show you the futility of your stubborn refusal to accept your fate.'

White Eyes turned around to face the valley beyond the rocks. The Grinning Dogs followed their Master's lead and turned to face the valley as well.

The Blue Cloud was still spread out wide just above the valley floor. White Eyes unfurled his wings and hovered above Frank's body. He pulled back his head and let out a shrieking howl. A white-tailed kite flying overhead scattered off in panic.

'Let me show you our victory! Let me show you our revenge,' he stormed. 'Then you will know there is no hope. Let me show you the open door to your world that beckons us.'

White Eyes glided over and floated in place just in front of the Blue Cloud. Carl, Henri, and Bird-Who-Hops crept silently to the hollow entrance and watched. Ben and Cora saw White Eyes fly off as well and stood there looking on not knowing what to expect.

The Blue Cloud collapsed in on itself once again. The valley floor shook and the intolerable booms like peels of thunder split the air. White Eyes waited until the Blue Cloud began to expand again. When it had spread out across the entire valley, he reached out both his arms toward it. Instantly, an image formed on the Blue Cloud as if it had become a gigantic movie screen.

A group of medicine men appeared on the Blue Cloud screen. Some stood there chanting and beating their ritual drums while others began drawing in the sky with Willing Stones in their hands.

White Eyes and the Grinning Dogs then appeared on the screen.

As the medicine men worked together, White Eyes began to back away from them toward the Blue Cloud horizon they were creating. His Grinning Dogs cowered and trembled in fear behind him. White Eyes howled in rage as the incanting of the medicine men forced him closer to the Blue Cloud. His Dogs bayed in discomfort at the incantations that tormented them and kept forcing their retreat. The medicine men continued chanting and drawing with their Willing Stones driving White Eyes and the Grinning Dogs back and back until they fell through the Blue Cloud trap created for them.

White Eyes looked on helplessly at the medicine men now on the other side of the Blue Cloud. He screeched in frightful fury as they persevered with their ritual. He looked on in impotence as the medicine men carried on chanting in unison and drawing with their Willing Stones until they and the world of light and time began to grow blurry and disappear. All White Eyes could now see was the ripple in the sky. The world from which he was banished faded from his view.

The Blue Cloud screen transformed back into its shimmering wrinkled state. The Brotherhood stood there mesmerized as White Eyes remained hovering at the Blue Cloud.

He placed his palms together and immediately a loud clattering sound like the shattering of glass rang out.

When he separated his palms again, the Blue Cloud began to split apart. A gap appeared to reveal the real world beyond. There was the Magic Valley in all its glorious color and tranquility. It shone like a glimmer of light in the darkness. It was a patch of brightness amid the dull drabness of White Eyes' realm.

The Grinning Dogs squealed in wicked delight. 'How great is our Master, Lord Remiel! All praise and glory to his name!'

White Eyes coasted back to rejoin the Grinning Dogs at the spot where they had desecrated Frank's body. He hung floating in the air just above the ground. He fluttered his wings and boasted shamelessly over his achievement.

'I have opened the door. Do you see? Look! There is the world from which you came. Can you not see its majesty? Look! Do you not long to walk in the world of light and time again? Does it not call you from your hiding? There is your home! There is your world of delight. Surrender yourself, Boy, and I will take you with us. I will take you home.'

CHAPTER
36

From the moment White Eyes parted the Blue Cloud to reveal the real world of time and space, it remained as it was. It no longer expanded across the sky nor did it collapse in on itself. The ground no longer shook with bone-jarring tremors and the crashing, shattering roar had stopped. The sliver of light to the world through the Blue Cloud and the glimpse of the passage back home endured. Through the gap White Eyes had created, time could be seen passing again. The shadows played across the ridges of the Magic Valley as the sun slowly began to slip below the horizon. The fading sunset dappled the landscape in gold.

After White Eyes had flown back to rejoin the Grinning Dogs, Carl and the others sat as far back in their hollows as they would allow. They stayed there as still and silent as possible. Carl tried not to listen as White Eyes spoke to him inside his head. He ignored the lies and promises that White Eyes would take him home. He refused to be fearful when White Eyes unexpectedly switched to taunts and threats and told him the unspeakable things he would do to him once he had him in his clutches. All he would let himself think about was Ben and Cora and how he might get to them and take them away from this horrific place.

White Eyes' impatience grew with his inability to vex

Carl. He was consumed by his rage and anger. His growing irritation boiled within him.

'Show me your fear again, Boy!' he squawked with venom.

He cried out in furious frustration. 'Your giant distracted me from claiming you as my prize. He let you slip away from me, but I know you are near!'

He kicked in outrage at what remained of Frank's body.

Ultimately, one of the Grinning Dogs said, 'My Lord, we do not sense him here. There is no fear. There is no sound. Shall we search elsewhere? Perhaps he has escaped us.'

White Eyes howled in his displeasure. 'Stay here!' he commanded.

White Eyes glided again over to the Blue Cloud. He landed on the valley floor and stretched his arms wide apart and then slowly brought them back together. As his palms touched, the gap in the Blue Cloud resealed itself. Immediately, a loud crashing cacophony rang out.

White Eyes shrieked with rage as he flew back to rejoin the Grinning Dogs.

'Go!' he commanded them. 'Find the boy! I will have him! I will make him fear me and serve me! I will turn him into my puppet!'

'My pardon, Lord Remiel,' one of the Grinning Dogs said as he bowed deeply. 'But why do we not leave? Why do you close the passage?' he asked.

'Let us all leave this place, My Lord. Let us all flee this prison now and then you may punish the boy for his impudence at your leisure.'

White Eyes glared momentarily in indignation and then all his pent-up anger and frustration finally exploded. He squeezed his hands firmly on either side of the Grinning Dog's head.

'Do you wish for me to destroy you? Will you defy me? I close the Blue Cloud so they may not escape! How dare you question me! I will have the boy now!'
The Grinning Dog fell to his knees and writhed in agony.

'Who is your Master?' White Eyes fumed. 'Will you take my place?'
'No, My Lord!' The Grinning Dog whimpered. 'You are my Master!'
'You dare question me, when it is I who sustain you?' White Eyes thundered in uncontrollable anger.

He then loosened his grasp and pushed the Grinning Dog away from him. The Grinning Dog crumpled to the ground and slowly got back to his feet.
'I will not be thwarted!' White Eyes raged.
'Find the boy! Then we shall go!'

The Grinning Dogs instantly changed into rapidly spinning columns of smoke. Together, they rose slowly upward and then shot off into the air. White Eyes watched them streaking through the sky in every direction.

'Find him!' he bawled up at them.
The bitter shouts of his frustration shook through the valley.
'Find the Boy!'

Before White Eyes flew off himself, he called out in fury in every direction.
'Your scent has grown faint, Boy,' he bellowed. 'But I have tasted your fear. I know its aroma. Fear me again and I will have you. For we can always smell fear.'

He too then made his eerie transfiguration into his black smoky form and rose into the sky to join in the search.

Once White Eyes had resealed the Blue Cloud, it again began to throb, expand, and then collapse repeatedly like storm waves smashing to the shore carrying a shattering roar in their wake.

Bird-Who-Hops looked out of the hollow. He peered up and scanned the sky. He turned back to the others and whispered, 'They fly above.'

He then looked straight at Carl. 'You must be quiet. You Pales cannot help yourselves from calling out like a cockerel. You nearly gave us all away.'

Carl nodded that he understood and then he calmly stood up and started to walk out of the hollow. Henri raced over to stop him.

'What do you think you're doing?' he asked softly. 'They are in the sky above us. They will hear you.'

Carl stood there with Henri and signaled to Bird-Who-Hops to come over and join them. He put an arm around each of them, drew them close, and then spoke as quietly as he could.

'Frank and I saw a Betrayer when we were making our way here. He said they tell White Eyes where we are, if they see or hear us or sense we are afraid. But he cannot see us himself, isn't that so?'

'That is what we think,' Henri said. 'White Eyes and his Dogs cannot see in the way in which we see.'

'But they can hear like a moth! They can hear the slightest of sounds,' Bird-Who-Hops reminded him. 'They 'see' by sound and fear.'

'Okay,' Carl agreed. 'But I wager that if we made no sound and showed no fear, they wouldn't know we were there. Just now, we were silent. We refused to be afraid and they've all gone off to look for me somewhere else.'

'That is why he creates Betrayers! Just as Frank told you,' Bird-Who-Hops objected. 'They can see us. They will betray us to him.'

'If there's one around they will. And not all of them can see us,' Carl replied.

'When we were waiting out a rockslide, Frank and I saw a young mother with no eyes. Frank said she was a Betrayer. She couldn't tell Frank and I were there and she stood right in front of us. Frank said if we weren't afraid and stayed quiet, she wouldn't notice us.'

'But there are others!' Bird-Who-Hops said as he shook his head. 'You are a New One! You do not know. Others do have eyes and can see us.'

'I know,' Carl said. 'Like Mad Tom. He saw me, when I first arrived, and I didn't know to hide from him. I do now.'

He stopped speaking and got them all to sit down on the ground.
'I have an idea,' he said softly. 'I say we go out there and look to see if there are any of these Betrayers around. If we don't see one, I'll go over to Ben and his mom, get them, come back here, and we'll all walk out of this nightmare through the Blue Cloud. We touch the Willing Stone together and go home. What do you think?'

Henri did not look convinced.
'They are directly overhead. If anyone makes a sound above a whisper, they will know. If there is a Betrayer out there, they will shout out and we are lost. It is too dangerous.'

Bird-Who-Hops agreed.
'If they catch us, they will scalp us and use our skins for a canoe.'

'We can't just sit here and let White Eyes and those creatures walk into our world, can we?' Carl asked. 'We have to take a risk. We must take our chance. The moment I arrived, White Eyes had all with the Gift here with him. He could open the Blue Cloud at anytime and go through. He showed us just now that he can open the Cloud right before they flew away, didn't he?' he said to refresh their memory.

'But White Eyes is vain and my dad taught me that vanity is a weakness. He won't leave until he finds me. He's stubborn. We'll use his weakness against him. We either get out of here ourselves or let him get out. If we stay here and do nothing, sooner or later he's going to find us. What do we have to lose? If he goes through the Cloud, we're all done for anyway. Everyone is.'

Bird-Who-Hops cocked his head to one side and looked at Carl. It was as if he were looking at him for the first time. He considered what Carl said and then began nodding in agreement.

'Your words are wise,' he said with respect. 'We cannot let White Eyes go on the warpath in the real world. He's right, Henri. We must not be afraid.' He looked at Carl again. 'Perhaps you are not a coward after all.'

'No, you were right,' Carl replied. 'I was a coward. I was afraid and it cost Frank his life. Let's try to make sure that he didn't sacrifice himself for nothing.'

'What do you want us to do?' Henri asked. 'How can we help?'

'You can help me look for these Betrayers,' Carl said. And as soon as he said that, Bird-Who-Hops started walking out of the hollow.

'Whoa! Now where do you think you're going?' Henri asked as he reached over to pull him back.

'I'm looking for Betrayers,' Bird-Who-Hops said proudly. 'You two come too and help me look.'

Henri managed to calm them down before they both brazenly marched out of the hollow.

'Bravery without forethought is recklessness,' he advised them.

Before they went out to scan the area for Betrayers, Henri suggested that they split up their search. After they agreed their plan, they left the hollow together.

Henri looked to the top of the ridge across the valley. Bird-Who-Hops scanned the area to his right and Carl to his left. Then they joined back together, turned around, and looked to the top of the ridge where they were hiding. They saw nothing, except for the black vapor trails of the Grinning Dogs still soaring through the sky. They stood together for a moment and stared and listened again for any signs or sounds of a Betrayer. When they were satisfied there were none in the area, they went back into the hollow.

'I'll leave the Willing Stone with you, so White Eyes won't get his mitts on it if he catches me,' Carl said.

'I'm going on my own. You're right. It's too dangerous for us all to go. If I can get over there safely, I'll tell Ben and Mrs. Cora about our plans and bring them back here. Once we're all together, we'll take the Stone with us and walk to the Blue Cloud.'

'Take your shoes off before you go,' Bird-Who-Hops suggested. 'You walk too loud. Like a buffalo.'
'Okay,' Carl laughed.

He took the Willing Stone in its suede leather case out of his jacket pocket and handed it to Henri.
Then Carl looked directly at both of them.
'We're going home,' he said.

Carl left the hollow. He stopped for a moment as he took a deep breath. Then he turned in the same direction Henri had shown him before his shouting had attracted White Eyes and the Grinning Dogs and forced their retreat. He started walking as quietly as he could to the hollow where Ben and Cora were waiting. He scanned the horizon carefully to check if a Betrayer was anywhere in sight. Even though he was trying not to look, he could still sense the trails of the intimidating black plumes flying above him out of the corner of his eye.

If only he could be quiet enough, if only he could completely master his fear, it would be a simple matter to reach Ben and Cora. But with each of his steps sounding to him like crockery crashing and with all his senses on full alert for any sign of danger, his journey there became a slow and careful trudge. He plodded on in his laborious and, to his mind, heavy-footed way. 'I'm in no hurry. I have all the time in the world,' he reminded himself as he slowly walked quietly forward.

Carl placed the palm of his hand on the flat ridge face to steady himself. He worried that he might fall noisily and attract the Grinning Dogs when the Blue Cloud collapsed and the tremors and ear-splitting din followed. He paused again and shut his eyes to hold himself together. He then took another deep breath and carried on.

Ben and Cora's hollow was only about fifty yards or so away. But at the pace Carl was walking, it would take him several minutes to get there. He weighed every footstep forward deliberately while trying not to make any sounds at all.
'There is no rush. There is no hurry. I have all the time in the world,' he mumbled to himself as he made his way forward step by silent step.

He ran over in his mind what he should do when he finally made it over to them. He decided that he would quickly rush in, grip them by their arms, and pull them as far back and away from their hollow entrance as he could. He thought, if he just walked in on them by surprise, they might scream in shock.

'They still don't know I'm here,' he reasoned. 'They might think White Eyes and his Dogs or a Betrayer found them.'

He wished now that he had spent more time thinking about what he should do when he got there before he set off.

As he crept ever closer to Ben and Cora, he could sense the smoky plumes still buzzing above him. Then finally he saw the entrance to their hollow just ahead. He could see neither Ben nor Cora though. He figured they were trying to avoid being noticed by White Eyes and his lackeys. When he did at last reach the hollow, he stopped. He listened for any sounds coming from within, but heard nothing.
He took a deep breath and rushed in.

As Carl imagined they would, Ben and Cora froze in shock. When they saw who it was, they both blinked at him in amazement. They could not believe who they were seeing. Carl grabbed each of them by the arm and pulled them far back into their hollow. He whispered very softly, 'We're going home. I have the Willing Stone. Follow me back to the other hollow. Trust me.'

Ben and Cora hugged Carl. Even though they knew they must be silent, the tears in their eyes and the beaming smiles on their faces spoke loudly enough. They were not yet sure what was going on, but their happiness at seeing him again was unbounded.

Carl spoke softly right into their ears.
'Come with me. Don't be afraid. Say nothing.'
Cora looked at Ben and then nodded to Carl that they understood.
'Trust me,' he said to them again.

Just as he had done before he set off to retrieve Ben and Cora, Carl first scrutinized the area for any sign of a Betrayer. After he convinced himself there were none around, they left the hollow.

Carl took the lead and Ben and Cora walked together right behind him. If anything, Carl walked at an even slower pace than he did when he walked over to fetch them.

Ben looked up to the sky and saw the Grinning Dogs crisscrossing directly over them. He turned around and started going back to their hollow, but Cora put an arm around him and kept him moving forward.

They followed Carl at his creeping pace. He thought for safety's sake to lead them forward only a few steps at a time and then stop. He would then turn back to them and put his hands up to signal to them to remain calm. They continued in this stop-start fashion as they made their way slowly back to where Henri and Bird-Who-Hops were waiting.

Carl tried his hardest not to be overly excited at seeing his friend and his mother again. He knew he must remain calm and fearless. He reminded himself again as he did all the way over to Ben and Cora's hollow. 'We've all the time in the world.'

He led them on step by careful step as soundlessly as possible. Every scrap of his attention was on getting everyone back safely.

Bird-Who-Hops started to fidget. He could not understand how it possibly could take so long for Carl to collect the others and get back to them.

Henri sat him down and said quietly, 'Be patient. He will come back.'
Bird-Who-Hops wanted to say that was exactly what Henri had said about Frank and look what happened to him, but he said nothing.
He sat with Henri and fretted.

Carl, Ben, and Cora finally began to approach the other hollow. When they were just outside of it, Carl stopped and gestured to Ben and Cora to wait. He thought it would be safer if he entered first and made a silent sign that he was successful in bringing the others back.

He went in the hollow, held a hand up, and nodded behind to indicate the others were with him. When he saw that Bird-Who-Hops and Henri understood, he went back out and brought Ben and Cora into the hollow with him. It was the first time that they had all been together, since the Blue Cloud quakes had destroyed their Gathering Place and the rockslides had chased them away from the rocky outcrop where they had taken refuge.

The hollow was far too small to accommodate the five of them. Carl wished now that he had given that some more thought too before he set off on his escapade. They all shoved back as far into the hollow as they could, but it was now possible for someone to notice the hollow was occupied.

Carl hoped no Betrayers would show up on the scene.

Henri handed the Willing Stone in its leather case back to Carl. He showed it to Ben and then whispered into his ear.
'We're going home, Ben. No sound. No fear. Just do as I say. Trust me.'

Carl then went over to Cora and, as quietly as he could, explained in more detail what they hoped to do.
'The Stone can get us out of here, Mrs. Crenshaw. We're walking to the Blue Cloud. Just do what I say and we'll stop White Eyes and get ourselves back where we're meant to be in the bargain.'

Cora wanted to ask him exactly how he planned to do that, but decided to trust him instead. She had never seen this confident side of Carl before. It made her put her faith in him.

Before they began their trek to the Blue Cloud, they first scouted for any sign of a Betrayer. They each left the hollow in turn and looked in different directions. When they were satisfied that no Betrayers were watching them, they went back inside the cramped hollow and waited.

Carl thought they would stand a better chance of making it safely across the valley to the Blue Cloud, if they all stayed together in one group. He put one arm over Ben's shoulder and the other one over Bird-Who-Hops. He indicated that Henri and Cora should do the same and whispered, 'Hold on to one another.'

Then, arm in arm, they walked out of the hollow and set off on their risky and dangerous escape.

As silently as possible, they made their way toward the Blue Cloud still spread out just above the valley floor. When they reached the spot where Frank's body lay on the rocks, they looked away. Everyone kept their eyes firmly fixed on the Blue Cloud in front of them.

When Ben looked up at the Grinning Dogs flying above, Carl squeezed his shoulder and pressed him forward. They walked together slowly and bravely with their focus straight ahead.

It was much farther to reach the Blue Cloud than it was to get to and from Ben and Cora's hollow, but Carl kept the pace as slow as before. They looked for Betrayers as they went along, but saw none. It dawned on Carl as they grew farther and farther away from their hollow haven that if a Betrayer did arrive on the scene, they would be caught out in the open. No escape from White Eyes would be possible and they would all be left at his mercy. He shook his head to chase away his fear and continued leading them all forward-first over the rocks and then across the valley floor.

The Blue Cloud continued to expand and then shrink to the size of a dime as they made their way to it. The sound of its collapse was deafening, but it did not deter them. The ground shifted in tremors too as they marched to the Cloud. They fell over time and time again, but they just dragged one another back to their feet and kept moving forward to their target together.

They carried on like this, slowly and surely, until they could see the Blue Cloud shimmering just in front of them.

They were almost at the Blue Cloud now. It seemed like the walk there was taking forever. They kept at their slow motion pace until they were almost close enough to the Blue Cloud to reach out and touch it.

When they did finally arrive at their destination, Carl lifted his arms off the shoulders of Ben and Bird-Who-Hops and nodded to Henri and Cora to separate too. He put his hand into his jacket pocket and took out the Willing Stone.

Carl was not really sure what to expect, when all with the Gift touched the Stone. Greyhawk neglected to discuss that in his book. He only hoped that when they did, it would get them out of this diabolical place and never to return.

Carl signaled to the others to gather around him. He had to fiddle around with the Willing Stone for a little while to get it out of its case without directly touching it. He eventually managed to put it in the palm of his hand atop its leather case. He held out his free hand and looked to the others to do the same. They were just about to place their hands on the Willing Stone, when a voice cried out.

'My Lord Remiel!' the voice screamed up at the smoky plumes flying above. 'The Brotherhood is trying to escape! Come, My Lord! Stop them!'

The Brotherhood quickly turned to where the voice was coming. They saw someone stumbling down the steep hill that led toward the hollows in the ridge.

'My Lord! Look below! They are at the Blue Cloud! Come before they get away,' the stranger yelled frantically while waving his arms up at the sky.

When the shouting stranger finally came to a stop, Carl and Ben recognized immediately who it was.
There, standing outside the hollow, was Greyhawk.

There were no signs at all of his injuries from Frank's attack. His bruised and battered face and his hair matted with streaks of blood had magically been wiped clean. He stood there hollering, 'My Lord, you must stop them! Come!'

Horrified, the Brotherhood watched as the dark columns of smoke began to descend rapidly.

'Who is that?' Bird-Who-Hops asked in a whisper. 'I've never seen that Betrayer before.'
But before Carl or Ben could answer, White Eyes and his Grinning Dogs had landed around them.

'My Lord!' Greyhawk continued to shout, 'The Last with the Gift is with them! He's there! The one known as Carl!'

White Eyes unfurled his wings to appear as intimidating as possible. He preened himself in his vanity and strutted around the Brotherhood with a sickening, smug smile on his face.

'So you wish to leave me?' White Eyes sneered. 'Without saying farewell? And after all my hospitality? Perhaps you should all be taught some manners!'

He looked at the Grinning Dogs and said coldly, 'Collect them all and bring them back to my Court. I will show them the price of their disrespect. And you, the Last with the Gift, will pay the highest price of all.'

The Grinning Dogs unfurled their wings and started laughing in their maniacal and joyless way. Then together, they began to descend on the Brotherhood.

The Brotherhood all stood there frozen in fear, when Carl suddenly shouted, 'Don't look at them! Look back to me! Touch the Stone! Now! Touch it now!'

Everyone turned back to look at Carl with the Willing Stone in his open palm. No one knew what might happen when they touched the Stone. All they knew was that if it did not save them now, all was lost. 'Touch the Stone!' Carl shouted again.

Carl felt the hand of one of the Grinning Dogs on his shoulder. He started to pull him away from the group. He saw the rest of the Dogs grabbing at the others and trying to drag them away. They were on top of them. 'Do it now!' he cried.

They squirmed away from the clutches of the Grinning Dogs and squeezed in a tight circle around Carl.

The Brotherhood looked at one another and then, as one, placed their hands together on the Willing Stone.

Instantly, everything lurched. It was as if the world had tilted on its axis and then rocked back again. The ground gave way beneath them and the Grinning Dogs fell back. All of the Brotherhood fell to their knees. A gripping spasm knotted Carl's stomach. He doubled over in pain. He struggled not to retch. He glanced up and saw the rest of the Brotherhood also bent over and gripped in nausea. And then just as quickly as the queasy feeling came, it passed.

They all looked around at one another as they slowly stood upright again. They were not at all sure what was happening. They did not know if they were safe or not. They could see the Grinning Dogs were still trying to get to them. They huddled together to try to avoid their hands reaching out to grab them. But even though the Grinning Dogs were close enough to seize them, they seemed unable to do so. It was as if something were blocking their way.

The Brotherhood stood there together afraid to move or make a sound. They shied away as the grasping hands of the Grinning Dogs continued to claw at them.

Cora had just reached over to Ben to pull him nearer to her, when a jolting bang made them all jump and a mysterious glistening bubble instantly materialized above them. It started to descend slowly around the Brotherhood and encase them.

They saw that White Eyes and the Grinning Dogs were still desperately reaching out for them, but their tormentors quickly began to fall out of focus. They could still see them, but they looked hazy and blurry.

They could no longer hear anything outside the bubble that now completely surrounded them. White Eyes stood there just a few feet away from them. It looked like he was shouting in fury, but they could not hear a word of his tirade. They saw the hands of the Grinning Dogs continuing to paw at them, but they became more and more indistinct as they slowly faded from view.

The Brotherhood all looked around in wonder. They could see one another perfectly well. They all heard Bird-Who-Hops ask, 'Where are we?'
But outside of their bubble sanctuary, both sight and sound died away.

A deafening noise like the shattering of glass within the encircling bubble forced them to fall again to their knees. They pressed their hands against their ears and shook their heads in an attempt to block out the sound. And then there was silence.

They slowly got back to their feet. They all looked at one another in the hope that someone might know what was going on. But no one knew. They stood there together dumb-founded, when suddenly Bird-Who-Hops began crying out wildly.

He pointed as he shouted, 'Look everyone! Turn around! There! There! Look!'

They all turned to where Bird-Who-Hops was pointing and saw the Blue Cloud in front of them. The gap within it, which White Eyes had created before, reappeared. The Blue Cloud had split apart again to reveal the real world beyond.

They all stood there numb and stunned in amazement. They kept looking back and forth to check if they were seeing what they thought they were seeing. No one could really believe their own eyes.

Henri stood there stupefied with his hand over his mouth. He kept staring and blinking at the gap in the Blue Cloud.
'The Blue Cloud is open,' he said in a daze.
Then he threw his arms around Bird-Who-Hops.
'My brave, young friend, it is open!'

Ben let out a roar of absolute delight.
'Mom, look! It's the Magic Valley! Just over there! Do you see it? Look, Carl! It's home!'

'No! No! It's my village!' Bird-Who-Hops beamed happily. He began to whoop and dance in unrestrained exuberance.
'Look everyone! Just over there on the right! My village is right there! Do you not see?'

'Nonsense! What are you saying?' Henri asked overwhelmed in his happiness. He pointed at the gap in the Blue Cloud.
'There to the left! That's the river I was navigating! Look over there! Sacré bleu! It's my canoe!'

'I almost gave up hope, Mom. I thought I'd never see the Magic Valley ever again,' Ben sighed happily. 'And now we're going home!'

Cora put her arm around Ben's shoulders. 'Never give up on hope, Ben,' she reminded him.
'It's hope that sees us home.'

And they all walked through the opened curtain in the Blue Cloud together.

CHAPTER
37

Noah, Stacey, Chief Marty, and Jimmy Junior waited together at the spot where Carl had walked through the Blue Cloud. They had not moved from there, since Chief Marty and Jimmy Junior tracked down Noah to tell him about Greyhawk's escape.

Jimmy Junior told Noah and Stacey that the State Police had not given up on finding Greyhawk, but they figured he had crossed the border into Nevada. He said they had informed the authorities there. Chief Marty told them what he had learned from the woman at the State University and what the museum curator had to say when he called him.

'The man's a total fraud, liar, and a thief too, Noah. We just have to accept that he played us all like a pack of rubes.'

'Orin and I think this craziness is all down to the Professor,' Jimmy Junior said. 'We're thinking Ben's going missing, this Cloud business, maybe even Cora's disappearing is all the Professor's doing. We're thinking he may be behind all of it. But the State Police don't want to hear it, because, I suppose, if you haven't seen this Cloud thing swallow someone up, you're not going to believe it.'

'That's right,' Chief Marty agreed. 'If we're going to get

our boys back, we're going to have to work it out for ourselves.'

He walked over to Jimmy Junior and tapped him on his shoulder.
'Come on,' he said. 'We better get ourselves back to the station. We've been out here quite a spell.'

Chief Marty looked over at Noah and Stacey while Jimmy Junior remounted his horse.
'You two staying out here? Why don't you head back with us? There's nothing out here to see.'
After he climbed back up on Daisy Mae, he added, 'You have my word, Noah. If I hear anything from now on, I'll be sure to let you know right away.'

Noah's heart sank after taking in what Chief Marty and Jimmy Junior shared with him. He felt what little hope he still held of ever seeing his wife and son again was slipping away from him.
'Hold up, Orin,' he said. 'Maybe we should head back with them, Stacey. We need to get Bess and Willy fed and watered anyway.'

Stacey stood there lost in her thoughts and staring out at the vista in front of her just as she had been doing most of the time they were out in the Magic Valley. She had stopped calling out for Carl, Ben, and Cora and looked out at the empty valley in silence.

She turned to Noah. 'All right then. Come on, Bess,' she said with a sigh. Let's go get you your grub.'

They got back up on their horses and started to follow Jimmy Junior and Chief Marty toward the steep trail that led out of the valley.

They had not yet reached the uphill path, when a frightful blast pulsed through the valley. Both Willy and Daisy Mae reared in panic and it was all Noah and Chief Marty could do to stay in the saddle and stop them from bolting off. Even placid Bess started bucking and Stacey slipped from her saddle and fell.
'Stacey!' Noah shouted. 'Are you all right?'

She got back to her feet and quickly grabbed Bess's reins. 'It's okay, Girl,' she kept repeating. 'It's okay.' She rubbed the lower left side of her back.
'Yeah, I'm fine, Uncle Noah. Bet I'll feel it in the morning though.'

Jimmy Junior quickly dismounted and turned back in the direction of the explosion. 'What in the thunder was that?' he asked. 'It sounded like something out of a war zone.'

Noah and Chief Marty hopped off their horses too and grabbed their reins to control them and try to calm them down.

Just as they finally began to settle their horses, a mighty tremor shook the valley floor. They all struggled with their mounts again to stop their panic.

'Is it an earthquake?' Stacey asked in confusion as she stroked Bess down her neck to reassure her.

'Don't know,' Jimmy Junior said. 'My buddy said there were some quakes over in Soda Springs. Maybe they're heading our way.'

Another head-splitting boom shuddered through the valley followed by a loud cracking sound like a mirror breaking. All the horses again started snorting and stamping fiercely. Their instinct was telling them to get as far away from the shocks and tremors as they could.

'I bet it's one of those military jets breaking the sound barrier,' Jimmy Junior suggested. 'They're not meant to do that so near where people live.'

As Noah fought to hold on to Willy's reins, he noticed something far out in the valley. At first he thought it was a group of animals, but they were too far away to discern clearly. He looked again as the group began moving and saw they were not animals at all. There were three people standing out there.

He blinked and narrowed his eyes to make sure that he was seeing what stood before him out there. He watched as the three people embraced one another and then began looking around at where they were.

Noah stood there staring and trying to figure out from where the people had come, when another jolting bang rang out. The valley floor began to shake with tremors accompanied by what sounded like the shattering of glass. Its epicenter seemed to be right at the spot where the three strangers were standing.

The ground around the mysterious trio shook violently. They fell heavily to the ground and slowly got back to their feet. They looked around again at where they were and held one another until the tremors passed.

Stacey observed Noah staring out into the valley. She walked over holding Bess by her reins and stood beside him. Then she saw the people too. Two of them were hopping up and down together like kids at Christmas.

'Are those people out there?' she asked. 'Where'd they come from?'
Noah shrugged his shoulders. 'I'm not sure. I was looking out across the valley. There wasn't anything out there and then suddenly there was. It's like they came out of nowhere.'

Chief Marty and Jimmy Junior joined them and all four of them stood there silently trying to make sense out of what they were witnessing.

Chief Marty told Jimmy Junior to ride out to them. 'See if they need help,' he said. 'Maybe their horses threw them and bolted when the ground shook. They could be injured.'

Jimmy Junior got back in his saddle and started to make his way out into the valley. The rest of them watched as he rode off at a canter until he reached the spot where the three people stood. When he got there, he did not dismount. He quickly turned his horse around, waved his hand frantically, and started shouting as he rode back like he was in a horse race.

'What's he yelling, Uncle Noah?' Stacey asked.
'Can you hear what he's saying?'
'Something's wrong,' Chief Marty said. 'Look.'

They stood there looking on together as Jimmy Junior galloped back toward them. They could see the dust kicking up behind his horse as he rode furiously. He kept shouting as he rode, but no one could distinguish anything he was saying.

They did not know what to think. From what they could see, the three people did not appear to be hurt. After Jimmy Junior galloped away, the mystifying strangers began calling out to them too. It was as if they were warning them of something. At least that is what it sounded like.

'Maybe they know what caused those blasts,' Chief Marty concluded. 'They could be trying to tell us to get out of here while we still can.'

Jimmy Junior eventually rode back within earshot, so they could finally hear what he was shouting, but all he said was 'Follow me!' He then turned his horse back around and began to gallop again toward the three people stranded out in the valley.

Chief Marty, Noah, and Stacey quickly hopped back in their saddles and galloped after him, but their horses were no match for Jimmy Junior's and he reached their destination well before they did.

This time he did get off his horse and they watched as

the three people all charged at him and threw their arms around him. When they finally got there themselves, they could see why.

'Carl!' Stacey shrieked with joy. 'Ben! Ben!'
She was so overwhelmed that she did not know what to do first.

She did a flying dismount, ran over to Carl, threw her arms around him, and kissed him. Her eyes were wet with tears.
'I told you I would be here waiting,' she reminded him. She then went over to Ben and squeezed him in a bear hug.

Chief Marty started weeping. 'My boy! Oh Carl! It's my boy!' he blubbered in his happiness. He went over and picked up Carl like he was a toddler.

Noah stood there numb and not believing his eyes.
'Noah?' Cora said caressing his face. 'It's me. It's your Cora. And look, there's our Ben!'
'Cora?' Noah asked as if he were dreaming. And then he promptly burst into tears. They reached out for one another and cuddled close together. They could not speak, because they were all crying so hard.

Jimmy Junior was the only one who seemed capable of knowing what to do next. Everyone else was weeping with joy and hopping up and down ecstatically or hugging one another.

There was never such a happy sight in this entire world.

Jimmy Junior took out his kerchief to dab his own eyes. 'We better get you all away from here. We got to get you to the hospital. You need to be checked that you're all right. Are you all right? Are any of you hurt? Come on now, everyone. Follow me.'
Then a thought hit him. 'Welcome home,' he said.

Carl went over to Jimmy Junior and handed him the Willing Stone.
'Thanks for keeping it safe, Carl. The museum is looking for that Stone. When you went missing, we found out that Professor stole it. They'll be happy to have it back.'

Carl got up on Daisy Mae with Chief Marty. Stacey took Ben with her on Bess and Noah and Cora rode together on Willy. It took a moment for Willy to settle. He was so excited to see Cora again himself. They then followed behind Jimmy Junior as he rode slowly along and led them to the trail back home.

They rode over to Groves Gas Station where Chief Marty and Jimmy Junior had left the patrol car before they rode to the Magic Valley to find Noah. They tied off the horses there.

Chief Marty asked Mr. Groves to call ahead to the medical center and inform them that they were coming. 'Tell them I'm bringing them over right now.'

Before they headed off to the hospital, Mr. Groves took Carl aside.

'Did you close that Cloud thing for good, Sonny?'

'I hope so, Mr. Groves,' he said. 'I hope we'll never see it again or what's behind it either.'

Carl and Stacey got into the patrol car with Chief Marty and Noah, Ben, and Cora went with Jimmy Junior in his pickup.

Everyone kept insisting that they were perfectly fine and healthy and just wanted to go home, but Chief Marty insisted that it was police procedure and they had to be medically examined first.

On the way to St. Luke's Medical Center, Ben asked Cora, 'Do you think the Blue Cloud trapped White Eyes? You don't think he can still get out, do you?'

'I hope not. I hope that dreadful creature never gets his clutches on another living thing ever again.'

'Me too, Mom.'

Ben wanted to ask about all the people who did not have the Gift of the Stone and were unaware that they were trapped behind the Blue Cloud, but there was no time. They had arrived at St. Luke's Medical Center and the medical staff were there waiting and ushered them quickly into the hospital.

While the doctors and nurses were checking to see if Carl, Ben, and Cora were injured or ill in any way, Chief Marty called his wife and then the police to let them know what had happened.

And after everyone was given the all-clear, they headed home.

Stacey called Annie as soon as she walked back in the house.

'Mom! They're home! They're all back home!' she squealed. Then after a pause to listen, she said, 'Yes! That's right. Ben and Aunt Cora too! Come right away, Mom! They're home!'

'What about Henri, Mom?' Ben asked. 'And Bird-Who-Hops? Do you think they made it home too?'

'Of course they did,' Cora said. 'Remember when the Blue Cloud parted? Everyone saw the home they hoped to see. Henri always thought that if we ever did escape, we'd go right back to the place where we went missing. I'm sure all of us went back to where we belong. Don't you worry about that. I know they're as happy as we are right now.'

A big smile suddenly crossed Ben's face.

'Mom!' he exclaimed. 'You know what? I'm hungry! Isn't that great? And tired too!'

'So am I, Ben! So am I! Doesn't it feel terrific?'

They fell into one another's arms, laughing and giggling, like they were one horseshoe shy of a full set.

Noah and Stacey looked at one another. They wanted to see if either of them had any notion why Ben and Cora would be so happy about being tired and hungry. They did not know what to think.

Cora stopped laughing for a moment, when she saw their confusion, and caught her breath.
'We'll explain everything later, but for now is there anything in the fridge?'

'Yes,' Ben giggled. 'I think I could eat a horse! And then I think I could sleep about twenty years or so!'
Both Ben and Cora started laughing again until they were wiping tears from their eyes.

When Carl walked through the door, his mother let out such a shriek of joy that his grandmother covered her ears. Mrs. Marty kept going back and forth from holding Carl close and kissing him to hugging and kissing her husband.

'You're my little hero,' she said to Carl as she kissed his forehead. 'And you! You're my big hero!' she said to Chief Marty while holding him like she would never let him go. 'Both of my heroes are here at home with me!'

Chief Marty then reminded her that Ben and Cora were back safely too.
'Everyone is back, Marian, safe and sound,' he said.
'And get this. Police reports are coming in from all over the area that some of the people who went missing are now suddenly reappearing right across the Magic Valley.'

Mrs. Marty was so pleased that she clapped her hands together and twirled in delight in a little circle around herself.

Chief Marty held his wife close to him and kissed her. 'Marian, if you hadn't insisted that I talk to Noah, I never would have been out there when it all happened.' And he kissed her again and put his arms around her and Carl and held them both close to him.

'Come over here, Carl!' his grandmother shouted. 'Your mother and I laid out some food for you.'

As Carl went to sit down, she patted his cheeks. 'You did it! I knew you would. I knew you'd make it back home! I never doubted it in all the time you were away from us.'

Everyone sat down at the table as Carl looked around at the feast spread out before him. He stared at the food for a moment and then promptly picked up a pitcher of water in front of him and drank every single drop. He then began to eat ravenously.

'This is the best fried chicken ever!' he said between mouthfuls.
'Slow down, Carl,' Mrs. Marty said as she watched him dig in. 'You'll make yourself sick.'

Then a thought struck Carl.
'Grandma, how long have I been away?' he asked her softly.

'Pardon, my dear? What did you say? It's impolite to mumble. You've been whispering ever since you got back like you're afraid to wake a baby!'

'Sorry, Grandma. I suppose I got myself used to whispering.'

And then Carl asked her again, 'How long was I behind the Blue Cloud?'

'Oh, must be coming up on two weeks or so by now,' she said.

'It was a terrible place where we were, Grandma. An awful place. No one will believe us, when we tell them what happened there and what it was like.'

'Well, I'll believe you, Carl,' she replied. 'Every word. Like I've been telling you ever since you were a little cowboy, there's all kind of strangeness in this world that we are yet to know.'

CHAPTER
38

(2019)

Jason and his friend, Larry, sat together in front of a computer screen in their dorm room.

'What do you think about this one?' Larry asked.
The Wendingo is an evil spirit who devours the innocent.
'Hmmm. Maybe,' Jason said. 'Let's keep looking.'

Their roommate, Ricky, walked in on them. He was with his girlfriend, Holly. They both had beers in their hands.

'What you two dogs doing?' Ricky asked scornfully.
'It's Halloween!' Holly said. 'What you studying for? School's out for the weekend! It's party time!'

Ricky went over to the computer. He read aloud over Jason's shoulder.
Rites and Rituals of Northwest Native American Tribes.
He shook his head. 'You doughnuts! Why you looking at that shit?'

'We're hunting for old Indian spells for the Halloween party,' Jason explained. 'We're going to light some candles and burn some incense. We'll put on some spooky music, perform an old spell to conjure up a dark spirit, and scare the pants off everybody.'

'Jason just wants to scare the pants off Melissa,' Larry said. 'He can't get her pants off any other way.'

'Why mess with all that bother?' Holly asked. 'Just get a couple pints of grain alcohol. That'll get the spirit into everybody damn fast.'
'Yeah, but first we want to freak everybody out,' Jason said. 'Spook them good, when they all get here, and scare the shit out of them. It'll be a laugh!'

'If Melissa's roommate, Cassie, shows up she's going to start crying,' Holly said. 'She believes in all that horseshit. She'll spend all night sage-smudging the dorm to protect us from evil spirits.'
'Great!' Jason said.

'What do you think about this one, Jase?' Larry asked. 'Get a load of this!' He chuckled to himself as he read aloud.

The Myth of the Evil Two Face. This two-faced demon has a good face and an evil face on the back of his head. Anyone who makes eye contact with his evil face will die.
'Can you believe people actually used to believe that crap?'

Ricky stood there sipping his beer and staring at the screen, when something caught his eye.

'Hold your horses, Dim-bulbs,' he said. 'Now here's one that will really get everyone going.'
He read aloud the name of the myth he discovered.
The Legend of the Blue Cloud.

'This one is right up your Shoshone family tree, Holly.'
'Tribal tree, Einstein,' she said struggling for patience.
'Tribal, yeah. Forgive me, Little White Dove.'

Ricky drank some more of his beer, coughed to clear his throat, and then read to them what he had found.

Contact with the dark spirit known as White Eyes may be made by the process of Thaumogenesis, when chanting a Resurrection Spell. It was created by an assembly of medicine men of the Shoshone, Bannock, and other local tribes. They cast out White Eyes behind the Blue Cloud centuries ago, when early European invaders brought their dark spirits with them.

'Oh yeah, I remember that story,' Holly said. 'My Aunt Stacey used to tell me and my brother about White Eyes and the Blue Cloud, when we were little kids. She claimed some relatives of hers down in the Magic Valley disappeared through the Cloud and then found their way back home. She's a bit of a joker, my auntie, and liked to scare us.'

'Then that's perfect!' Jason replied. 'And look! The spell is right here! Wicked! What else does it say about this White Eyes guy? Move over Ricky. Let me read it. This is way cool!'

The imprisonment of the malevolent spirit, White Eyes, was achieved by a conference of medicine men, when they enchanted Willing Stones and used them to draw a Blue Cloud barrier beyond which White Eyes could not cross. One with the Gift of the Stone can have a vision beyond the Blue Cloud and witness White Eyes' prison.

Incanting the following Resurrection Spell will contact White Eyes and reveal the Blue Cloud to all who possess the Gift of the Stone.

Jason read on in silence for a moment.

'It says we have to form a 'Domboni',' he said uncertainly. 'Hey, Holly! What's a domboni? You're the language major.'

'It means form a circle,' she said. 'And I'm a linguistics major, Numb-nuts.'

'Thanks.'

Jason then said to the others, 'It says we form a circle. We form this domboni thing and then we say this.' Jason recited the Resurrection Spell in a spooky voice.

My Lord Remiel! Hear my voice. I call out to you through the Blue Cloud. I am at your service, My Lord. I will do your bidding. Reveal your glory to me and show me the entrance to your world. Speak to me. Make your will known to me. I have the Gift of the Stone, My Lord. Let me untie you from your bonds and set you free!

'I tell you again. I warn you. If you do that shit in front of Cassie, she's going to pee herself,' Holly said unimpressed.

'Awesome!' Jason said. 'Let me print this off. Come on. Let's rehearse it, you know, like we know all about it before they get here. Who's got some candles and incense? Right, we'll get that stuff later. Everybody sit on the floor in a circle. We got to practice. Otherwise we'll all start laughing and screw it up.'

'Okay, Lard-ass,' Ricky said. 'Let me get another beer first.'

They all sat on the floor in a circle.
'You read it, Holly. It'll sound more authentic if you do it,' Ricky said. 'You're part Indian.'
'Part Shoshone,' she corrected him.
He had another swig of his beer.
'Whatever,' he mumbled.

They made several attempts to get through the ritual, because someone or other kept making wisecracks.
'Can we get on with this?' Holly asked while rolling her eyes.

She then read the Resurrection Spell in its entirety without interruption.

After she had finished, she said, 'All right. I'll do it, Jason, but if Cassie or someone else loses it, you've only got yourself to blame.'

They all got up from the floor. Larry took a six-pack out of the mini-fridge and handed a beer to Holly.
'Anybody else?' he asked holding up what was left of the six-pack and waving it in front of the others.

Holly popped the tab of her beer, looked up, and then narrowed her eyes at something.
'What is that?' She said peering at a spot across the room.
'What's what?' Larry asked as he took a sip of beer.

'Over there! Don't you see it?' Holly asked. 'Have you gone stupid or something?'

'See what? I don't see squat,' Larry said.

'It's right there!' Holly said as she walked over to what she was seeing.

Larry gave her an uncertain look. Then he smiled and said, 'Nice one, Holly! You had me going there for a minute. But cut it out, will you? Stop horsing around. Save it for the party.'

'How much have you been drinking? Have you gone blind? Are you high?' Holly asked laughing in disbelief. 'Are you saying you can't see these rippling waves shimmering in the air? How can you not see it? Stop being stupid. It's right in front of your eyes!'

'Very funny, Holly,' Ricky snorted. 'You should be on Comedy Central. Larry, you gullible horse's ass, there's nothing there. What you think, Holly? I'm going to fall for that Indian mumbo jumbo too?'

Jason got up from the desk. 'Come on, Larry,' he said. 'Let's go rustle up some candles. We'll stop by Melanie's room and get some incense. I want to get everything together before everyone gets here.'

Larry followed Jason out the dorm room door. Ricky raced over and shouted down the hall after them. 'Dudes! Make a beer run too!'

'Doughnuts!' Ricky said with a shake of his head as he closed the door.

'Can you believe those guys, Holly? Party games! Total dweebs or what?!'

He turned back around and walked into the room, but he did not see Holly. He figured she was in the bathroom. He walked over to the bathroom door.

'Holly!' he shouted through the door. 'You hungry? What you say we grab a pizza or something before this whole shebang kicks off?'
But there was no answer.

'Holly? You in there?' Ricky asked as he rapped on the door. He saw the door was not entirely shut and peeked in.
'Holly?' he asked looking around inside.
But the bathroom was empty.

He turned back to the room and glanced around for a moment, but there was no sign of her.

'Huh!' he grunted to himself with some surprise. 'Now where the hell did she get to?'

ABOUT CHARLES SERIO

Charles Serio is artistic director of Serio Ensemble. The Ensemble focuses on new writing and performing arts. Six of his published plays have been produced and performed in the United Kingdom and America.

He is a former finalist in the London Writers' Competition-poetry division and a former prize winner of the British New Plays Competition. He works as a professional actor, teacher, and director.

He is a previous winner of an Emmy award for his scriptwriting on the CBS television series, *In Our Lives*.

He also leads highly acclaimed corporate presentation skills workshops internationally.

Charles lives in London.

This is his second novel. His first novel, *The Lies I've Told,* was published in 2015.
www.charlesserio.com